Arsonist's Lullaby

Ever Chace Chronicles
Book 7

SUSAN HARRIS

ARSONIST'S LULLABY
Copyright ©2020 Susan Harris
All rights reserved.

Summary: The past, present, and future collide in the penultimate book in The Ever Chace Chronicles. Life just got complicated for the agents of P.I.T as Ashlyn, Derek and Ever's teenage daughter, makes her entrance. And with Odin poised to attack, Ever will have to decide if she can survive another personal sacrifice in order to save the world.

ISBN: 978-1-63422-429-1 (paperback)
ISBN: 978-1-63422-398-0 (e-book)
Cover Design by: Marya Heidel
Typography by: Courtney Spencer
Editing by: Chelsea Brimmer

This book is dedicated to Helen,
My partner in crime, the Kylie to my Jason.
My world is a brighter place because you are in it and
I love you to infinity and beyond.
(You're still the bad influence though)

PROLOGUE

L ightning crackled through the sky as thunder boomed like thousands of hoofbeats in the air. An eerie mist gathered around Yggdrasil, the tree of life, bringing a sense of foreboding to the night. A flash of blue streaked across the sky as past, present, and future collided, unfolding themselves before three women who had watched time and time again how the world was shaped and reshaped.

The strands of time had been unraveled, and the preordained future was once again uncertain, made precarious by choices made and chances taken.

Gathering around the tree, its connection to the nine realms flaring a bright green, Urðr, Verðandi, and Skuld greeted one another for the first time in over a century. Not since a Valkyrie queen was born and the road to Ragnarök had turned as clear as ice had they seen one another.

Urðr inclined her head toward Verðandi. "The past has come calling for the present, Sister."

"The present lingers on the verge of change."

Skuld regarded her sisters, eyes white as the mist that surrounded them. "The future is unclear. It has been altered, and I see no sign as to whether the nine realms will survive."

"If the future now lies uncertain, we must wait to see what strands these warriors unravel." Verðandi sighed, impatient as always for the past to become present and present to become future.

Searching deep within for the future she'd once seen as clear as the waters of Valhalla, Skuld felt a sense of foreboding. Even as she braced a hand against the trunk of Yggdrasil, hoping the tree would feed her magic, she could not see what was to be.

The Sky rumbled as if the former God of Thunder himself were trying to send them a sign as the three sisters placed all their hope on a visitor to the present who was not meant to be there.

It would seem, for now, that fate was out of their hands.

CHAPTER ONE

Ash's best friend had always told her she had a flair for the dramatic. When they'd devised the plan to go into the past, all the advice she had gotten from Z was to be chill, don't be extra, and don't take things up a notch. Ash had punched him in the arm, earning a grin before she'd gone back in time. Now, she was standing in front of her parents and their family once again.

"There is a war coming. The fate of the world has fallen to all of you, but the future is changeable. Free will leads to paths that alter the course of destiny and change how the future unfolds."

Ash was surprised her voice didn't waver under the intense gaze of those she admired most. She had to use every ounce of her will not to squirm.

Steeling her resolve, Ash let her eyes wander down the line as she continued. "The vampire queen and her consort, the god of mischief and his goddess of war, the seeker of truth and her not-so-vampire husband." Ash let her eyes rest on her mother once again and swept her arms out in a mock bow. "The Valkyrie princess who has not yet claimed her crown and her champion, the alpha wolf with a collection of non-wolves in his pack. All have parts to play. Can you withstand the impending storm? Are you ready to save the world?"

"Who are you?" The tone of his voice was a familiar one, and her dad looked as formidable as ever as he took a step toward her.

Amber flooded her eyes, brighter than before. Ash loosened the grip on her powers and halted her dad's step. When a roar of thunder rolled overhead, Ash grinned.

Bowing low once again, Ash then rose to her full height, filling her voice with the confidence and pride that came from being chosen by Thor to wield Mjölnir. "My name is Ashlyn Kyria Doyle, and someone is about to fuck up the future."

There was a collective gasp at her declaration, and her dad looked shocked as he stumbled backward. His eyes darted to her mother. The Valkyrie queen's hand rested firmly on her stomach, and Ever blew out a breath. "She will be worthy."

Thor had deemed her worthy. And Ever Chace was about to take the life Ash had built away from her.

Ash inclined her head to Ever. "Hey, Mom."

Ash tried not to react as her father paled, and her mother's eyes widened in surprise. Ever looked the same as she always had—beautiful, strong, fierce—except now she looked a little scared, too. Her mom was never scared of anything.

Derek stepped forward. "How do we know what you say is the truth? How is this all possible?"

"Well, Dad, when two people love each other very much…"

The growl that rumbled from her father's throat brought her own she-wolf to the surface, and Ash snarled back at the alpha wolf in front of her.

"Yeesh… Aunt Erika said you always had a stick up your ass; I guess she was right. If you don't believe me, then ask the truth seeker."

Ash folded her arms across her chest as Derek glanced at

Melanie, the vampire nodding her head, her flame-red hair glinting in the moonlight. When Derek ran his eyes back over her, Ash shrugged and blew out a breath.

She felt the shields in her mind buzz as someone tried to get inside her head, and Ash grinned as she dropped her mental walls and let Donnie inside her head, her gaze running the length of him as he explored her mind.

Damn, she thought, *no matter if it's the future or the past, the vampire is hot. He's looking all like Tom Hardy... Now all I need is for Donnie to take off his clothes, and this would be my teenage fantasy come to life.*

Donnie choked back a laugh and shook his head, bending to whisper in Caitlyn's ear. One of her favorite people in the nine realms eyed her with suspicion, and Ash just shrugged her shoulders.

"Don't worry, Auntie Caity, we had a long midnight stroll where we discussed how my teenage crush on Donald made him feel a little uneasy. We're all good. But next time he wants to dig around in my head, your boy toy should ask first."

A small ball of fur ducked under his father's legs and bolted toward Ash. A wave of elation washed over her as she sank to the ground, resting Mjölnir beside her as sparks flashed and a little naked boy stood in front of her.

The adults cried out as Ash held up a hand. Ignoring Ricky's urging for little Zach to come back, Ash bent her head down and grinned.

"Hello, Big Brother. This is the only time I've ever been taller than you. Do you mind if your dad gets you a T-shirt? I've seen enough of your naked butt over the years that I am totally going to tease you about this when I go home."

Zach grinned and climbed into Ash's lap, resting his head in the crook of her arm. Ash stroked down Zach's hair, and the little guy purred. "The last time we did this, when you had your head in my lap and I stroked your hair, you had the galaxy's worst hangover after we raided your dad and Uncle Donnie's homebrew."

Silence surrounded her now, and she forgot her parents were watching her. All she cared about was the little cat in her arms, who trusted her without knowing her in this time, and who Ash loved with all her heart.

Tapping Zach on the nose, Ash ruffled his hair. "You and me, Z, we take on the world together. You are my best friend in the whole world, you know that, kid? You and I are family. Now, before they all pounce on me, go back to your dad. We can play later."

Ash lifted Zach and nipped at his nose, the little boy swiping at her with his tiny hands. Getting to her feet, she set him down on the ground. The little boy hesitated before strolling back to his dad.

Ricky scooped up the little boy. "You've seen him naked?" he asked, raising a brow suggestively.

Ash wrinkled her nose. "Ew, that's gross. He's my brother. That's all kinds of nasty."

Ricky chuckled. The tension eased from his shoulders, but then he licked his lips and took a step backward. "Jesus Christ, Derek, the power from your kid is making me hungry. I need to back off."

Ash dusted off the grass on her butt and walked toward Ricky. She cupped his cheek as Melanie grabbed Zach and Ricky let out a low groan. Removing her hand, Ash gave him a small smile.

Ricky glanced at Loki. "Dude, compared to her, you got nothing. This kid has some serious mojo."

"I can feel it," Loki drawled.

Ash glanced over her shoulder at her uncle. "Don't be jealous, Loki. I'm a tri-breed, so I pack a punch."

"What do you mean, tri-breed?" Ever muttered, the first time she had spoken since Ash introduced herself.

Ash quirked a brow. "Has no one seen *Legacies*? I am Valkyrie, I am goddess, and I am wolf."

Emphasizing her final point, Ash let the magic of her she-wolf wash over her. One minute, she stood on two legs. The next, she was on four, complete with paws. The scents, the sights, all poured over her in a rush of adrenaline. Lifting her head, she flashed her teeth at her father as he stared at her in wonderment. Quick as a flash, she was back on two legs, righting her clothes.

"The change..." her father murmured. "It doesn't hurt you."

"My father," Ash said, staring pointedly at him, "told me years ago, back when I was a pup, that you have to be one with your wolf or it will control you. At first, I used to panic when I changed because everything was so overwhelming. Still, you were with me and stayed until it became second nature. Full moons are still my favorite time because I get to spend them with you."

Ash wasn't sure if it was the tone of her voice or the words she spoke, but her dad was starting to believe her. She could hear it in his voice. But others were wary of her. Kenzie had begun to stalk her, the wicked scythe glinting in the moonlight as the girl inched closer.

Ash sent out a sliver of her power. Thunder rumbled in the sky, and it froze Kenzie in her path. "Kenz, I love you, girl, but if you take one more step toward me with that scythe of yours, I'm gonna have to make you bleed. Let's not get off on the wrong foot here, 'kay?"

But the menace in Ash's tone didn't deter Kenzie, and she swiped out with her scythe despite Caitlyn's sharp cry. Ducking out of the way, Ash lunged forward and grabbed the handle of the scythe, using her foot to kick Kenzie in the stomach and send the girl flying backward. Ash flashed to where Kenzie landed and pressed the top of the weapon against the flesh under her neck with a snarl.

"Ashlyn."

The wolf in her squirmed, wanting to roll over and show its belly to her alpha father; however, Ash wasn't about to roll over right then and show weakness.

"Ash," she said without turning from Kenzie. "Call me Ash. It's what Uncle Ricky called me from the day I was born."

Derek rolled his eyes. With a smirk, Ash pulled the scythe away and held out her hand to help Kenzie up. The other girl grabbed her hand. Soon, she stood on her own feet. Ash handed her the scythe as Kenzie inclined her head toward Caitlyn.

"She train you?" Kenzie asked, a hint of amusement in her tone.

"You know it. She and Auntie Erika trained us all."

Ash broke off with a grimace. Zach had warned her about sharing too much about the future so as not to overly influence the present. She was only to reveal enough to ensure that she, Ash, was born, and then she would go back to the future and fulfill her own destiny.

"And who is 'us all'?" Caitlyn asked, stepping forward.

Ash inclined her head in respect. "Auntie Caity, I am limited in what I can reveal and what I have to keep to myself." Switching to Caitlyn's native tongue, Ash smiled and added, "The burden you carry lessens in time. You do learn to be happy without feeling guilty. The love you have for those who are feasting in the great halls of Valhalla never goes away. It is their light that will guide you on your path to happiness."

Confusion and sadness in her eyes, Caitlyn replied in English. "Your French is almost perfect. Who taught you?"

Ash grinned and shrugged her shoulders. "You did, of course. I learned from everyone standing around here."

Ash reached down and wrapped her fingers around Mjölnir. It's comforting thrum of power ran through her veins as she lifted the infamous hammer and rested it over her shoulder.

"How are you here now? Why did you come here?"

Her mother's voice was soft, almost a whisper against the night. Her hands had yet to leave her abdomen, and Ash tried to not feel animosity toward the woman standing in front of her, someone unlike the mother she had grown up wanting to become.

"I was in the middle of a case," Ash replied, "and I suddenly started to disappear. We thought it was a new power; I've been getting some new ones lately. But then the others started losing memories of me like I was being erased. Then I got a visit from the Goddess of Death, who told me she had come to take me."

Ash shifted her weight on her feet before she continued. "So, Z manipulated the Bifrost to send me back in time instead of just to Midgard. And here I am, hoping the fact that your teenage daughter standing in front of you convinces you not to kill me."

Ever gasped at the harshness in Ash's tone, but Ash didn't care. She tried to rein in her temper, but there was so much more at jeopardy than just her mother's hurt feelings.

"At this stage in your belly, I can feel your emotions. You are farther along than you think. You mated with a wolf, which makes me part wolf, and you're about three months along, which is the full gestation period for a wolf. Being a Valkyrie, you've been able to hide the pregnancy through a glamor, but if my timing is right, you have about four weeks until I pop out of there."

Everyone was looking from Ash to Ever and back again, but Ash was watching her dad and the hurt in his eyes. Ash set the hammer down and took a step toward the man she idolized. She was more like him, or so people told her. Her father once a legend, and even though Ash was on her way to becoming just as famous as her parents, she always felt she paled in comparison.

"Hey, Dad."

Derek's eyes snapped to hers at the sound of her voice, and he looked like a deer caught in the path of a very hungry wolf.

"Would you prefer I call you Derek? I mean, it's weird even to suggest that because the last time I tried that, when I was pissed off and gave you sass, slamming my door to keep you out, you removed the door and made me work off my anger in a run."

Her dad cleared his throat. "No, dad is grand."

"Then can I have a hug, Dad? I really need a hug right now."

The moment Derek opened his arms, Ash flashed into them and rested her cheek on his chest, inhaling deeply. His scent was all wolf and forest, and it eased her soul. Z teased her that she was a daddy's girl, but Ash had never denied it. As Derek pulled her closer, Ash sniffed back her tears and, with one final squeeze, stepped back from his embrace.

Her dad's eyes were amber, his wolf recognizing its offspring even though she was merely a pup in her mother's belly.

"This can't be happening. This is all some weird dream that I'm going to wake up from soon. You just can't be standing here right now."

"Well, if I'd been a few hours later, then maybe not. Correct me if I'm wrong, but isn't that an Asgardian medicine in Erika's pocket? For the love of the gods, Mam, did grandma not explain anything about Valkyrie pregnancy to you?"

"Grandma? Why would Samhain explain things to me? She doesn't even know what I am."

Ash rolled her eyes. "Not Grandma S, Grandma Freya. I mean, she would know all about Valkyrie pregnancies, right?"

Ever let out a harsh laugh. "Freya? Do you mean the woman who handed us daggers when we were mere babies? The woman who sent us out into the forest with no food or water to fend for ourselves? Who pitted us against one another? Now I *know* this is a dream, because no one would take mothering advice from Freya."

Ever's words lit the fuse on Ash's temper, and she stalked over to her mother with a growl that rumbled low in her chest. "And the woman who is about to kill her unborn child wants to criticize someone else's mothering skills? Let me tell you something, *Ever.* Do you know why Auntie Caity and Auntie Erika— hell, even Aunt Melanie—all trained me? Because you refused to. You decided that my destiny wasn't something *you* wanted for me. And that was when I saw you, which was rarely. So, before you scoff at my grandmother—who, for your information, baked cookies with me, watched stupid horror movies with me, and braided my hair for me—remember that you are no prize of a mom, either."

Ever sucked in a breath and flinched liked Ash had hit her.

Good, Ash thought. *Let her feel a molecule of the pain that has plagued me since we figured out why I was disappearing.*

"Hey, Ash. Take it down a notch, eh?"

"Uncle Ricky, with all due respect, fuck off."

"Language," her dad growled, and Ricky stifled a smirk.

Ash turned to Erika, who was studying her as if she were a battle plan. "This is why you call him Boyband, right? Why you throw insults at each other? He really was this uptight?"

Erika quirked a brow. "Are you saying that he isn't in the future?"

Ash shook her head. "Not with me. Not with us. Dad's always laughing, messing around. He dressed up as a Disney princess for one of my birthday parties and made Ricky and Donnie do it, too. You told me a few times that having me changed him, loosened the uptightness... but I never saw this side of him."

"Hold on a minute, what princesses did they dress up as?" Melanie asked, her grin showing her fangs.

Ash tapped her nose with a smile. "Can't reveal all my secrets just yet."

Silence filled the space, and Ash watched as her parents

actively avoided one another. She knew things would get worse before they got better, and Ash couldn't leave until she knew she would actually be born.

Ever might be the one to end her curse, but Ash had her own destiny to live up to, and she would use whatever power she had to make sure she was alive to achieve it.

The fate of the world might be in Ever and the gang's hands, but the fate of the nine realms rested on her and her own team. There would be no point in saving the world if Ash wasn't there in sixteen years to make sure her parents' sacrifices hadn't been for nothing.

CHAPTER TWO

EVER

T his can't be real... This can't be bloody real.
Ever stared at the young woman in front of her. Even though she knew deep down in her marrow that this beautiful, powerful girl was hers, this was far too much to let sink in. The reason she'd been able to pick up Thor's beloved hammer was that his successor was already growing inside her. Ever hadn't understood at the time, but her brother had known before her.

"Well, I need a change of clothes if I'm gonna fit in around here," Ash said. "Mel? You still have clothes here, right? Hey Z, wanna help me find something to wear?"

When Ash made to walk away, Loki stepped out and grabbed her elbow.

Ash gave her adopted uncle a sinister grin. "You might wanna take your hands off me, *Uncle*. Or perhaps you would like to know how it feels to have a broken hand?"

"Child, we have not finished discussing why you are here. And I am not afraid of you."

"You should be. You are wiser in the future." Ash yanked her arm in, bringing Loki so close their noses almost touched.

"Word of advice for the future—don't bother trying to bind my powers when Ever asks you to. It doesn't work, and it makes me very angry. Healing your shattered hand takes a while."

"*Stop*," Ever shouted, but neither paid her much heed.

Ash slowly peeled Loki's fingers off her arm, and when Loki made to grasp her tightly again, Ever heard the unmistakable sound of a bone snapping. Loki hissed out a breath.

Erika pulled Loki away from Ash and clutched a dagger.

"Erika, no."

At Ever's command, Erika immediately sheathed the blade.

Ash patted her head. "Good little warrior."

With a snarl, Erika snapped, fists clenched as she went for Ash, but Ash was ready for her and vanished, popping back into view inside the house with a grin.

"Not fun being patronized, is it? Remember that in the future."

The hammer that rested in the grass trembled as Ash held out her hand, and the group ducked out of the way as it sailed through the air into Ash's palm. Without a backward glance, Ash turned and stomped away. Zach chased after her, and Ricky's look of concern relaxed when he heard Zach's peal of laughter. The team turned to look at Ever and Derek, wondering what they could do or say.

This can't be real... This can't be bloody real.

Lifting her gaze, Ever tried to ignore the look of hurt in Derek's eyes. Turning to Melanie, she asked, "Is what she says the entire truth? Is she our daughter?"

"Ash is definitely hiding something, but what she says feels like the truth. That being said, I get the feeling she could probably lie her ass off and I wouldn't know the difference."

Ever inclined her head before looking at Donnie. She didn't even need to ask; the mind reader simply shrugged. "Compared to the rest of us, Ash is pretty much an open book. Her mind is fascinating. I managed to get glimpses, feelings mostly, and that kid is terrified. The bravado is just that—she's cocky and powerful and she knows it, but she's terrified of failing."

"Well, we all know where she gets that from, right?" Derek said bitterly.

Ever finally braved looking at him. "I'm so sorry," she said. "I thought I was doing what was right."

"And again, you decided without even asking my opinion."

Ricky cleared his throat, steering Melanie toward the door. "Well, my wife and I are gonna track down our furball and make sure your daughter isn't leading him astray."

As they left, the rest of the team followed suit, with Erika and Loki being the last to leave. Loki looked like someone had slapped him.

"I cannot understand why she dislikes me so."

"You did grab her arm, babe. Maybe we need to work on your communication skills."

Loki ignored Erika's attempt to alleviate the tension and frowned, his handsome features furrowing as he pursed his lips. "No, I saw it in her eyes. My own niece hates me, and I need to know why."

Erika huffed out a breath as Loki vanished. "I'll go after him… unless you want me to stay, Ever?"

Derek growled, his lips curling back into a snarl. "Go after your mate, Erika. I need a few words with my own."

Erika folded her arms across her chest, ignoring Derek until Ever responded.

"Go, Erika," Ever said with a sigh. "I'll be okay."

With a glare at Derek, Erika winked out of view and left them alone. Neither spoke for a long time, and Derek frequently glanced toward the house as if he wanted to bolt inside and make sure Ash was still there.

"She looks just like you," Ever said as she exhaled a breath.

"And I see so much of you in her."

Derek's tone was sharp, though his expression was a mask of

indifference as he glanced down at his mate's belly, noting she had yet to take her hands away from her stomach. "You weren't going to tell me, were you?"

Ever wanted to reassure him that she would have one day, but seeing the pain in her mate's eyes, she knew it would have been a lie. She would have borne the knowledge alone until the end of days.

"I'm not going to lie to you, Derek. With Odin trying to kill me, I didn't think it was the right time to bring a child into this world. It was just another person for me to be worried about trying to keep alive."

Derek shook his head, scratching the stubble on his jaw. "*She*, not *it*. She is ours, Ever, and you were going to make it so she never took a breath. She is beautiful, funny, strong, and too much of a smartass. And you almost made it so I never got to hold her in my arms. Did you just not want to have our child?"

Ever wrapped her arms around herself as she shook her head furiously. "By the gods, *no*. I wanted her so badly it broke my heart to make the decision. But being pregnant made me weaker. I was sick, Derek, and I'm never sick. She's so powerful she's zapping my energy. If Odin knew I had a weakness, he'd strike immediately, and you'd lose us both."

"I'd have lost you both anyway if you'd not been found out." Derek inhaled, and amber flashed in his eyes. "I should have known. Your scent changed, but I've never been around a Valkyrie who was pregnant before. Has she changed your mind now, our daughter?"

Ever wanted to tell him that yes, laying eyes on their teenage daughter had instantly changed her mind about being a mother. And Derek knew it from his darkened expression.

"Don't look at me like that, Derek. I don't know how to be a mother. Freya wasn't the best role model unless you were killing something, and Samhain … she tried her best and I love her for raising me, but I don't know how to be a mom to *her*." She pointed toward the house.

Derek's eyes flashed. "Does any parent, Ever? You just do the best you can and hope they turn out better than you did. I'm absolutely terrified because I can see Ash already thinks of me as a hero, and how can I live up to that? You just try and be the best."

When Ever didn't reply, Derek snarled and shook his head, turning away from her. "I'm going to get to know our daughter, Ever. Maybe if you did the same, the girl might forget you were willing to kill her for your own selfish reasons." He walked toward the house, muttering, "And you say you aren't like your father."

Ever felt anger well up inside her, and she spun to face Derek. "I am *nothing* like him. How dare you throw that at me? Odin has killed me numerous times over. Can you imagine what he'd do if he got his hands on her power? If he realized she might be as powerful as he is? Did you feel it, Derek? She's even more powerful than Loki, and he's one of the strongest gods I know. If you think I made this decision lightly, then you don't fucking know me at all."

"Now this is a familiar sight," Ash's voice drawled from the patio doors.

Ever and Derek both turned, watching the girl step out wearing black yoga pants and one of Melanie's Marvel tees. Her hair was pulled back into a long braid, and Ever thought it made her look her age. Derek was staring at the girl's arms, covered in Norse tattoos and runes that Ever could read.

Derek quirked a brow. "Tattoos, young lady?" he said in a teasing tone.

Ever marveled at how easy this came for him, how Derek had accepted the young girl instantly without question, and even though she hated herself a little for it, she was already jealous of their relationship.

"Relax, Dad," Ash said with a smile. "They appeared on my skin, slowly, as I grew up. I didn't even feel anything. They're gifts from Thor—the story of him and me."

Stepping out into the night air, Ash inhaled a breath. "Full moon's coming next week. If I'm still here, can we go running together? Unless you want to go alone, Dad?"

Derek grinned, and Ever felt like she was intruding on a private moment. "There is nothing I would rather do," he said.

Ash beamed, obviously delighted with Derek's response. Her expression changed when she glanced at Ever and then back to Derek. Folding her arms across her chest, Ash gave her father a small smile.

"Dad, I'd murder one of your hot chocolates right now. You mind giving Mom and me a minute?"

Derek let his eyes drift to Ever's and then back to their daughter before nodding. Turning to leave, his step faltered.

"I don't know how you like it. I need to learn."

"Sure you do, Dad," Ash replied.

Derek left them alone, and Ash turned to Ever. They held each other's gaze for an age before Ever decided she would be the first to speak. But when she opened her mouth to speak, not a single word came out.

"I get it, Mom. It's all good."

The hurt in Ash's voice was unmistakable, and Ever remembered how much she, as a teen, had wanted her mother's approval—her love and a sliver of a bond. How had she ended up with her own child feeling the same as she once had?

"It's not. It's really not, Ash. I'm sorry. You came all this way to stop me from making the biggest mistake of my life, and I haven't been very welcoming."

Ash scrunched her nose. "Do you mean that? Look, I don't want the reason you and Dad are fighting to be me. The only time you guys fight is when it comes to me, and..."

Her words trailed off as Ash clamped her mouth shut. Ever

took a step forward and took her daughter's hands in her own. "What I was doing had nothing to do with whether or not I was in love with you—it was because I couldn't let Odin use you against me. My first emotion when I found out I was pregnant was delight, but that changed to dread when I thought of my father."

Ash gave Ever a small smile. "It is what it is, Mom. It's what you do from now on that matters. The end is coming. Things will be harder before they get better. There will be losses that feel like too much to bear, but don't let it make you cold. Talking to Caitlyn will help; the darkness she carries with her sometimes threatens to drag her to hell. Whatever happens next, you and Dad need to stick together, okay?"

"What's going to happen, Ash? Tell me."

Ash shook her head, taking a step backward. "I've said too much already. Revealing anything risks altering the fabric of time beyond repair. The less I tell you, the better, but don't worry—I promise you'll know when it happens."

Ever opened her mouth to argue, but Ash was already making her way back inside the house, so Ever followed her toward the sound of voices coming from Caitlyn's kitchen. As she stood in the doorway, Ever studied those she considered family. Ash may have just charged into their lives unannounced, but she already seemed to fit in more than Ever did.

Derek glanced over at her, his eyes full of love for the child they had created. Donnie nudged his shoulder as Ash and Caitlyn embarked on a conversation in French, Zach nestling into the crook of Caitlyn's arm.

"She is more than you could have expected."

Ever turned to Loki. "I'm not sure how to respond to that."

"Look at her, Ever. She's your child, and she's come a long way to stay alive. She may dislike me for some perplexing reason, but do you not feel who's aura flows from her?"

Ever concentrated, letting Loki's words sink in, and then she felt it—the same aura that had been a comforting hand to help her on her way.

"She feels like Thor, as if part of him is with her."

"And if the thundering oaf deemed her worthy, then who are we to argue with him? Especially when we cannot hear his side of the story."

Ever sighed as Loki squeezed her shoulder and blinked out of view again, leaving her alone with her thoughts. Leaning against the doorframe, Ever rested her head against the timber and simply watched as Ash embedded herself into the present like she was always meant to be here.

She will be worthy...

Thor's voice in her head filled her with reassurance and allowed Ever to let herself finally feel. Tears streamed down her face, and her knees threatened to buckle as the loss of Thor and the fact that she'd almost taken this remarkable girl from the world hit her like a tidal wave. She stifled back a sob, but in a room full of supernaturals, there was no hiding her loss.

Her legs gave way, and she would have hit the ground if Derek hadn't caught her. Ever buried her face in his chest and cried and cried until she could cry no more.

"What did I almost do, Derek? How could I almost have done that?"

Derek scooped her up and carried her into the living room, sinking into a chair, his hand snaking into her hair as he whispered in her ear, "But you didn't. And now—now, you won't."

No, she wouldn't. Even if she knew the child inside of her and the one from the future were in grave danger, far more danger than Ever was in. Ash was even more unique than Kenzie or Ricky or Melanie—some would hurt her just to get a taste of her power.

"I will kill anyone who dares harm her, Derek. I won't even flinch."

Derek pressed his lips to her forehead, and she felt a weird sensation in her stomach. When Derek cupped her cheek, the flutter happened again, and Ever let out a gasp.

Derek snapped to attention. "What's wrong? Are you okay?"

"She kicked. You kissed me, and she kicked. I've never felt that. I didn't know what it was."

Derek rested his palm on her stomach, but nothing happened, so his wolf pressed his mouth to Ever's and gently nibbled on her lip. When Ever did the same to him, he growled, and Ash kicked with a fierceness that caused Ever to gasp again.

Derek pulled away and grinned. "That's our girl."

Shifting, Ever took his face in her hands and kissed him some more, until a throat cleared. They sprang apart, discovering their daughter looking at them with a flush to her cheeks.

"I'll go," Ash said quickly. "I didn't mean to upset you. And now I'll never get the image of my parents sucking face out of my head."

Ash turned to go and only hesitated when Ever called her name.

"Please don't go. It's not you, Ash. I just let myself feel Thor's loss and your almost-loss, and it overwhelmed me."

"I get it. But can you please climb off my dad's lap before I'm permanently scarred for life?"

Derek chuckled as he lifted Ever to her feet. Ash sidestepped and let them walk past her. Ever felt Ash's eyes on her as she strolled into the kitchen and took the cup that Caitlyn handed her.

"It's decaf," the vampire said with a knowing smile.

"Thank you."

"It is nothing."

Ever made to answer when she saw Ash freeze, and her eyes flare amber.

Ash suddenly yelled at them to get Zach and Ever out of the kitchen, reaching out for the hammer that was in her hand a second later. Derek called for Ash as their daughter snarled.

Glass shattered. Ash swung her hammer, hitting some creature square in the face before another came into view. Ash continued to swing her hammer again and again. Ever made to help her when Erika appeared and blocked her path.

"Let the girl show us what she knows. It's my job to keep you safe."

Derek had pulled out his gun and fired off a shot, hitting one creature right in the forehead and dropping the beast immediately.

Ash dove through the shattered glass and, quick as lightning, took down the small contingent of Dokkalfar. She strode over to one that was still alive and crawling away, trying to reach the surrounding forest to escape. Save for the whites of its eyes, the creature was entirely black.

Ash stalked around the creature, smirking as she set her hammer down on its back. It screamed—the sound so harsh it could break glass—but the sound only intensified Ash's grin.

"Well, well, well... what's a filthy Dokkalfar assassin doing on Midgard? Better to answer me than face my wrath."

When the elf didn't respond, Ash pressed the hammer down harder, and the creature begged her to stop.

"He told us he would make us gods in his new world if we killed the queen," it gasped. "We wanted to rule our own realm... he promised us Midgard now that Thor is gone."

Ash lifted the hammer and kicked the elf over onto his back just as Ever and Derek reached them.

Once the elf noted the hammer Ash was holding, his black eyes widened. "You wield Thor's hammer? Who are you?"

Ash inclined her head toward her parents. "I'm their kid. And Thor's niece. And you won't get to tell a soul."

Ever and Derek stood mesmerized as they watched their daughter pull a dagger from thin air and stab the elf right in the head, much like Derek had shot the other assassin. Yanking the blade free, Ash wiped it across the dead elf's clothes before rising.

Turning to her parents, she flashed a wolfish grin and shrugged. "I'm starving... got anything to eat?"

THE COUPLE TIED TO THE CHAIRS IN THE MIDDLE OF THEIR KITCHEN begged and pleaded with the man whose hair was the same color as the flames dancing in his hands. Eyes filled with hunger, the arsonist leaned in and blew warm breath into the woman's face as sweat ran down her cheeks. When he leaned in and pressed his lips to hers, she screamed as her mouth began to burn.

Back to back, the couple held each other's hands tightly as the monster flicked his wrists and sent sparks flying, igniting the living room curtains and setting the couch ablaze. A line of fire snaked toward them as the arsonist grinned and walked to the door, pausing to watch as the couple's chairs caught fire, along with their skin.

He stayed and watched as they screamed and tried to escape, but there would be no escape. It wasn't personal; he didn't know this couple at all. It was simply part of his master plan, one that would see Derek Doyle on his knees.

He'd already taken away his mentor—now he would take everything from him until Doyle had nothing left to lose. That made men and monsters unpredictable.

As he felt the life leave the couple's bodies, the man held his palms over the fire. The flames obeyed his command and flooded into his bloodstream, steam rising from his flesh.

Charles Harrington and Diane O'Connor died because Derek Doyle lived.

And their deaths would haunt him for the rest of his short life.

CHAPTER THREE

DEREK

D erek watched in awe as his daughter sat at Ever's breakfast bar, devouring a mountain of bacon like she hadn't eaten in weeks. Derek understood the hunger; his own wolf was used to eating vast amounts after exerting energy. Ash had nearly singlehandedly taken down a group of assassins. He marveled at how like Ever she was, but he could still see himself in certain expressions.

Ash glanced up and paused. "You're staring."

And he was. He'd been staring at her since she'd crashed into his life last night. It was hard to believe she was his, his and Ever's, but then she smiled, and he knew exactly who she was.

Derek gave her a small smile. "I'm sorry. It's hard not to."

"I know it's a lot. I'm a lot. Zach tells me all the time. I mean, I could have handled things better. Instead, I gate-crashed a wedding and smashed shit up."

Derek sipped his coffee, hiding a smile before he spoke. "It *is* a lot. But you are everything I ever wanted in a kid. I just went from not knowing I was going to be a dad to having a teenage daughter."

Ash swallowed a mouthful of bacon. "Well, hopefully now that Mom seems to have changed her mind, you'll get all the good stuff that comes in between like night feedings and diaper changes."

"I'm down for that."

Ash returned his grin and blew a stray strand of hair off her face. Picking at her nails, she glanced up at Derek. "Is Mom okay?"

"She's just tired. And a little sad, but not about you. She told me last night that she can feel Thor in your essence, and she's letting herself grieve for him now."

Ash went silent, chewing on her lip just like Ever did when she was thinking. Derek was just about to ask his daughter what was on her mind when he heard Ever shriek. Dropping his cup, he bolted for Ever's room.

Skidding to a stop just inside the room, Derek suppressed a grin as he saw Ever staring at her own reflection in the mirror, her stomach having grown to an unmistakable bump overnight.

"Oh, by the gods, there's no hiding her now."

"You look very bitable," Derek said with a grin.

Ever rolled her eyes at him just as a throat cleared behind them.

"Your mind has accepted the pregnancy, so the glamour has fallen. Others will sense the baby… me… now."

Ever let her top fall, but it did little to hide the sudden bump. Ash turned and walked away, leaving Derek and Ever standing alone in the room. Last night as Ever slept, Derek had spent the night sleepless, wandering from Ever's bedroom to the couch where Ash had fallen asleep.

His emotions had gone from anger to elation, from fear to trepidation. He was absolutely terrified and didn't know what to do to calm himself. He wanted not to be angry at Ever, and how could he be now, when the woman he loved stood in front of him carrying his child?

"What's on your mind?" Ever asked. "You have that look on your face when you're thinking too hard."

"I'm just wondering how I got so lucky."

"Smooth talker."

Derek snorted and shook his head. "Not so sure about that, but you asked, so I told you. However, I do think you need a bigger top to conceal that bump."

Ever glared at him in mock outrage. "Are you calling me fat?"

"Never, darling. I've already said you look bitable."

Lust flared in Ever's eyes, and Derek took a step toward her like a moth to a flame.

"Daughter with long-range hearing about to lose her breakfast down here. Please refrain from coupling until I've at least left the building. Or just forever…"

Derek pulled Ever close and chuckled into her hair, happiness swelling his chest. "I guess we have to get used to being interrupted, don't we?"

"She's not too old for sleepovers, right?"

Derek let loose a burst of laughter, taking her hand and leading her down into the front room. Ash was not alone; sitting at the other side of the room, Loki held his niece's stare, his hand cupping Erika's calf as she rested on the arm of the chair. Erika's eyes wandered to Ever's stomach.

"That's an impressive bump you've got going on there."

"I'll remember to be just as complimentary when it's your turn."

Ever sighed as she lowered herself down beside Ash. Erika paled at the thought and, as Loki squeezed her thigh, she pinned Ash with a stare.

Most people would have balked at a stare from the Valkyrie general, but Ash simply shrugged. "I'm limited as to what I can and will say. Besides, I have enough to contend with just handling his already-psychotic offspring. I don't have time to worry about how your kid will turn out."

Loki leaned forward in his chair, resting his chin in his hand as he asked Ash what she meant. When Ash shook her head, Loki let loose a wave of power. Derek saw Ash shudder, then flash Loki a grin. "That tickled."

Loki sat back in absolute amazement as Derek growled at his mate's brother. "I would ask you to refrain from using your magic against my kid, Loki, or you and my wolf are going to have words."

Dismissing Derek's warning with a wave of his hand, Loki continued to study Ash with a level of interest that made Derek uneasy. Ash got to her feet, stopping to press a kiss to her mother's head, then patted Derek on the shoulder.

"It's okay, Dad. Uncle Loki and I actually do like each other in the future, but what's the saying... 'blood is thicker than water?'" Ash turned back to Loki, and Derek felt her wolf rise to the surface. "If you want us to get along, *Uncle*, then do me a massive favor. Keep your kids well away from me and mine."

Loki tapped his chin with his fingers and tilted his head slightly. "And why is that, Niece?"

"That's a story for another day. Now, I promised Auntie Caity I'd stop by, so I'm gonna bounce and let y'all talk about me while I'm not here."

"Wait a second, kid," Erika huffed, looking at Ever. "The secret is out."

Derek tensed as a figure appeared behind Ever, and his mate instantly sagged her shoulders. Not one single person looked happy to see Freya standing in the room; well, apart from Ash.

"*Grandma*," she exclaimed and rushed forward to embrace the centuries-old Valkyrie who looked appalled at being called 'grandma.' The moment Ash felt Freya's indifference, Ash backed away confused.

Freya's eyes wandered from Ever's belly to Ash and back again. "Well, you've gotten yourself into one hell of a predicament, haven't you, Daughter?"

The coldness in Freya's tone seemed to come as a great surprise to Ash, who looked as if Freya had clocked her one, her eyes widening at the utter look of disgust on Freya's face.

Derek rose, beckoning his daughter to him, but Ash did not come. She held her ground and faced off against Freya.

"Predicament? How can you be so cold? Who the hell are you?"

"Sit down, child, and respect your betters," Freya chided as she made to step past her.

Ash growled. Her hands changed to claws and her teeth lengthened, but she did not fully shift. Derek stood amazed as his daughter morphed into a movie version of a werewolf before his eyes.

Ash looked down at her hands and stumbled back as if she were surprised. Derek saw her close her eyes, and then he felt her calm her wolf, speaking to it as if it were separate from herself. Soon enough, her features returned to human.

Freya regarded her with disdain, then turned back to Ever. "Look what getting on your back for a wolf got you—a child who is part monster and doesn't even feel like a Valkyrie."

"You just wait a *damn* minute," Derek growled, but Ever got to her feet and held up a hand to silence him.

"I do not need or want parenting advice from you, Mother. If you cannot hold a civil tongue in your head, then you are free to leave. My family and I are not your concern. I'm happy to see you on your feet, though. Now, get the hell out of my house before I ask my mate to toss you out on your ass."

Derek almost growled with pride as Ever stood up to her own mother, finally accepting her new role. As Freya and Ever locked eyes, he watched Ever step around and place herself in front of Ash. Derek rested a hand on Ash's shoulder in solidarity, the three of them squaring off against Freya.

"And just so you know, Mother," Ever continued, "Ash is perfect just the way she is. She is both Valkyrie and wolf, and she is also Thor's chosen guardian of Midgard. Your opinion matters little, and I realize now it never did."

With one more glance in Ash's direction, Freya left as suddenly as she came.

Ash shook her head. "That's not the woman who baked cookies with me and braided my hair. I don't know who she is."

Ever turned to face her daughter and rested a palm on her cheek. "I'm sorry. I truly am. Maybe the Freya you know is changed because of you. I can't say. You changed our lives in an instant, so it's possible to change her."

"I've gotta go. I'll see you later."

Ash flashed from the room, but the scent of her lingered as Derek pulled out his phone. A text flashed from Caitlyn, saying Ash had just arrived and was fine.

Derek shot off a quick reply saying he knew his kid was in capable hands before turning back to Ever.

Once she sat back down, Derek looked at Erika. "If I'm not with her, I want you at her side."

"Agreed."

"We keep her on lockdown as much as possible until the baby is born, and she has round-the-clock protection."

Erika bowed her head. "I've already requested the Valkyrie come and guard Ever. They will camp out in the garden and train while keeping an eye on her. She will need to be visited by a Völva, just to check her over."

"I'll need to meet them first, or my wolf won't let her anywhere near Ever. He's relaxed now because he trusts that you both will keep Ever and Ash safe. Strangers are another matter."

Ever raised her hand. "Does anyone want to listen to what I have to say?"

Derek smirked, ready to tease his pregnant mate a little when the doorbell sounded. Holding up his hand, Derek stood and went to answer the door, his wolf on edge as he opened it.

What met Derek was a familiar sight, though he'd never been at the receiving end of such a call.

Dread washed over him as two officers in dress uniform took off their hats. Derek knew the tall, thin, warlock with hair skimmed down to the skull, standing in front of him; he was part of the Major Crimes Division, and Derek had worked with him a time or two.

"Agent Doyle, I'm not sure if you remember me, but I'm Detective Pierce of Major Crimes, and this is my colleague, Detective Kiely."

Derek nodded at the female detective but kept his expression blank. "What brings you to our door, Detective?"

The cop looked around. "May we step inside, sir? It's quite a delicate matter we need to discuss with you and your mate."

"My mate is heavily pregnant, and if this is as bad as I expect, I wish to help soften the blow to her."

Pierce swallowed hard. "Then I am sorry if the news causes her distress. At exactly eight o'clock this morning, members of the major crimes unit were called to a house fire where, on arrival, officers came across the body of a man who had been burned from the inside out. The person who called us gave us your details and your mate's as the next of kin. It is with great sadness that I must tell you that Sergeant Delaney was murdered at his residence last night. I am very sorry for your loss."

Derek's wolf howled inside his head, and Derek stumbled, clutching the doorframe so he wouldn't fall. Overcome with grief, he lifted his head to the sky and howled, man and wolf united in their loss.

He needed to control himself; he needed to tell the team and work the case.

"Agent Doyle? We think the murder is tied to something Major Crimes has been investigating for a few days. Once you and your team are ready, Major Crimes is ready to assist you in any way. We've held the scene for your team."

"Where is he?" Derek asked, his voice hoarse and thick with emotion.

"We've taken him to headquarters, and Anna is tending to him. She asked for you to come whenever you're ready."

"My team and I will be at the scene after sundown. We'll see you there."

The detectives nodded and offered their condolences again as Derek stepped back inside and almost ran into Ever. She was pale, her hands braced on the wall.

"I felt it—the loss—in my head, and heard your wolf call out. It's not true, is it? Tell me it's not true. He can't be gone."

And then she was falling, and Derek caught her, falling to his own knees as Ever sobbed in his arms and beat her fists against his chest. Feeling eyes on them, Derek glanced up. His eyes, now fully amber, collided with ones the color of whiskey. Erika looked just how he felt—as if the world had tilted and lost all sense of meaning.

"Go and bring the team here. See if Ash can help, and Loki. Bring Donnie first because he'll hear your thoughts. It's on me to tell them."

"You got it."

And then she was gone, and Derek lifted Ever into his arms and walked with her into her bedroom.

Loki offered Derek no words, simply pressed his lips to Ever's forehead. "Sleep now, sister mine."

Ever's head lolled to the side, and Derek lay her on the bed. He was torn as he heard Erika arrive with the team and Ash calling out for him. His eyes wandered back to where his mate lay sleeping.

"I will keep watch over her, wolf. No harm will come to her while I have air in my lungs."

Derek nodded and made his way downstairs, walking into

the room full of people they had chosen as their own family. And it had all been possible because of Sarge. They had become who they were because of him.

Ash watched him with a sadness Derek knew came from the knowledge she could have shared but didn't. He couldn't blame her; if Ash had stopped this wave from dragging them out to sea, then maybe someone else would have had to die in Sarge's place.

As if she'd read his mind, Ash shook her head. "Everything is as it should be. Stopping it would have led to the deaths of many, according to the fates." Ash glanced over at Caitlyn and Melanie, and Derek knew his daughter had made the right choice, even if it was a painful one.

Donnie stood closest to him, and the big man's eyes were clamped shut as he tried not to let on what was happening. Derek glanced around the room at the supes gathered in Ever's living room. Caitlyn sat still with one hand on the back of Donnie's thigh and the other resting on Kenzie's arm. Ricky and Melanie stood off to the side watching Erika, trying to make out what had the Valkyrie so glum.

"Where's Zach?" Derek asked his best friend.

"With my mom," Ricky replied, his face full of concern. "What's up, D?"

Derek blew out a breath as Caitlyn lifted her gaze to him. He wondered if his oldest friend could survive another loss. He needed to be strong now, for his team, for his family, and for Sarge.

"About half an hour ago," Derek began, "Major Crimes knocked on our door to inform us that we lost a fellow cop—murdered in his home by a supernatural creature who burned him from the inside out. It's going to hurt. This will knock you for six, and you will feel like you can't go on. But we have to... for him... because he would do—and has done—it for us."

Caitlyn sucked in a breath as Derek continued. "We will find his killer and bring him to justice, and when we do, we'll lay him to rest and mourn his loss. But now we need to be the team he built, the family he created. So let it out now—cry, scream, and rage at the world—but then get your asses straight and let's do what we do best. Let's catch a killer."

"I need you to say the words, Derek," Melanie said in disbelief. "I'm not going to believe it until you say them, and I taste the truth. Stop beating around the goddamn bush and just *say it*," Melanie finished in a scream.

Derek could almost hear her heart breaking as she covered her mouth, and Ricky wrapped his arm around her. Slowly, he steeled himself to say the words he'd never wanted to say, not until the old bear had become an old man and his life could be celebrated.

"Sergeant Thomas Delaney was murdered in his home last night, and it's up to the team he built to find out who took him from us."

Caitlyn

Caitlyn was no stranger to loss. Every fiber of her being was engrained with it, an unyielding force that had driven her for a very long time. When she lost Sebastian and her babies, Caitlyn had not felt she could ever recover from the pain or open her heart ever again. But thanks to Thomas Delaney, Caitlyn had not only found the capacity to let people see past her hard exterior, but she had also learned to love once again.

Donnie has been a shock to her system, a jolt in her chest when she'd found him dying on a Dublin street, and her vampire instincts had screamed at her to turn him. For a moment, she'd rebelled against it, *need* being a foreign concept to her, but then she'd let herself want for the first time in an age.

Standing in Ever's kitchen, waiting for the sun to set and night to befall the city, Caitlyn took a moment to grieve for a man who had meant so much to her. In many ways, Sarge had reminded her of her own father. He'd given Caitlyn a purpose, a family, and even if she found it hard to allow herself to be so, a happiness with her mate that sometimes made her feel guilty for those no longer with her.

But Caitlyn hadn't made it easy for Sarge. A faint smile ghosted her lips as she closed her eyes and recalled the first time she'd met him.

Despite the throng of people packed into the backstreet bar, the patrons gave Caitlyn a wide birth, as if a 'don't come near me' vibe scented off her skin. By now, she'd already earned quite the reputation for herself, slaying those associated with her maker—the scum of the vampire race—with a coldness that frightened most who knew of her.

She'd arrived in Ireland barely a year ago, having received some information that a vampire who liked to hear his victims scream while he toyed with them had set up a cult where some poor humans had agreed to be scarred—mentally and physically—because they thought him a god.

Caitlyn spent a year searching for the vampire, but her search had resulted in nothing but frustration and anger. Now, sitting in a shitty bar in Cork, Caitlyn snarled at the bartender and lifted her glass.

She was six whiskeys in, something that wouldn't normally affect a vampire. Still, this bar was known for its blood-laced alcohol, and Caitlyn was a little buzzed and feeling extremely off-kilter tonight. It had crossed her mind many a time that in a couple of hours she could simply walk into the sun and end her suffering.

Today would have been her beloved daughter's birthday.

Downing the whiskey, Caitlyn ignored the admiring glances in her direction. Without a second thought, she reached over the bar and lifted a bottle of whiskey from under the counter. Chester, the owner of the bar, said not a word. He simply sighed and shook his head, though his eyes sparkled with intrigue.

Chester liked to collect unique things, and Caitlyn was a unique treasure whose maker had seen her with breath in her lungs and life in her veins and thought her beautiful enough to decide she had to be his. Caitlyn despised she was considered beautiful and had only accepted such a compliment from the man who had stolen her heart with paint on his face and sunshine in his smile.

But now she was utterly alone, and the only thrill she felt was when she killed.

Cain had made her into an effective assassin. Still, the moment the adrenaline of the chase left her veins, she remembered her losses and the wounds cracked open once again.

Slugging from the bottle, Caitlyn dropped her head and stared at the oak-stained bar as she felt a presence at her back.

"I can make you feel better, babe."

"I doubt that. Fuck off."

The other vampire snarled as Caitlyn drank deeply from her bottle once more, her entire body on edge as she waited for what would come next. The stupid vampire grabbed her arm, and the entire bar held its breath as Caitlyn lifted her gaze to the mirror in front of her. The sudden spark of fear wafting from the vampire as they locked eyes in the mirror sent a cheap thrill through her.

A sadistic smile curved Caitlyn's lips as she tossed the whiskey bottle in the air, caught it by the neck, and smashed the base on the counter. Whipping around, she drove the bottle into the vampire's neck, relishing the blood gushing from him as she yanked out the bottle again. She swayed a little on her feet as another vampire lunged forward, the sound of Chester's shout ringing in her ears, but Caitlyn wasn't done yet.

She took the shoulder to the gut, ignoring the surge of nausea from her over-drinking as she dropped and rolled into a crouch. Reaching under her jacket, Caitlyn yanked out two small daggers, and as the other vampire staggered to his feet, she plunged both daggers upward into his throat.

The vampire staggered back, blood gurgling from his throat as his friends came to pull him out of Caitlyn's reach. Coolly lifting one of her daggers to her mouth, Caitlyn licked the blood from the blade, a silent challenge to anyone else looking to join the fray. The rest of the patrons backed away, and some went back to their drinking.

She wanted to kill—she wanted to bathe in blood. Instead, she staggered forward and slapped a wad of cash on the counter, muttering, "For the damage," as she retook her seat.

Her French accent was more pronounced whenever she was drunk, and she'd been drunk more nights than not recently. Chester slid her a coffee with a cautious frown, and Caitlyn pushed it back with a growl. Chester made to speak but stopped, distracted by something over Caitlyn's shoulder.

Or someone.

Caitlyn glanced up into kind, hazel-colored eyes and a smile just as warm. She smelled the scent of the woods on his skin and knew this kind man was a shifter. He was relatively good looking and appeared to be in his mid-forties, but she never really could tell a shifter's age.

The man set a whiskey down in front of her, taking a sip of his own as he sat on the stool next to hers, and then he spoke.

"Before you tell me to fuck off, too, I have something you've been looking for."

The shifter slipped her a folded piece of paper. When she opened it and read what was on the page, her eyes widened.

Turning herself to stare at the shifter's profile, Caitlyn pursed her lips. "How did you find him?"

The shifter smiled. "I'm part of a new task force set up by the garda to deal with paranormal crime and supernaturals that the human police cannot hunt. We stumbled across who you've been looking for, and I thought you might like to be involved when we arrest him."

"I work alone. And I don't plan on leaving him alive."

"I know that, too. But I've had my eye on you for a while, Ms. Hardi, and I would very much like to recruit you to my team."

Caitlyn snorted at the shifter as she slipped the paper into her pocket. "If you knew exactly who and what I was, you would not be recruiting me to join your silly team."

"I know exactly who and what you are, Caitlyn," he said, leaning close, "and that is why I'm willing to offer you anything in my power to join our team."

"I cannot be police. I am not exactly a law-abiding citizen. I'm a murderer."

"Someone who kills monsters and rapists is not a murderer. A vigilante, perhaps, but from what I've heard, you have no unjustified kills under your belt."

Caitlyn regarded the man once more before draining the last of her drink and standing. "I thank you for the information. I am not who you are looking for. I do not play nice with others." She inclined her head and made to leave.

"Grief is the price we pay for love."

"Pardon?"

The man spun his chair around to face Caitlyn. "I know what happened to you. What you have lost and what you still must struggle with daily. I can't imagine the pain and loneliness, Caitlyn. I'm not even going to try."

The man stood, and Caitlyn was surprised at how much shorter he was than his presence. She had met men like him before, but none who'd instantly made her feel at ease like this.

"I'm offering a chance to be part of something bigger than your grief. To help us help the innocent. We could use someone with your skills and talent."

Caitlyn remained silent, so the shifter continued. "Think it over. Here's my card. Meet some of the others before you decide. We have someone inside your monster's camp. We'll retrieve him in three nights. If you want to walk away after meeting the team, no harm, no foul."

Taking the small card in her fingers, Caitlyn turned it over and read the embossed lettering.

THOMAS DELANEY

SUPERNATURAL ENFORCEMENT OFFICER

With a snort, she rolled her eyes. "You should call it 'Paranormal Investigations Team.' Supernatural Enforcement Officer sounds stupid."

The shifter, Thomas, grinned and tipped his imaginary hat. "See? That's why we need you on the team. It took the boys and me a month to come up with that. Come see us tomorrow, Caitlyn. It could be the turning point in your downward spiral."

"What makes you think I'm on a downward spiral?" she asked.

"Been thinking of walking into the sun lately?"

Caitlyn jerked back in surprise and flashed her fangs. The shifter held up a hand in apology.

"Think it over, Caitlyn. You've spent a year hunting a monster that took us two months to find. We can be helpful to one another. I'll see you tomorrow night. Sober, if you can manage it."

The man walked away, and Caitlyn called after him. When he glanced over his shoulder, she asked, "What makes you think I will show up, Thomas?"

The man smiled. "I see something special in you, Caitlyn Hardi. It's one of my many talents. And please, call me Sarge. Everyone else does."

And Sarge had been right, Caitlyn had shown up that night and never looked back. Derek was the first of the team she'd met, and she instantly took a liking to the werewolf who seemed just as haunted by personal demons as she was. Sarge partnered them together for the first couple of years, and she found herself becoming his friend quickly.

She felt her mate approach, his presence overwhelming her senses as she popped open her eyes and caught sight of him in the glass. Had she not taken Sarge up on his offer that night, Donnie may have died in that dirty street, and she would not have found him.

Fate was a fickle bitch.

From the look in his eyes, her extremely gifted mate had seen inside her mind and memories. Had she wanted to, Caitlyn could have shielded her thoughts from him. But Caitlyn had hidden so much from her mate for so many years that she'd almost driven him away. She didn't want to hide any more… and that was in part due to the man who'd shown her what it was to find purpose once more.

"I never knew the full story. Thank you for sharing that with me." Donnie wrapped his arms around her waist and rested his chin on the top of her head. "And I remember you telling me you've never been tipsy…" he teased.

Leaning into his embrace, something she would not have done even a year ago, Caitlyn sighed. "Sarge is responsible for the person I've become. I was unhinged and simply waiting for someone to kill me. Then Sarge came striding in with all his bravado, and his offer intrigued me. Then I met Derek, and the rest is history."

"And then you stumbled across a drunk rugby player who was so handsome even with his face kicked in that you had to have him." He said it with a tease in his tone, trying to soothe her soul and her heart.

"You reminded me of me, and you know I wanted you even then. I've told you."

"Gods, Cait. I can't believe you actually say that to me so freely now."

Neither could she. It had taken her a long time to, as Derek once said, get out of her own way and realize that Sebastian would have wanted her to be happy. And that he would have really liked Donnie.

"That means a lot, Cait."

She smiled despite the grief in her chest. And she was grateful he'd allowed her the space to gather her thoughts. Everyone was distraught at the loss of Sarge, especially since he'd been taken from them so suddenly, so cruelly, and just when they were celebrating such a happy moment.

Donnie huffed out a breath, and Caitlyn turned in his arms to face him. "Are you okay?"

Donnie winced. "I can't seem to differentiate my own grief from everyone else's. I'm finding it hard to deal, and, man, my head pounding. It's not their fault. They can't help it. It's just a lot."

Caitlyn reached up and cupped his cheek. "Is there anything I can do to help you?"

Donnie gave her a genuine smile that sent flutters into her stomach. "Kiss me and make me forget for even just a second."

Sliding her hands up, she tugged slightly on the overgrown lengths of his hair—hair that he grew out simply because she liked to run her fingers through it—then raised on her toes to kiss along his stubbled jaw. She felt him relax as she pressed her lips gently to his.

Donnie deepened the kiss instantly, and Caitlyn let him take what he needed, her entire body coming to life as his hands roamed over her, stopping to cup her ass as he backed her against the glass. He nipped gently on her bottom lip, and Caitlyn smiled against his mouth as he purred.

Before they got caught in a very compromising position, one they would be teased for mercilessly, Caitlyn gently pushed against Donnie's chest, and he backed away. Almost immediately, his eyes filled with bloodred tears. As her mate finally broke, Caitlyn pulled him to her and let him cry until he could not do so anymore.

When Donnie finally lifted his head, Caitlyn brushed her thumbs under his eyes to wipe away the tears. *"Je t'aime, mon âme soeur."*

Donnie pressed his lips to hers again. "I love you, too, mate of mine."

Hearing him repeat her words back to her brought a rare smile to Caitlyn's lips. A throat cleared behind them, and Caitlyn stepped back out of habit. When Donnie glanced at her, she gave him an apologetic smile and reached for his hand.

Lifting her hand, he kissed her knuckles. He then excused himself, making sure he walked around Ash, who grinned at Donnie, highly amused by his embarrassment at revealing his crush.

Caitlyn looked at her friend's daughter, remembering her own, and inclined her head toward the retreating vampire. "You enjoy making him nervous."

"He's so calm all the time. I like ruffling feathers."

Caitlyn chuckled at the thought of Donnie being calm. Her mate liked to give that impression, but he was as passionate and explicit with his emotions as anyone else when he was around those who he was comfortable with. Caitlyn couldn't imagine him any other way. She loved him. Perhaps she had always loved him.

Returning her attention to Ash, she inclined her head again, and the girl wiggled a finger at her.

"Oh, *hell* no," she exclaimed. "Anytime you look at me like that, I always end up in trouble."

Caitlyn smiled again. "We are close in the future, *oui?*"

Ash strode over to the counter and hoisted herself up, a habit she'd no doubt learned from Erika. "You are, like, one of my favorite people *ever*. I mean, you and Zach have this insane bond, but I try not to get jealous. I had a hard time dealing with some things. My dad told me that when he was struggling, he went on walks with you, and it helped."

"I am certain I could care for you both exactly the same." Caitlyn felt the need to reassure the young woman, but Ash waved her hand in the air.

"I'm made of tough stuff. Though I'm not used to seeing you like this, you know. Feeling your aura like this. Zach told me what you were like when he first met you, but I never believed him."

Caitlyn did not want to know what the future held, she wanted to see where life took her, but she couldn't hide the fact that she was intrigued about who she may become.

"And what did Zach tell you? What was I like?"

Ash considered her for a moment before she sighed. "Sad. He said you smelled sad all the time. And he also said that Uncle Donnie sometimes made the sadness go to sleep. But it always came back."

Children, Caitlyn believed, were far superior to adults at understanding emotions. Walking to the counter, she hoisted herself up beside Ash. Swinging her legs, Caitlyn smiled. "Zach is right. I can sometimes find myself lost in sadness when I remember what I have lost, but then I remember what I have found. And it seems I gain more people to love as time goes by."

A flush tinged Ash's cheek, and a stray strand of hair fell across her face. Caitlyn tried to ignore the tremble in her hands as she reached out to tuck the strand behind Ash's ear. The action didn't feel at all strange, which was the very reason it gave Caitlyn an uneasy feeling.

Ash may have sensed her unease, and the girl smiled. Caitlyn imagined Ash hid behind a guise of making others feel at ease.

"I lost someone close to me in the future, and it was my fault. I got cocky and she died, and I cried and cried because I spent my whole life dreaming of being a hero just like all of you. You gave me the biggest hug and told me that a hero is an ordinary person who finds the strength to persevere and endure despite overwhelming obstacles."

Caitlyn sucked in a breath as Donnie sauntered back into the kitchen. "Why is Girl Thor quoting Christopher Reeve?" he asked casually.

Another memory flashed in Caitlyn's mind, of Sarge telling her that she could be a hero. After he'd told her that, she'd laughed at him and said she didn't know how to be a hero. Sarge had gripped her shoulder and uttered the words Ash had just said. Then the bear had smiled, saying that Caitlyn should listen to the wise words of an old man.

Caitlyn had spent all these years thinking that bear was the wisest person she knew, and the quote hadn't even been his.

She barked out a laugh that startled even herself, and, as tears rolled down her cheeks, her laughter turned to sobs as strong arms wrapped around her and she cried into her mate's shoulder.

CHAPTER
FOUR

DEREK

D erek stood outside the door of the morgue, taking a minute to summon up the courage to go inside. Caitlyn leaned against the wall, her own eyes closed, arms wrapped around her waist as she waited for him to make the first move.

Donnie and Ricky had gone to Sarge's house to check out the scene; Ricky's magic and affinity for fire were more useful there. Derek hadn't wanted any of the team to see Sarge like this. Still, considering it had been himself and Caitlyn who'd been here since the beginning—two broken souls united by this man's vision—it seemed fitting they were the ones to come see him.

None of the others had argued, the younger ones still fighting against their emotions a little too hard to help just yet. Derek knew how they felt. His emotions were a bit on edge as well, his wolf lingering very close to the surface. But he had a responsibility to remain calm now, to keep his emotions in check. Sarge had always been the calm one, and Derek was not ready to do this without him.

Neither man nor wolf wanted to leave his pregnant mate at

home, but Erika and Loki promised to stay with her, Loki working some magic to keep Ever asleep. Ash had gone with Melanie and Kenzie to settle Zach at Ricky's mom's, and Derek had witnessed the sadness in his daughter's eyes as she watched them grieve for Sarge.

As his fists clenched and unclenched, Derek recalled how he'd first come face-to-face with Sarge, back when he'd been forced to leave the garda. After a few years of not aging, his fellow officers had become suspicious. It wasn't until he'd gotten a phone call from Sarge and was invited to the station that Derek had found purpose.

Derek pushed open the door with a creak and stepped inside the small room, his nose wrinkling at the smell of shifter. When the door closed behind him, he waited for the other man to face him before he made another move.

Until he had received the phone call last night, Derek had been adamant that he was moving on, leaving Ireland, with no destination in mind. Since being forced to retire, Derek felt he needed a fresh start, somewhere no one knew him. And with rumblings that the leaders of the supernatural world were going to reveal themselves to the human world, it might be for the best.

As the man continued to ignore him, Derek's eyes were drawn to the freestanding corkboard covered in pictures. He inched closer, studying the jagged marks on the body in the photos, the sheen of white behind his eyes, and the unmistakable toothmarks on the man's collarbone.

"Tell me what you see, son."

Derek wanted to stay quiet, find out why the infamous Thomas Delaney had called him in when he'd just been about to walk out the door. However, Derek felt compelled to answer.

"The victim was obviously bitten, looks like a werewolf bite, and the gashes along his torso look like claw marks. I'd have to scent the body, but I'd say the man died in a dominance fight with another wolf.

He got sloppy, though, and left the body for anyone to find because the fight probably wasn't sanctioned."

Sarge clapped him on the shoulder and grinned. "This is why I need you on my team."

Derek eyed him with suspicion. "I've left the garda, sir. People had begun to get suspicious of me."

The other man pulled out a chair and sat down, resting his hands in his lap, and motioned for Derek to take a seat. Flipping a chair around, Derek sat and rested his arms on the back of the chair as he faced the sergeant.

"Some of the head garda, especially the commissioner, are well aware there are creatures who go bump in the night, and they want a special task force set up to deal with the deadlier criminals of Ireland. They have allowed me to form my own team, and I need you on it."

"Why me, sir? I'm nothing special."

Picking up a file, Sarge started to read out facts about his past. "Lieutenant Derek Doyle, honorably discharged by the Irish army after your entire unit was killed in a secret mission labeled Project Alpha.*" Sarge rolled his eyes." Not subtle, were they? I mean, they should have just called it* Project Wolfman *or something."*

Derek huffed out a breath as Sarge continued to read off his accomplishments, most of which felt like having dirt thrown in his face because his supervising officer hadn't considered any of that when he'd suggested Derek leave due to his predicament.

"We have a different set of rules to run with on this task force. The powers granted to us by the suits mean we have the authority to use deadly force. We police the supernatural community so that if and when humans find out we exist, we already have a proven record of being able to keep people safe."

Lifting his gaze from the file, Sarge gave him a wide grin. "What do you say, Derek? Are you in?"

Of course he'd said yes, and the rest had been history. It took a year before they were fully operational, with some bad team-mate choices made before Caitlyn came along, and the team started to take form. Sarge had used that time to teach Derek all he knew, including how to be a leader worthy of respect.

"I can go in myself, should you not feel able to see him like so."

Caitlyn's voice shattered his thoughts, and Derek glanced over at his friend. "He would never forgive me if it wasn't us who went to him. We both know he'd do the same for us. He already did."

Steeling his resolve, Derek pushed open the door to the morgue and stepped inside, holding it open for Caitlyn as she stepped inside and hissed at the smell of burnt flesh. The stench was powerful enough to make even hardened supes like him and Caitlyn want to vomit.

Anna was not only their resident witch with an affinity for magic that told cause of death, but she had also been dating Sarge, and the old bear had been quite smitten with her. Anna's eyes were swollen and red, but her face was determined.

Derek made to step to her, but the witch held up her hand.

"Derek Doyle, if you so much as try to comfort me right now, I'll break, and Tom deserves to have the best figure this out."

"Tell me what we got, Anna."

Anna cleared her throat as Caitlyn inched closer to the body. They'd been told that Sarge had burnt to death, his house engulfed in flames, but Sarge looked like he was sleeping. The only inclination that anything was wrong was the burn print on his chest.

"He was burned on the inside," Anna said. "His organs are ash, and he died quickly as his heart gave out. He'd been having some issues with his heart lately, and it's probably the only reason he didn't suffer."

Caitlyn brushed her fingers over Sarge's salt-and-pepper hair. "He never told us."

Anna gave Caitlyn a small smile. "He said he planned to, but he needed to make sure you all could cope without him. He worried about you like you were his own damn cubs."

Anna hiccupped, dashing off before Derek could stop her, leaving himself and Caitlyn alone with Sarge.

"We will find out who did this, Sarge," Derek said, "and we will have justice. I swear it."

Caitlyn leaned in and pressed her lips to Sarge's forehead. Then she straightened and nodded to Derek. Reaching for the sheet, Derek pulled it over Sarge, resting his palm on his forehead before turning and walking out of the room.

Caitlyn remained inside for a while, and then she came out and rested a hand on Derek's arm. "The person who did this, Derek, doesn't get to live."

"Agreed. It's up to us to lead the team now, Caitlyn."

"No, *mon loupe*, the team is yours. Sarge was molding you to take over when he stepped down. The team is yours. But I have and will always have your six."

Derek gave her a weak smile. "Donnie's been making you watch his shows again."

"I find David Boreanez to be quite handsome."

Derek's phone buzzed, and he pulled it from his pocket.

"D, you need to get your ass over here. This shit is weird even for me."

Derek inclined his head to Caitlyn and made his way out the back to where his car waited, telling Ricky they would be there in ten minutes.

As they drove, Derek and Caitlyn sat in silence for ages before Caitlyn spoke.

"So, Ash?"

Derek blew out a breath. "I knew the moment she said her name that she was mine. My wolf knew it before I did. She's not what I would have expected."

"Our children rarely ever are. Look at Melanie—she has put us all to shame with how easy she makes being a vampire look."

Derek smiled as he thought of the former tech girl who was now as badass as the vampire who sired her. "Does she know you speak as if she's your child? I think that would mean so much to her."

"She does, or so Donnie has told me."

"I'm not sure what to do with Ash. I mean, she's my kid, but she came from the goddamn future, Caitlyn. How crazy is that?"

"We will solve this murder and lay Sarge to rest, and then you can bond with your daughter. I have a feeling Ash is hiding more than we could possibly know."

Derek didn't have time to contemplate Caitlyn's words as they pulled into the little wooded lot where Sarge's house had once stood.

Only one side of the house was still standing; the rest was nothing but ash and ruin. Donnie and Ricky were waiting for them outside, Ricky looking tired and not at all like the man who'd been married barely twenty-four hours ago. His friend scrubbed a hand down his face and frowned.

Donnie walked over and pressed a kiss to his mate's lips before he stepped back. Ricky called Derek over and then went into what remained of the house.

Ricky waited until Derek was inside before speaking. "The fire needed to collapse a house like this has to be nuclear, D—I mean, me losing my control over my magic and blowing up a hotel kinda heat. There should be nothing left... but this wall is perfectly intact."

Motioning with his head, Ricky focused Derek's attention on the wall.

Derek Doyle is the reason I'm dead.

Written in ash, the words were still smoldering. Derek swallowed hard, his wolf snarling as the words sank into his head. Derek's stomach sank.

"D, this could be any one of hundreds of unsubs we've

arrested *or* their families. And the only person who is responsible for Sarge's is death is the firebug who killed him."

Derek wasn't convinced by Ricky's words. However, the hairs on the back of his neck stood to attention just then, and Derek darted out of the house and ran toward the woods without a second thought.

Someone was watching them from the woods, and Derek ground to a halt just before he charged headlong into the forest following his gut. He couldn't just go running into danger anymore. He had a mate and a child on the way. He was now responsible for a team. He had to be patient.

"Come out and face us, you coward!"

His words echoed through the forest. The sense he was being watched still lingered, and his wolf growled in his head. So did Derek.

Finally dismissing the feeling with a wave of his hand, Derek went back to his team. "There are eyes on us," he said. "Whoever did this wants to see our suffering. We won't give him or her the satisfaction. You hear me?"

Donnie, Caitlyn, and Ricky all nodded.

"We need to go see Detective Pierce at major crimes. This is our case to work, but he mentioned that a case he's working on might be linked to Sarge's death. Gather the team and let's go find out what they know."

Ricky had already pulled out his phone and called Melanie as they headed back to their cars. Donnie and Caitlyn left together, and Ricky slipped into Derek's passenger seat like he'd done so many times before. Derek glanced at the house one more time, guilt eating at him as if he'd been the one to burn away Sarge's life.

"I can see you turning the blame on yourself, D, and you need to cut that shit out. This team, myself included, has a fucking uncanny ability to blame ourselves for anything and everything that goes wrong. I mean, Sarge saw something in us and recruited us to this team. We gotta respect that. I'll burn the bastard alive when I get my hands on him."

Derek felt the heat of Ricky's rage—it mirrored his own—and felt the need to pour some water on it before it got out of control.

"You don't know this," Derek began, "but Sarge and I came to watch you when we were deciding on whether or not to bring you onto the team. There was a training exercise for new recruits. While everyone was all serious and stoic, you stood there grinning like an idiot."

A similar grin spread across Ricky's face. "We were told it would help the top brass decide where to place us. I wanted P.I.T.; nothing else would have satisfied me."

"You had to chase down an invisible perp. Everyone else was running around like headless chickens, and what did you do? You studied him every time he became visible, ripped an extinguisher off the wall, and emptied it on him."

"And then I cuffed him and handed him off to the training officer."

Eyes on the road, Derek huffed. "Sarge looked at me and said, 'We need him.' I worried you were reckless, having read your file, and I didn't want someone on the team who may endanger it."

"I didn't know that," Ricky replied, a hint of disappointment in his voice.

"Sarge slapped me on the back and told me that was why he was making you my partner. That I could learn to be a little reckless, and you needed to learn how to be serious. He said we would complement each other, and since you sauntered into the room on Day One, after chasing a goblin dressed as a homeless man, I've never been more grateful that Sarge forced us together."

"I asked him once," Ricky said, a sadness in his tone, "why he made us partners, and he told me that you had trust issues and needed to learn to trust someone. He asked me to look out for you."

It was Derek's turn to allow his lips to curve into a small smile. "He wasn't wrong, though, was he?"

"Nope. He rarely was."

They lapsed into silence for the remainder of the journey. Pulling into the station on Angelsea Street, they found the entire —and Ash—waiting for them.

Derek got out of the car and strode over to where the team waited, the mood somber as they waited for Derek and Ricky to catch up with them. Derek glanced around at his team and knew, without a shadow of a doubt, that they would get their killer.

"I know we're all feeling the loss. Sarge was one of the greatest men we all knew. But he formed this team knowing we were the best there was, and we owe it to him to put aside our feelings and give him peace. If any of you can't do that, then let me know now. No one will think less of you."

Kenzie stepped forward. "I didn't know Sarge as well as the rest of you, but he was kind to me and made me feel like I belonged here. My scythe is yours."

Derek nodded his thanks to the blood-kissed girl, and she stepped back.

"Sarge wouldn't want us to let his killer slip by because we're sad. We do this as a family," Donnie growled. Caitlyn gently ran her hand up and down his shoulder.

Melanie and Ricky nodded in agreement as Derek turned to face his daughter. He opened his mouth to ask her to go home, to look after her mother even though Ever was being looked after by the most bloodthirsty creatures Derek knew. His mate was in safe hands.

His daughter glared at him with a look he was famous for giving and folded her arms across her chest. "Before you go all dad on me," Ash growled, her eyes flashing a little as she held

Derek's gaze without looking away, "I know I didn't know Sarge personally, but you all spoke so highly of him that I feel like I knew him. I have skills, some that you wouldn't believe until you see them. I can be an asset."

Derek's wolf was amused at his daughter's spunk, but the newly developed parent in him didn't want his daughter anywhere near danger.

"C'mon Dad, don't send me home."

Derek shook his head. "This is a police matter, Ash, and no matter how much I'd like to keep you close, the guards won't let a teenager get involved just because we say so."

Ash grinned, her entire face coming alive with mischief. "You see, Dad, I'm Ever Chace's daughter, too. I finished school at fifteen, and despite your and her reservations, I followed in my father's and my aunts' and uncles' footsteps." Reaching into her back pocket, Ash pulled out and flashed a badge at her father. "Agent Ashlyn Doyle of the Paranormal Investigations Team, at your service."

Derek's breath hitched, and his jaw almost hit the floor.

Ash shrugged her shoulders. "It's the family business, Dad. Even though my partner isn't here to help me, I'm sure I can be of use. I've learned from the best."

"Who's your partner?" Ricky asked, the hopeful gleam in his eyes making Derek smile a little.

Ash turned to him and winked. "I'm not the only one who went into the family business."

Derek Doyle had been within reach; he could have burned him where he stood and ended this century-long grudge he'd held against the wolf. While his little pack of vampires watched, he could have toyed with Doyle, prolonging the torture until Doyle begged him for mercy.

And he wanted him to beg.

The wolf had called him a coward, and if it weren't for direct orders from his leader, Derek would be writhing in pain right now. Or even better, dead.

Striding from the forest, the murderer felt his phone vibrate and answered it.

"Boss."

"How is Derek?"

"Not as broken as I want him to be."

The voice on the other end chuckled. "Soon, my boy, soon."

He smiled. "When do you arrive in Cork?"

"Tomorrow night. Come meet us on the tarmac."

"I'll see you then, boss."

"You will. I'm looking forward to seeing what destruction you have caused in our Derek's life."

The phone line disconnected, and the murderer smiled before getting into his car and driving toward the city he couldn't wait to burn to the ground.

CHAPTER FIVE

MELANIE

M elanie couldn't stop her leg from bouncing up and down as they waited for Detective Pierce to finish up his meeting and come to speak with them. Her leg kept on bouncing until Ricky put his hand on her knee to stop it from moving.

"Sorry," she muttered to her new husband, giving him a small smile that he returned. His handsome face nearly caught her breath as she reached over and patted his cheek.

"No need for apologies, babe. This isn't easy for any of us."

No, this wasn't easy for anyone in this room, and Melanie wondered if any would ever be the same again once it was over. Sarge had been the glue that bound them all together, and now... Now, she felt as if they were barely holding on.

When Melanie thought of Sarge, she was reminded of the life she'd almost had, the one behind bars for a crime she didn't commit. Sarge had given her an out. She'd never regretted saying yes to his offer to come work for him, even though she'd been the only human on a supe squad, even though it got her kidnapped and killed and reborn as a vampire. She couldn't regret it one bit; she was happier than she possibly could have imagined.

Turning her head, she looked into eyes of emerald green. "I love you."

A mischievous smile toyed on his lips. "I know," Ricky teased as he squeezed her knee. "I plan on showing you how much I love you, *wife*, once we get a second alone."

If Melanie had been able to blush, she would have at the promise in his words. Instead, she ducked her head until she regained her composure. Once calm again, Melanie lifted her head and looked around at the team. She was about to ask if anyone wanted a coffee when Detective Pierce came into the room, and everyone went alert.

Small in stature, Pierce had dark hair, dark skin, and a warm smile that put Melanie at ease. He ran his fingers through his dark, unruly hair before turning to Derek, shaking hands, and offering his condolences once again. He then faced the team, eying Ash with silent suspicion, and picked up a remote. With the press of a button, the wall in front of Melanie became awash with photos of corpses and burnt houses.

"We've been hunting an arsonist for weeks now who leaves no evidence of himself at the scene. All the victims were couples, killed at night, woken from their sleep, though our ME confirmed they were all still alive when they were burned. All were burned from the inside out."

"How did this end up with Major Crimes and not P.I.T.?" Derek asked, folding his arms across his broad chest.

Pierce didn't even blink at the steely gaze from the werewolf. "I called Sarge in about two weeks ago and asked for your help, but he said you were dealing with a drug case and had people undercover, so he came by himself and offered his thoughts. It might be why the unsub targeted him."

Ash was studying the board intently, and that made Melanie sit up and pay attention. Something about the names on the board struck a chord with Melanie, and it was starting to annoy her.

Getting to her feet, Melanie went to stand by Ash. The young woman nodded at her as Melanie tuned out the noise around her and stared at the board. The most recent couple had been tied to a chair, scorch marks all around the floor circling them, and oh, the fear in their faces.

"All the victims were human, all killed in various locations around the city. We're used to dealing with arsonists of the human variety, but this is above what we can handle. I'll hand over everything we have to you, but we can help if you need us."

"What did Sarge say?" Derek asked with a rough edge to his voice.

"He said that the best team in Ireland to catch the killer was his team. He was planning on calling you all in after the wedding. Congratulations," he added, turning to Ricky.

Melanie was too busy staring at the screen to pay any attention, though she did smirk when she heard Ricky say, "Thanks, I married up."

Leaning in closer to Melanie, Ash said, "Say what you see. Try and make sense of it." Then she stepped back as Ricky came up to stand beside his bride.

Melanie asked for a list of the victims, and Detective Pierce obliged. Pieces clicked into place as Melanie read the names of the victims out loud.

"First couple: Evan Cantwell and Dawn Day..." Grabbing a marker, she circled their initials, then continued reading. "Martin Nash and Regina Mason, and Charles Harrington and Diane O'Connor." She turned to the group. "Do you spot what I do?"

The team stared blankly, so Melanie circled the initials of the other couples and then pointed at the names. "I don't think these were random. I think this has been about us from the beginning."

"Tell us what you see, Lanie," Ricky coaxed. He could tell she was hesitating, hoping that her hunch was wrong.

"Evan Cantwell and Dawn Day. If you cut out the names and leave the initials, you get E.C. and D.D.—Ever Chace and Derek Doyle."

Donnie stepped up, then pointed to the names Charles Harrington and Diane O'Connor. "Caitlyn Hardi and Donald O'Carroll."

Melanie nodded, tapping the pen at the last names. "Martin Nash and Regina Mason are Melanie Newton and Ricky Moore. The killer is targeting substitutes for us and killing them to taunt us."

Pierce shook his head as if he couldn't believe he hadn't seen it before. "The case is P.I.T.'s. Major Crimes will step back."

He shared a few words with Derek before leaving to arrange the transfer of the files to their precinct. Kenzie walked up to Melanie and nudged her friend in the shoulder. "I suppose there's one good thing about being single."

Melanie barked out a laugh, and it eased the tension in the room a little. Then she heard Ricky hiss out a breath between clenched teeth that dropped to a rumble in his chest, and she spun, instantly alert.

"There's someone in the room watching us," Ricky said.

Everyone braced for an attack except for Ash. Melanie watched as the girl stalked the room and then snapped her arm out, grabbing at what looked like thin air. Suddenly a figure blinked into view firmly within Ash's grasp.

Loki's daughter, the goddess Hel, coughed and tried to pry Ash's fingers from her throat.

Melanie held up her hands and walked toward Ash. "Hey Ash," she said gently, "it's all good. I know her—she's kind of a friend... *and* the reason why Ricky is alive right now."

"I could squeeze the life out of you right now and save myself a lot of grief," Ash growled, ignoring Melanie.

"C'mon Ash, let her go. Whatever she did to you in the future, she hasn't done it yet. She's kind of a friend, so please let her go."

Ash yanked back her hand, but Hel—or Helen as she liked to be called now—didn't so much as blink at Ash's reaction. Instead, she licked her lips and grinned.

"Hello, gorgeous."

Ash snarled, her wolf rising in her eyes unbidden before she snapped her head around and stalked to the other end of the room, as far away from the death goddess as possible.

Dressed in pink leggings with unicorns and a bright yellow T-shirt, Loki's daughter waved at Melanie before she winked at Ash. Thunder rumbled in the night as Ash growled, and Melanie hurried to defuse the situation.

"Not that I'm not happy to see you," she said with a smile, "but we're kinda in the middle of something."

"That's why I came. So much death… I was drawn here." Helen's eyes wandered around the room until they landed on Caitlyn, and then she licked her lips. "Oh, death is in her blood. I like her."

"Well, she is happily mated and my sire, so please stay away from her."

"You guys are no fun," Helen said with a pout. "I'm going to go annoy my dad a little. Laters!"

She disappeared, and Ash let loose a shuddering breath. Derek asked if she was okay, and Ash said she was fine. Melanie swallowed her lie and cringed a little at how bad it tasted. Ash glared at her in warning, but there was no need. Melanie thought it best to keep Ash's secrets to herself.

"Getting back on track," Derek said, "we now know that the arsonist has a grudge against us. There's a long list of suspects, but I can't recall any with an affinity for fire. We need to go back and look at Sarge's notes to see if he had any leads."

"D, I need to go make sure Zach and my mom are safe. Ward

the house against intruders." The worry in his voice was one Derek understood all too well now as he glanced at his own daughter.

"Do what you have to do," he said. "We'll regroup at Caitlyn's. Her place is the most secure. I'll get Ever and bring her over."

Ricky gave Melanie a quick kiss and muttered for her to be careful before he ducked from the room. Derek guided Ash out of the room, leaving Melanie alone with Kenzie, Caitlyn, and Donnie.

"Does anyone else feel like life just got batshit crazy right now?" Kenzie mused as they began to make their way out the door.

"I think our lives have always been batshit crazy, Kenz. This is just extra crazy."

When they were all inside the car, Melanie swallowed hard and exhaled. She may be nearly indestructible now, but after the crash where she almost lost Ricky, Melanie felt uneasy whenever she got into a car. She knew it was an irrational fear, but hey, the love of her life had almost died in a car wreck; she could be a little skittish if she wanted.

On the drive back to Caitlyn and Donnie's home, the one where Melanie had learned all about being a vampire, Melanie sensed an unease. Kenzie dozed in the seat beside her, her jacket pulled over her face as her breathing deepened, so Melanie turned to the pair in front.

"Hey, what's up?" she asked quietly.

"I will not say nothing, little vampire, and lie to you," Caitlyn replied, "however, now is not the time for such discussions."

Melanie leaned forward and rested her head against Donnie's seat. "I need a distraction. Humor me."

Caitlyn chuckled softly as Donnie raised his brows. "It's up to you, Cait."

"Dudes! Now you *have* to tell me."

Caitlyn moistened her lip, and if Melanie's heart could beat, it would have been thundering in her chest.

Caitlyn turned around in her seat to face Melanie. "When I finally saw sense and allowed myself to be with Donnie, we decided that as our—how would you say it?"

"Well," Donnie said, "as Caitlyn's only sired vampire apart from her mate, we decided that, should anything happen to us, we wanted to leave you and Kenzie everything in our wills."

Melanie sat back. "Um, that's not something we need to talk about right now. And since when did vampires need wills?"

Caitlyn sighed and glanced at Donnie, who shrugged.

"Little sister, just listen to us for a second. It's important after everything that's happened. We needed to make sure you, Kenzie, and even Ricky and Zach were looked after. Caitlyn has amassed a tidy sum over the years, and there are plenty who would try to lay claim to it. As the oldest of Caitlyn's line, if we are gone, you will become the head of the line."

"Well, you guys aren't going anywhere, so this is not a conversation that needs to happen." Melanie pulled her headphones out of her pocket as she slumped back in her seat and tried to ignore her sort-of parents. She didn't press Play on the music but knew they'd understand the gesture. She did not want to have this conversation with them right now.

"I don't want to sell the house," Caitlyn said suddenly.

Donnie smiled over at his mate. "I know."

"Of course you do," Caitlyn said dryly as Donnie chuckled. "I've decided that Cain cannot spoil what I—what we—built in that house. We can redecorate our wing like we'd planned to do with the warehouse. But as Melanie won't be living with us anymore, we do not need a massive warehouse."

Yanking the buds from her ears, Melanie leaned forward. "Um, why wouldn't I be living with you guys? Are you kicking me out?"

"I assumed you would be moving in with your husband, Melanie."

Melanie's mouth hung open at Caitlyn's words. Well shit... she *would* be moving in with Ricky and Zach, but she didn't want to leave Caitlyn and Donnie and even Kenzie. Their house was the first place where she'd felt truly at home, and she and Ricky hadn't even thought about living arrangements, let alone spoken about them.

She was still reeling when they arrived at the house and found Ricky leaned against the hood of his car, waiting for them. Getting out of the car, Melanie waited until Caitlyn and Donnie had gone inside before joining Ricky. Kenzie was still asleep in the backseat.

Reaching for her, Ricky placed both hands on the sides of her face. "What's wrong, babe?"

"I think I've just been evicted from my home."

Ricky chuckled and ran his thumb across her bottom lip. "Considering how embarrassed you got when Cait and Donnie caught us making out in alleyways, I assumed you'd prefer we had a place of our own. Less chance of us being overheard when you're moaning my name."

Melanie punched him in the shoulder, but her sexy warlock/kinda-vampire only grinned. "Arrogant much?"

Ricky leaned in close, and Melanie suppressed a shudder as he tugged gently on her ear with his teeth. "Confident, but arrogantly so."

Melanie laughed and then covered her mouth. She felt as if she shouldn't be laughing when their lives were in danger, and Sarge was dead in the morgue.

"It's okay to laugh, Lanie. Sarge wanted us to be happy. And in regards to our living arrangements, the cottage is far too small for three of us and not very vampire friendly. I spoke to Caitlyn about what a house would need to protect you during the day, and we came to an agreement."

"What are you up to, mister?"

Grabbing her hand, Ricky all but dragged her 'round the side of Caitlyn's home and pointed to the field next to it. Melanie's gaze narrowed as Ricky grinned.

"Caitlyn has agreed to sell me the land next to her house so we can build our own house together. We'll be far enough away for privacy and close enough that if we need a babysitter, Caitlyn is right here."

"When did you plan all this?"

"When I realized I was in love with you and wanted only to make you happy. When I went and asked your sire for your hand in marriage and she said that if you said yes, that would be enough of a blessing."

Wrapping her arms around his neck, Melanie dragged him down for a claiming kiss that had her entire body ablaze. When Ricky swept his tongue under one of her fangs, nicking the flesh, Melanie tasted blood and groaned.

Ricky's hands wandered down to her hips, holding her firmly against him, and Melanie could feel him smile against her mouth.

"Dude, stop manhandling my sister and get your asses in here."

Ricky dragged his lips away from Melanie's, grinning wickedly when she chased after them—a grin that did all kinds of things to her insides.

"I've barely been able to consummate my marriage, bro," Ricky yelled over his shoulder. "Give me a break."

"They have pills for that, mate, if you're having problems," Donnie retorted, causing Melanie to duck her head and groan.

Ricky laughed and flipped him off as Melanie asked, "Is this what it's gonna be like, living next door to them?"

"Probably... are you okay with that?"

"I can't wait."

They walked back to the house hand in hand, slipping inside

and into the living room. Melanie heard Caitlyn humming along to a song on the radio as Donnie put the kettle on in the kitchen. As Ricky dragged her down into his lap, she rested her head on his shoulder and closed her eyes.

"I can't believe he's really gone," Ricky said suddenly as Melanie toyed with the ends of his hair. "He was more of a father to me than my old man," he added softly, tightening his grip on her hip.

"He gave me my shot. Me and Derek and Donnie and Caitlyn. He sent them after me when I went on a downward spiral and again when I almost ruined my life being an idiot on drugs."

"Ricky."

"I know how to be a dad because of him," Ricky continued as if he hadn't heard her say his name. Melanie didn't need him to hear her; she just had to listen.

"The first time I saw you, it was because of Sarge. He'd hauled me in to reprimand me for getting drunk and being late to work again. He handed me my ass and then told me to go and check if the newest recruit was still in the hall. I walked outside, and you looked up at me with those green eyes hidden under those sexy-as-sin glasses, and I was a goner."

"As if he knew we'd end up together."

Caitlyn strode into the room with Donnie, carrying a tray of coffee. "It was Sarge who sent me to Dublin, told me that Temple Bar was full of predators eager to take advantage of humans. I was on a case, but I kept being lured back to Temple Bar."

"I always wondered if the man could see into the future," Donnie said with a grin. "He seemed to know everything."

"He was a regular matchmaker, was our Sarge," Ricky said as he smiled at Melanie.

Donnie lifted his mug. "Not a proper drink like you deserve, old man, but here's to you."

Ricky tipped his head. "To Sarge."

They sipped their coffee, lost in thought and memory, grateful for the man who'd brought them all together.

"So, are you ready to be our neighbors?" Melanie asked after some time.

Donnie grinned.

CHAPTER SIX

EVER

E ver walked barefoot through familiar halls, wind whipping around her, lifting the ends of her white gown. She shivered against the chill, her fingers grazing the crumbling pillars and broken tiles as she passed. The ground underneath her feet trembled as lightning flashed against a rainless sky.

Instinct drove her, and she watched in amazement as a memory flickered of Thor chasing her through these very hallways on one of her visits. There was laughter and joy as Frigg and Odin stood side by side, love shining in their eyes.

The man who had killed her six times over was not in this memory, and Ever found it hard to reconcile this man with her father of now. Odin was a broken man about to shatter the world because he'd lost the woman he loved.

Ever wanted to be repulsed by his need, but she found herself feeling pity for him. She knew what it was like to love with an all-consuming madness.

"Daughter, I need not your pity!"

Her father's voice boomed throughout the palace, and Ever kept her *feet moving until she arrived at the throne room and faced her father. Odin did not spare her a glance as she came into view; in fact, he jerked his head to peer out the window.*

"It is hard not to pity you, Odin, for you seem lonely and lost, a thing of great pity."

Lightning ripped through the blue skies outside, the only indication that Ever's words had affected him. He turned slowly to face her, ignoring the flutter of wings as Huginn and Muginn flew in to perch on Odin's shoulders, their beady eyes studying Ever as if she were prey.

"You turned my son against me."

"That was a feat you managed all on your own, Father. Thor loved the Midgardians with every beat of his heart, and you threatened to rid them from the world by ushering in Ragnarök. You were not content to let fate take care of itself; you had to force its hand."

Odin stroked his ice-white beard as he regarded her. "I wish this were real so I could rid the world of you once and for all."

"You forget I have amassed a pack, Father. They are more than allies; they are family. They do not aid me out of fear but love and loyalty. Can you say that?"

"I will enjoy watching your face as I eviscerate them one by one," Odin sneered. "I will leave that mongrel Úlfheðinn for the very end and rip out his heart in front of you." Ever shook her head. "I knew very little of Frigg, but she was kind and caring, and she would despise you for what you have done. Do not dishonor her name like this, Father. Stop this foolish war and let Loki unbind the ties of this oath. Let me have Valhalla and Midgard."

"I made a mistake the night I lay with your mother. Look at the weakling we created."

Ever was not fazed by his words; she was spurred on by them. "Many have called me weak, Odin, and I have proven them all wrong. I shall do the same with you."

"The path you walk on, Ever, will see you lose. Let me show you."

Odin waved his hand, and a scene of battle flared to life in front of her. Ever clasped a hand over her mouth as Erika rode into battle, sword held high, astride a white stallion with wings leading her on her charge. Her battle cry was cut short, however, as Tyr plunged his sword into her chest, bellowing mournfully as she tumbled from her horse.

There was so much blood and death that Ever did not know where to look. Everywhere she turned, she saw another life lost. She heard her name and turned to see Derek racing toward her, fighting against Odin's soldiers to reach her. Then, Odin himself stepped into his path, and she knew Derek didn't stand a chance against the father of all.

Odin held Derek off the ground as his wolf looked at her, screamed that he loved her, but the words were cut off by the unmistakable sound of bones cracking as Odin snapped Derek's neck and tossed him aside as if he were an inconvenience.

Then her father turned on her and lunged with his staff.

The vision disappeared as Odin stood and came down from his dais, his footsteps like thunder as he came nearer. "That is how you all end, dearest Ever. Bend the knee, and, perhaps, after a century of confinement, I will decide not to kill you."

"I challenge the fates. Here I stand, declaring that I will, until my last breath, strive to end your reign of terror. You have time, Odin, to redeem yourself."

"Monsters cannot be redeemed, child."

Ever smiled at her father. "You will always be a monster. You have done too much; there is no turning back from it. But what type of monster you continue to be is entirely up to you."

Odin reached for her, gripping her around the neck and lifting her off the ground with a sneer as darkness engulfed her.

Ever shot up in bed, gulped in a breath, and instantly reached for her stomach. Relief washed over her as the baby kicked as if to comfort her.

"Are you all right?"

Ever lifted her chin and looked to the corner of the room

where Loki sat. He appeared to be the epitome of calm, reclined in the chair with his hands folded in his lap. His eyes were a galaxy of stars the reminded Ever of the night sky in Valhalla.

"I dream-walked with my father. Even in my dreams, he kills me."

"Well, at least he is consistent."

Ever shuffled back to lean against the headboard, the weight in her chest heavy when she remembered Tom was gone.

"I am sorry for your loss, Ever. I knew him not at all, but everyone speaks of him with such warmth that I know he was a good man."

"He was the best, Loki. I wish you could have known him."

Loki got to his feet and tilted his head to the side. "Your wolf is here. As is your child."

Her child. There was an underlying tone in Loki's words, and Ever pinned him with her stare. "Are you miffed because she doesn't seem to like you?"

"I'm miffed because she seems to know more about my children than I do."

"Then ask her. She may just tell you."

Derek popped his head around the door as Loki vanished, leaving her alone with her mate. He came to stand by her bed, sitting down and pausing before he rested his palm on her stomach.

"That kid is as amazing as you are. Smart, beautiful, fierce. We did good, Ever."

Not wanting to dredge up the fact that a mere two days ago Ever was convinced she couldn't be a mother, she smiled and asked Derek about her godfather's death.

"We think the arsonist is targeting the team. His other victims were substitutes for us all, and he left a message on Sarge's wall that I was the reason he was dead."

Despair ran through her as she reached out and put her hand

over Derek's. "The only person responsible for this is the person who killed Tom."

Derek gave her a small smile. "That's what Ricky said."

"Ricky's a smart guy."

Derek chuckled softly and then sighed. "We need to start telling people that Tom has passed. You need to go and tell Samhain."

"I guess I do. Not sure how to explain all this," she said, waving a hand over her belly, "but Samhain should hear it from me."

"We can stop by on the way to Caitlyn's, if you like."

Ever nodded, moving to get out of bed. She threw on a fluffy cardigan, then wrapped it around her before waddling over to the door. When she turned, she saw Derek grinning at her.

"What?" she asked.

"You're sexy when you waddle."

Ever laughed. "I'd hit you, but I don't think I can manage it without hurting myself."

"Part of me wants to lock you indoors until she's born so nothing can happen to either of you. The other part wants me to keep you by my side so I can protect you, especially with everything going on."

"I know, and I love you for it. But neither of us is going to sit inside this house when Tom's killer is out there. Let's go and tell my parents. Hopefully, the shock of this doesn't give them a heart attack."

Ever went downstairs to find Ash looking out the window as rain pelted the ground, and thunder rumbled in the distance. Watching Ash staring out the window reminded her of stormy days on the shores of Valhalla, when Thor used to stand out in the rain even during the worst storms.

Ash caught her watching and smiled coyly back at her.

"Thor used to do that. Stand still whenever there was natural thunder."

"It calls to me, even from so far away. I find myself longing for it. It's strange to know that he used to feel the same. I wish I had known him."

Ever slipped her feet into her shoes. "One day, when we're all feasting with our loved ones in the part of Valhalla where our greatest warriors go, Thor will greet you, and you will know he knew you were worthy before I even knew you existed."

"Are you going to tell Samhain and Conrad about Tom and, well, me?"

"I have to."

"Listen, I'll flash to Caitlyn's. I'm not sure they would understand mini-me in there *and* future me walking around the place. Too many shocks and all that."

Ever leaned against the doorframe. "I'm not ashamed of you, Ash. If you want to come, you can."

The girl blinked in surprise as if she'd expected to be rejected. After a minute, she shook her head. "Nah, I think I'll go make Uncle Donnie uncomfortable for a while. He doesn't like it when I picture him naked in my head."

Ever laughed as Derek strode into the room. "And neither does your father. Do we need to have a talk about boys?"

"Donnie's not a boy. He's all man."

Derek's face paled as Ash grinned and flashed from the room. He glanced at Ever, and she saw absolute love in his gaze.

"I'm not sure how to respond to the fact that she has a crush on Donnie."

Ever patted his cheek as she walked toward the front door. "You have sixteen years to get used to it."

The drive to Ever's childhood home didn't take too long. The Chace estate was as big as Ever remembered it, and as Derek pulled up in front of the house, Ever released a breath. She wasn't quite ready to reveal all her secrets to the people who'd raised her. Samhain hadn't been as welcoming to Derek, and Ever had avoided Conrad's calls for months because the truth of who she was, the look of disappointment that Samhain had shown her, was not one she wanted from her adopted father.

Before she had time to think, Derek had opened the car door and held out his arm to her. She took it without hesitation as her muscles groaned, and she sucked in a breath.

"I swear since I admitted I was pregnant, this kid has grown ten feet."

Derek chuckled. "Ash is quite tall, and you are a little vertically challenged."

"Shut up and knock on the door."

Derek rapped his fingers on the door as Ever bit her lip, glancing at her watch. "Derek, it's kinda late. We can come back tomorrow."

The front door opened, and Conrad blinked in surprise as he spied her. To let Ever recover, Derek, bless him, held out his hand to Conrad.

"Mr. Chace, my name is Derek Doyle, Ever's mate. It's nice to finally meet you."

"And you, too, Derek. My daughter has kept you away for so long I worried she was ashamed of us."

"It's not like that, Dad. You know how Samhain is."

"I do. I love her, but she does not speak for me. Come inside; it's cold out there."

Conrad held open the door, stepping back so Ever and Derek could follow him in. At Ever's profile, his brows quirked as he regarded her stomach.

"That is *quite* a surprise."

Derek chuckled softly. "You have no idea."

He and Ever shared a smile as Conrad ushered them into the good sitting room reserved for guests. Samhain was already there, reading a book, which she closed upon their arrival.

"It's a little late for guests, Ever."

"I hadn't realized I'd been demoted to a guest in this house.

You have my apologies," Ever remarked with a dry tone. Ash chose that moment to kick her, and Ever winced, a hand falling to her stomach.

Samhain's gaze followed her daughter's hand, and she huffed out her breath. "There'll be no getting rid of the wolf now."

"I'm rather fond of him, Samhain. I'd prefer to keep him."

Derek cleared his throat, and Ever silently begged him to be the one to say the words. He was used to explaining death to victims' families. She was just used to death.

"Mr. and Mrs. Chace, this is an official call, so please take a seat."

Perhaps it was Derek's tone, but Conrad did as he was instructed, and Ever noticed that he chose not to sit beside his wife. When they looked suitably comfortable, Derek sat down across from them.

"I'm sorry to be the one to tell you that Thomas Delaney was murdered last night at his home. He died quickly if that is any consolation. I loved Sarge like a father, and I will not stop until his killer is brought to justice.

Samhain was quiet for a moment before she stood and left the room. Ever heard her door upstairs close, and she frowned.

Rising to his feet, Conrad shook Derek's hand. "Thank you for telling us. You will inform us of the arrangements once they are set?"

"I will."

Conrad walked toward Ever, and her heart pounded in her chest.

"You and I will speak next week. We have a lot to catch up on." Glancing down at her rounded belly, Conrad flashed her a grin. "I'm very much looking forward to spoiling my grandchild."

"I'm sure she will love that."

Smiling, Conrad gazed at Derek before he glanced downward to show it was not in aggression. "Daughters are a blessing," he said. "Treasure her."

"I intend to."

They left the house then and made their way down the road a short distance to where Caitlyn resided. A clap of thunder rumbled in the air, and as they both leaned forward to check the sky for clouds, they were blasted by another rumble of thunder so loud it rattled the car. Derek increased his speed, barely grinding to a halt in Caitlyn's drive to see Ash squaring off against Erika, a bloody Loki on the ground behind her.

Ash swung her hammer toward Erika, who managed to duck just as the weapon sailed over her head. Erika twirled her daggers in her hands and blocked Ash's next blow.

Before either could strike again, Derek was out of the car. Pouring every ounce of power into his voice, he bellowed, "Ashlyn Kyria Doyle, *stop!*"

Ash froze at the sound of his voice, as did Erika. Ever's best friend met her eyes and gritted her teeth. Ever slowly got out of the car as Derek stormed over and held out his hand to help Loki off the ground. The god of mischief accepted his hand, and when he was upright once again, dusted the dirt off his tailored suit pants.

Ash shook off Derek's command. "I almost had her, Dad," she said, her tone sharp.

"Boyband, rein in your brat, or I will."

Derek glowered at Erika, who went to check on Loki. Turning to his daughter, he could see the wolf in her eyes. "Control her," he growled.

Ever was stunned as she watched Ash's eyes illuminate before they returned to their unusual shade of amber.

"I know how to control my fucking wolf, Dad."

"Then act like it," Derek snapped. "Whatever the hell grudge you have with Loki, you bench it while we try and deal with everything else going on. You listening to me?"

"It's very hard not to when you're wailing like a banshee."

Derek's nostrils flared, and he took a step toward Ash. Ever realized Derek's grief was finally slipping through in the form of anger, and she needed to step in before he said something he'd regret.

"Ash," Ever said quickly, "you need to walk it off or scream it out, but whatever you do, you walk away. Derek, my ankles are swollen, and I'm starving. Please, help me in the house. Take a step back before you say or do something you'll regret."

Instead of coming toward her, Derek growled and stalked off to the side of the house as Donnie came forward and held out his arm. "M'lady."

Taking his elbow, Ever sighed. "Thank you."

Donnie escorted her into the house, followed by Loki and Erika, as father and daughter stormed off in different directions.

"Well, she certainly inherited Thor's temper," Ever muttered. "Of that, I am sure."

Donnie helped her into a seat as Erika flopped down next to her. "And she definitely went through the Erika Sands school of how to kick ass. I haven't been that winded in ages."

"Does anyone know what set her off?" Ever glanced at Loki, and her adopted brother simply shrugged.

"I asked her why she tried to kill my daughter today and why she disliked me. I pushed a little hard, and she punched me. Her fist is almost as hard as her hammer. Erika was merely protecting my honor, and Ashlyn snapped. We were lucky we were outside when this happened, or we may have broken Lady Caitlyn's house."

"That's okay, we were planning on knocking down that wall anyway," Donnie said with a grin.

When Ever looked toward the door, Donnie patted her shoulder. "Cait's got her. She's pretty good with stubborn supernaturals. She's known Derek long enough."

Ever returned his smile, but she was determined to find out why Ash hated Loki so much when he'd always been one of Ever's favorite people.

Her daughter was hiding things, and Ever would find out exactly what.

CHAPTER SEVEN

DEREK

Derek prided himself on having ironclad control over his wolf.

Not since he was a pup had he slipped the leash on his anger, his wolf's main fuel. The past year had tested his control, though, and his mating with Ever had loosened the grip. And now, losing Sarge and clashing with a teenage daughter who seemed to have inherited his stubbornness was messing with his head.

He had taken an aggressive step toward his daughter, and the shame coursed through his body. His wolf, however, was lurking just under his skin, growling, urging Derek to spin on his heels and go and make Ash see who the alpha really was.

When he'd called her name, the goddamn power in his tone was something he'd hoped he would never feel. Derek had been a lone wolf for a reason; he hadn't wanted the power that came with being an alpha. Perhaps he'd always known he was an alpha, but he'd never felt the raw power of it, always happy to follow Sarge's lead.

"The alpha wolf with a collection of non-wolves in his pack."

Ash had spoken those words to them when she'd crashed into their lives, and now that everyone had looked to him to fill Sarge's shoes, Derek feared he would never be able to take even one step in them.

"I wouldn't have hurt her."

Derek didn't even glance over his shoulder at the voice. "I know."

"You wouldn't have hurt her either, Boyband."

Huffing out a breath, Derek inclined his body slightly as the petite Valkyrie came to stand beside him. His relationship with Erika was tenuous at the best of times; however, her loyalty to Ever was never in question. This warrior would die protecting her best friend and her friend's child.

"How do you know that?" The question sprang from his lips before he could halt them.

Erika glanced up at him with her whiskey-colored eyes. "Well, you've wanted to kill me for months now and haven't done it. I mean, if you can stop yourself from harming the woman who's killed you more times in the last few centuries than anyone or anything else, then I'd say you're solid, Boyband."

Derek's lips twitched as he raised a brow. "What you did, you did out of duty. I never faulted you for that, Erika. I never understood why you hated me so much, but I think I understand now."

With a snort, Erika glanced away, and Derek felt she did not want to meet his gaze. "Care to enlighten me, O Wise Wolf?"

Derek lowered himself to the ground and stretched out his legs. He waited until Erika did the same, hugging her knees to her chest as she looked out over the city.

"You thought you were in love with Ever, and you hated that she was in love with me, or past me. You've had to kill the person that your sister in all but blood loved, over and over again. And despite your early reservations, you'd rather not kill me this time."

"Didn't know you had a degree in psychology all these years, Boyband."

Derek ignored her flippant remark and continued. "You like being part of this team, but you try to distance yourself because if we lose, you don't want to face them if you have to kill me this last time. You love Loki and fear losing him, so now you understand what it might have been like for Ever to lose me all those times."

"Can't I just go back to pretending to hate you? All this touchy-feely crap is making me uncomfortable."

Derek barked out a laugh, startling Erika as she tilted her head to look at him. The knot in his chest loosened a little as he smiled at her.

"I'm glad Ever has you. And Ash."

His smile slipped as thoughts of his daughter came to the forefront of his mind again. He wasn't sure he could do this right now, lead the team and try to remember that Ash had come from the future and had sixteen years to deal with Derek.

When would he be the type of dad who dressed up as a Disney princess for his kid?

"Listen, Boyband. You're gonna make mistakes. No one is perfect. But Ash looks like she was loved and safe. She has fire because she was allowed to be independent as she grew. Take it from someone who is absolutely terrified of meeting her father —especially now, when I see how Ricky looks at Zach, how Caitlyn looks at Melanie, and how you look at that bump... and Ash herself."

Erika got to her feet. "If I meet him and he looks at me like Odin looks at Ever, having seen how you guys look at family, I think it would break me. I've always craved a family of my own, and I'm not sure I can handle that kind of rejection."

For the first time, as if seeing through new eyes, Derek held a newfound respect for the warrior. She may drive Derek up the walls, but Erika was as much a part of the team, the family, as any of them. Maybe she needed to hear him say it to believe it herself.

Derek shoved himself off the ground and faced Erika. "If you meet your father and he rejects you, then *he's* the fool." Pointing to the house. "Everyone inside that house is my family—yours, too, if you'll have them. We always say that family isn't always about blood, and that's our fucking bond. We are your family, Erika, even if you are the bratty little sister that gives me gray hairs."

Erika stood staring at him, swallowing hard before flipping her braid off her shoulder. "If you tell anyone we've been having a warm and fuzzy chat, I'll shave your hair in such a way that when you turn into a wolf, you'll have bald patches of fur."

Derek chuckled as Erika took a few steps toward the house and then paused, looking up at the night sky before casting a glance at him over her shoulder. "I always wanted a brother to torment."

And then she flashed from sight as Derek rolled his eyes, the tension between him and Erika hopefully wiped away in one short conversation. He made to stride back to the house, when blinding pain suddenly shot through his forehead. Derek gripped the side of his head, a growl slipping through gritted teeth as the pain intensified and dropped him to his knees.

Shutting down the mating bond to protect Ever, Derek flung a scream toward Donnie, hoping the vampire would hear him before darkness flooded his vision and his body crumpled on the ground.

He stood on the shores of a beach, water lapping at his booted feet. The sun shining down on him was hot enough to blister skin. Glancing around, Derek saw a gathering of lush green trees just over the dunes. It seemed familiar, yet Derek knew he'd never been here before.

Stepping back, Derek's heavy boots sank in the sand. Lifting his hand to shield his eyes from the sun, Derek scanned the beach for signs of life and wondered how the hell he'd gotten here.

"We rarely get to speak, son. I wanted to finally get the chance to have a conversation before the general killed you one last time."

Derek spun around at the sound of the voice, his eyes widening as he beheld a sight he never imagined he would see until the final battle.

Odin stood a short distance from him. He wore a patch over his right eye. His beard was long and the color of snow, his hair equally so. Eyes full of knowledge and wisdom were darkened by a coldness that caused Derek to shiver.

Odin strode toward him, using his staff as a walking stick, and Derek remained rooted to the spot. "Why am I here?" he snarled.

Odin's lips curved into a sardonic smile. "I wanted to speak to my son-in-law, grant him a boon. You are more levelheaded than my daughter, and I wished to speak to you, give you a chance to end this before I destroy Midgard."

"No boon you could offer me would be great enough for me to make a deal with you."

"Not even if it meant you and Ever could still be together, even after she is dead?"

Derek grunted. He didn't need Melanie's powers to taste that lie. Folding his arms across his chest, Derek glared at Odin, who didn't seem intimidated by Derek at all.

"Would you not like to hear my terms? I assure you they are quite reasonable."

"No matter what you say, Odin, it will be wasted on me."

Odin walked in a circle around him, his feet barely making a dent in the sand. Derek knew the god had knocked him unconscious to try and manipulate him.

"It's quite a good offer, I believe. When Ever is dead, she will be enslaved on Valhalla, in the veil between this world and the next, where all my warriors go. I've always been fond of the Greek gods, so just like Persephone, six months of the year, you will be able to visit her, feel her, scent her. *The other six months you belong to me and will do anything I ask."*

Derek regarded Odin and smirked, much to Odin's chagrin. "A sadistic bastard once owned me," he said. "I will not bow to another. Perhaps I should offer you the same. When Ever kills you, we will keep you in Valhalla, forever on the fringes, never able to meddle in our affairs anymore. Watching but unable to experience joy or love, laughter or song."

Odin answered with a snarl of his own, his hands around Derek's throat as the god lifted Derek off the sand and tightened his grip around his windpipe. Derek wanted to gasp for breath, to struggle against the hold, but Derek knew none of this was real, so there was no need to panic.

"I could reach inside your body and rip out your wolf, make you nothing but human. Your bones would weaken, and you would age quickly. Death would come calling soon enough. I could snap that mating bond with nothing more than a click of my fingers. Would my daughter love you then? When you are weak and pitiful?"

Derek lifted his gaze to Odin's, let the wolf rise in his eyes. "She would still love me. She would still be mine. You could take away my wolf—take a part of me—but the man and the wolf are both hers. Even if you rip part of me away, the other half will still fight for her. Who will fight for you when you are a shell of the man you used to be?"

With a yell of anger, Odin tossed Derek away like he were nothing, but Derek rolled when he landed and crouched low with a growl. Raising his staff, Odin coiled back his arm, ready to strike out and pierce Derek's chest with the sharpened end of the staff.

Derek lunged forward, his change from man to wolf instantaneous, between one breath and the next. He sank his sharp incisors into Odin's arm, tasting blood and magic. Derek felt a sharp pull on his power. Even as his teeth grazed bone, Derek felt Odin reach for him.

Derek came back to the present with a yell, jerking upright despite his pounding head. Donnie was crouched over him, careful not to touch Derek in case he hurt him. Ricky stood off to the side, his eyes closed as Melanie rubbed circles on his back in comfort.

A hand reached out for him and he took it, nodding his thanks to Caitlyn as he stood, his legs a bit shaky. Derek looked at his hands and saw his claws. His vision was shrouded in amber, his senses sharper as he pulled back the wolf and regarded his team.

"Is Ever okay?"

Donnie nodded. "When she sensed something was wrong, Loki sent her to sleep before she could panic."

Derek inclined his head to Ricky. "What's up with him?"

"When you called out to Donnie," Caitlyn replied, "we rushed out to help, and while we tried to rouse you, you suddenly started giving off immense waves of power. Like any newborn vampire, Ricky was overwhelmed with hunger. He is being over hard on himself."

Derek watched as his partner and best friend lowered his head further, ignoring Derek as he called out to him. Caitlyn held out a tissue and indicated to his mouth. Derek wiped his mouth, surprised as blood stained the white.

"What happened?" she asked.

"I had a visit from my father-in-law. He wanted to make a deal."

Ricky turned to face him, coming a little closer before halting just shy of the group. Derek walked over to him as Ricky tried to look anywhere but at Derek's face. When his friend got too close, Ricky reached out and shoved him, hard.

"D, don't come near me, please. I saw you lying there, and I forgot to push down the hunger. You fucking glowed, D, and I couldn't help myself."

Placing a hand on his friend's shoulder, Derek looked him straight in the eye. "You pulling on that power is probably what saved my life and woke me up."

Ricky brushed off his hand, and Derek left his friend to

reconcile with himself. Turning back to Donnie and Caitlyn, Derek blew out a breath. "Odin must be desperate if he's trying to make deals with me. He promised to allow me to see Ever if I agreed to be his for six months of the year."

"I take it from the blood on your lips you told him to piss off," Donnie said with a toothy grin.

"Hell yeah I did. Now, let's go inside so I can hold my mate and we can get back to solving a crime."

Derek strode off across the driveway and headed inside Caitlyn's house, making a beeline for Ever, who was just fluttering her eyes open at the snap of Loki's fingers.

"I could snap that mating bond with nothing more than a click of my fingers."

Derek held back a shudder as he regarded Loki with new eyes as the god of mischief looked back at him. A smile toyed on his lips, amusement in his eyes.

"I am not our father. I would not do anything hurt Ever. Breaking a bond like that, ripping it from two souls, would be excruciating—not only for the bonded, but for the person foolish enough to mess with the bonds of fate, as well. Even I am not so much of a masochist as to inflict that upon myself. Not even for the greater good."

"Where's Ash?" asked Ever. "Does he know about her? Oh my god, Derek, he could go after her."

Panic flooded his veins as he glanced at Erika, who immediately disappeared. She came back a second later, a stupid grin on her face.

"Ash is currently playing Legos with Zach. She's good."

Ever immediately relaxed, then let out a hiss of pain. Derek crossed the room and crouched in front of her, concern in his eyes. She flashed him a small smile. "I'm okay. She just decided I needed a kick to the ribs to remind me that she's here."

Derek quickly pressed his lips to Ever's. "I love you."

Ever smiled, and it was if the sun were shining down on him. "I love you, too."

Everyone looked exhausted. Dawn was only an hour or two away, so Derek heard himself decree that they all needed to get some rest, even as Kenzie stumbled in from her nap in the car. She bypassed everyone and headed straight for the hallway leading to her own bedroom.

Caitlyn invited them all to stay the night, saying it was a day the family should spend under the same roof. While Caitlyn busied herself readying beds for them all, Donnie led Ever to a room where she could rest in peace. Derek followed them, keeping a little distance but staying close enough to hear their conversation.

"Can you hear her in there?" asked Ever.

Donnie laughed softly. "It's more feelings and pictures than thoughts. She's happy, loved, impatient—but having met her, I can see that's not going to change."

Derek could feel Ever's smile through the mating bond, and it warmed his soul. Then he heard Ever speak again. "You can hide out in here with me if you want. I know it must be over-whelming, having to deal with all of our sadness and your own."

The thought hadn't even occurred to Derek. Donnie had always had to deal with hearing people's thoughts, and this must be torture for him.

"While I appreciate the offer, Ever—and I truly do—I think our mates need us right now. Thank you for thinking of me."

He heard the sheets shifting as Ever moved in the bed. "When I thought I was going crazy, you kept my secrets until I was ready. I'll always be grateful for that. Anytime you want to come to me and just listen to baby feelings, day or night, you come to me."

"Yes, ma'am."

Derek stood back as Donnie slipped from the room and gently closed the door behind him. When he turned, Derek grinned at him. "Hey, isn't it enough that my daughter is enamored with you, now you gotta have my mate thinking all warm and fuzzy things about you, too?"

Donnie looked at him, startled. When he spied Derek's smile, he shook his head. "That's not even funny, Derek."

"Kind of is."

Donnie punched him gently in the shoulder before he left Derek standing there, listening to his mate's breathing as it evened out until he felt her fall asleep.

Loki stepped out of the shadows and inclined his head. "I've weaved some magic around the room so that she will sleep a dreamless sleep for a while. Should you need me before then, simply call for me and I will be here."

Derek thanked him, telling him that Ever was lucky to have a brother like him.

The god offered Derek a smile. "No, it is I who am lucky to have her. She was always the best of us, and perhaps that is something Odin cannot look past."

As Loki vanished, Derek thought back to his interaction with Odin and pushed thoughts of the impending apocalypse from his mind. He had a she-wolf to hunt down and make amends with.

Ash

"Look, Ash! Look what I made!"

Ash grinned as Zach showed her the spaceship he had built from his Legos, a proud look of achievement on his little face. It made it easier, being here with little Zach, because she missed her best friend and partner in crime like she was missing a limb.

She had begged him to come with her, to travel across time

and space, but Zach had told her this was her journey, her path, and that she had to take it alone.

Sometimes, Ash despised that he was so smart. Well, only kind of.

Turning her attention back to Zach, Ash high-fived him, watching as the little boy's eyes grew tired, his energy waning. When his eyes drooped, Ash cradled him close to her as she lifted him with barely any fuss and laid him down in his bed. She tucked the covers right up to his chin, the way her best friend still slept, and ran her fingers through his dark locks.

Zach purred, unashamed at the fact that he enjoyed it. As Ash got up to leave, Zach said her name softly, sitting up in the bed again.

"Tell me a story, Ash."

Pushing him gently back down into bed, Ash ruffled his hair. "Maybe another night, Z."

"Please."

Ah, but Ash was a sucker and knew she couldn't resist a request from this little kid. Flopping down on the bed beside him, Ash felt a tug on her heart as Zach snuggled into her. It was surreal, having him being this small, because she'd only known him as this protective older brother. She wondered what he was doing now, if he missed her as much as she missed him.

Some people didn't understand their bond, and sometimes, neither did they.

"Ash."

Zach's impatient tone sparked joy in her, his exasperated tone one she was overtly familiar with. The last time she had heard it was when Zach had begged her to come for a spin in one of Auntie Caitlyn's prized cars. At least they hadn't damaged it... much.

Snuggling down into the bed, Ash crossed her legs before she began to speak. "Right. Storytime. Once upon a time, there was a princess and her bestest friend in the whole world. The princess's best friend was older than her, and even though they were not blood-related, they loved one another like brother and sister."

Ash felt her father's presence outside Zach's room, and not wanting to deal with that just yet, she continued with her story.

"One day, the princess started to vanish, and her brother forgot who she was for an entire day. She tried to get him to remember by telling him stories of all the times they had been very naughty and up to mischief and their parents had not been happy. Her brother didn't believe her, and this made the princess sad because half of her heart belonged to her brother."

Ash sighed, wetting her lips before she continued. "So the princess continued to disappear and then, one day when she was out fighting a monster, the brother suddenly remembered her and they slayed the monster together. They cried as they decided that the princess needed to be sent far, far away from him, not sure if they would ever lay eyes on one another ever again."

A snore alerted her to the fact Zach was already asleep. Still, Ash needed her father to understand what was at stake for her even when she couldn't exactly tell him what the future would bring them all.

"So the princess left her brother and went in search of the magic that had made her brother forget her, because she could survive so much—and had done so already—but if she lost her brother, then she would lose half of herself."

Leaning down, she pressed her lips to Zach's warm cheek. "Don't ever forget me, big brother. We have galaxies to discover and monsters to slay. Promise me you will never forget me."

Of course, Zach did not answer her, lost in slumber. Ash gently eased off the bed and padded across the carpet. Opening the door, she glanced over her shoulder at his sleeping form before stepping out to face her father.

Derek Doyle was always an imposing figure, especially to

those he trained. To her, he was always just Dad, and she had triggered something in him that had uncorked a power he didn't know was now etched into his aura.

"You guys are close in the future." It was a whispered statement because anyone could see how much she cared for Z.

"Just like you and Ricky."

"Then I'm glad you have someone like I do."

Ash waited for him to chastise her for losing her temper with Loki and Erika. It wasn't something she wanted to discuss with her dad, and especially not with her mom or even Loki. Talking it over wouldn't change the other reason she'd been so eager to fling herself into the past, and she would deal with that when and if she made it home.

"I'm walking back to Caitlyn's now. Walk with me?"

Ash said nothing, just bobbed her head and followed her dad down the stairs. Derek gave Mrs. Moore a quick hug, had a few words with Killian, Ricky's brother, and then he ushered Ash outside into the breaking dawn.

Of all the worlds and galaxies that Ash had seen, and perhaps because she considered herself to be Irish, having been born here, Ireland had always been one of her favorite places. Most tourists who came to Ireland marveled at just how magical the island seemed, but Ash could feel the magic beneath her feet, scent it in the air.

There was a reason why most supernatural creatures were lured to Ireland... but that was a story for another day.

Ash kept in step with her dad's long strides, listening to the steady beat of his heart as they walked down the hill toward Caitlyn's home. This home was different from the one where she and Zach had run around. She worshipped them for being such awe-inspiring figures, but it was nice to know that the perfect heroes she worshipped hadn't been as perfect as she had thought growing up.

"Is Mom okay?"

"Yeah, she's sleeping right now, and I didn't want to disturb her. Besides, you and I need to talk."

Ash rolled her eyes. "Can we just pretend you've lectured me about controlling my wolf and let that awkwardness be over? Been there, got the T-shirt."

Derek chuckled softly, and Ash found herself smiling back.

"Humor me. What got you so mad at me?"

Ash halted her movements, forcing her dad to look at her. His face was impassive, devoid of emotion, but Ash wanted to shake him.

"Dad, I wasn't mad at you; I was pissed off at myself. I mean, it's not like we don't argue; I am a teenager. There are things I can't say as to why I have issues with my uncle and aunt, recent things that trigger me. I was never mad at you."

"Oh."

That was all he said, so Ash began to walk again. With a few quick strides, her dad was back to walking by her side. They continued down the hill silently until her dad cleared his throat.

"You must have been so scared and alone."

Ash didn't need to ask what he was referring to, she heard it in his tone, having listened to her story. She shrugged. "It is what it is. I'm here, and now that Mom's decided to keep me, I'm not sure why I'm still here. The plan was to come back, guilt trip Mom into having me, and then go back home."

"Maybe you haven't done all that you were supposed to do."

"Maybe."

They walked into the courtyard, her dad narrowing his gaze as if he wanted to ask her something that was going to embarrass them both. He kicked at the dirt with his boot, and Ash sighed.

"Go ahead, ask the question. You look like your head might explode if you don't ask."

A dazzling smile lit up his face, and Ash's heart kicked like a drum.

"You and Zach? That's not something I need to worry about, right?"

Ash let loose a bark of laughter, but when she saw her dad's face, she held up a hand. "No, Zach and I are just friends. If you really must know, we had wondered that ourselves. Everyone was wondering, and it started to freak us out. But having recently tested the theory, I can assure you we have zero romantic chemistry."

Her dad blew out a breath of relief, but Ash didn't have the heart to tell him that a relationship with Zach would have been the safer bet. The one they all could have dealt with.

As if his thoughts finally managed to catch up with him, Derek growled. "Hang on a damn minute, Zach is five years older than you."

"It was just a kiss, Dad, and it's not like it was my first kiss."

Groaning, Derek rubbed his temples, shaking his head as if he couldn't believe he was having this conversation.

Stepping into his body, Ash rested her head on his chest. "It's okay, Daddy. You'll always be my hero."

Arms wrapped around her tightly, and Ash inhaled the scent of him, the scent of home and love. She had hugged him like this right before she left, not telling him she was embarking on this mission. She imagined he was going out of his damn mind now that she was missing.

She hoped Zach wasn't in too much trouble right now.

Ash heard the whistle on the wind as she twisted and shoved her dad out of the path of the bullet meant for his chest. The shot slammed into her left shoulder, and Ash hissed at the burn, ignoring the sensation of blood dripping down her back as she whirled around and flung out her hand.

Mjölnir sailed through the air and was nestled in the palm of her hand as the next bullet was fired. Ash knocked it aside with a growl, reaching the hammer of the gods into the sky. The bright morning sun disappeared as thunderclouds gathered, the rumble so loud Ash felt the ground shake.

She tracked the path of the shots to their origin, and with one motion, slammed Mjölnir into the ground. The dirt beneath her feet cracked, the tremors traveling across the road and through the field where another shot was fired.

Her dad screamed her name, but she was Ashlyn Kyria Doyle, protector of Midgard, chosen by Thor himself, and a mere bullet could not fell her. Reaching across the fields, she yanked on the shooter's aura and gave him a mental punch as another bullet ripped into her flesh.

She held Mjölnir out in front of her, ready to fly to the person who had tried to steal her father away, when a strong hand latched around her ankle.

"Ash, don't."

His pleading tone tore her concentration away from the shooter. Cursing, Ash growled as the clouds overhead dissipated. As her dad scrambled to his feet, Ash clutched Mjölnir and flashed to where she thought the shots had come from.

Eyes scanning as she solidified inside a barn overlooking Caitlyn's house, she was careful not to disturb the scene, the shooter had disappeared. Crouching, Ash saw indentations in the strewn-about hay from a sniper rifle. Flashing back to Caitlyn's, she'd barely reappeared when her dad engulfed her in a hug, unwittingly sending a flare of pain through her injured shoulder.

"Jesus Christ, Ash, what the hell were you thinking?"

"I thought that even you might not survive a bullet to the chest."

Derek pulled away from her and examined the wounds in her shoulder. Growling, he led her inside and called for help. Ash heard the rushed sounds of feet as Derek strode into Caitlyn's kitchen, yanked out a chair, and demanded she sit her ass down, Mjölnir resting on the floor beside her.

Ash rolled her eyes but obliged as the pain in her shoulder intensified. Caitlyn and Donnie were first to come across them, and Caitlyn's eyes widened for a second before she rushed to action. Melanie and Ricky came in next, Melanie coming to crouch in front of her, concern all over her features.

"Listen, there's no need to fuss. It's not like it's the first time I've been shot."

When her dad let loose a growl so fierce it rivaled her own thunder, Ash grimaced at Melanie. She tried to yank off her T-shirt, but her arm was starting to go numb as the adrenaline wore off. Melanie helped her out of her shirt, her eyes wandering over the tattoos ingrained in her skin from neck to wrist.

"The bullet's not silver," Ash muttered quietly as the team fussed over her. When no one answered her, Ash sighed and reached into the wound with a grunt. Blood poured from the opening, coating her fingers, making them too slick to get a firm grip on the bullet.

"*Mon Dieu!* What are you doing?" Caitlyn gently moved Melanie out of the way, the vampire going to find some clothes for Ash and sat down in the chair in front of Ash.

"I'm getting the bullets out so I can go find out who just tried to kill my dad."

"Patience, little wolf. Patience."

Caitlyn set some utensils in a tray on the table, dousing them in antiseptic cleaner before turning to face her. Ash sucked in a breath as Caitlyn dug into her arm with a pair of forceps. Ash growled, her wolf flashing in her eyes from the pain. The moment Caitlyn pulled the bullet free and set it down on the table with a clang, Ash felt a release from the pain.

"One more to go, little wolf."

This time, when Caitlyn went in search of the second bullet, Ash let loose a stream of swear words in every bloody language she spoke. Derek paced in front of her, and Ash hissed as Caitlyn slowly removed the bullet.

"Dad, stop pacing. You're giving me a headache."

Derek froze as Caitlyn poured some solution onto a gauze pad and pressed it over the wounds. Ash closed her eyes so as not to betray the sting of pain. The house was too quiet; everyone was so quiet she could hear the rush of her own blood.

"Shooter was a sniper, long-range, and an excellent shot," Ash said to fill the silence. "Bullets weren't silver, so he didn't mean to kill Dad, just give him a nasty itch. He's also supernatural and left no trace apart from an imprint in the hay where he set up his rifle."

Ash opened her eyes and saw everyone looking at her like she'd grown an extra head.

Ricky grinned and nudged Derek's arm. "Chip off the old block, eh, D?"

Her dad shot Ricky a look that made her wince.

"Did I hurt you too much?" Caitlyn asked, mistaking Ash's wince for pain. Worry in her tone, she quickly checked the bandages she'd taped over Ash's wounds to make sure they weren't too tight.

Ash gathered up her bloody tee and pulled it over her head, letting Caitlyn help her. "Nah, you were far gentler than the last person who pulled a bullet from me. It was from the thigh, though, and shoulders hurt like a mother—"

Cutting off the curse, Ash smiled sheepishly at Caitlyn, who simply patted her cheek and got to her feet. Ash rolled her shoulder, breathing through the pain. She knew she'd be fine in a few hours.

"Who was the last person you took a bullet for? And who pulled it out?"

Ash lifted her amber gaze to Ricky. She knew he already had the answer, but she thought distracting her dad with a story might be a good idea. He looked like he was going to go all *Exorcist* and spin his head three hundred and sixty degrees.

"We were chasing down an unsub, and the dope pulled out a gun instead of using his powers. He pointed it at Zach, I got in the way, the idiot dropped the gun, and it went off—bang—bullet in my thigh. I made Z pull it out because I'd saved his ass. I kinda think he enjoyed it, the jerk. Plus, we didn't want to report back to our commanding officers that I'd been shot. We'd already been chewed out for always coming back bleeding."

A smile tugged her lips upward as Ricky grinned, but her dad had gone deathly quiet. His eyes were glued to the bullets Caitlyn was rinsing clean. Ash could scent the change in him, his eerily calm predator rising to just beneath the surface.

"What is it, Dad?"

A haunted expression fell over her dad's handsome features, his eyes glazed over, and the only inclination he was feeling anything was the tick of his jaw. Moving closer, his eyes never strayed from the bullets Caitlyn had set down on the table.

Ash thought he was worried about her, that he was angry she'd gotten between him and a bullet. "Dad, I'm sorry if you're angry at me for pushing you out of the way. I mean, I just reacted, and I knew that I could take a few bullets."

Eyes flashing amber, her dad glanced at her before turning back to the bullets. "I'm not mad that you took a bullet for me, Ash. I'm sorry that you were shot by a bullet that belonged to me."

Confused, Ash watched as her dad plucked one of the bullets from the table, his eyes focused on the slug as if it were a ghost.

Etched on the old bullet were the initials *DD*.

CURSING AT THE PAIN IN HIS HEAD AND THE UNPREDICTABLE ELEMENT he hadn't anticipated, he leaned against the hood of his car. He waited while the plane taxied into the hanger. He couldn't wait to tell his boss about the girl who'd taken a bullet for Derek Doyle; none had antici- pated anything like this.

He wondered if Derek had gotten his little present, or if he'd been too blinded by his own self-importance to notice that the mysterious teenager had been shot with Derek's own bullets. He hadn't wanted to kill Derek—not yet anyway. But he was enjoying making his life miserable.

The plane's engines shut down. He straightened as the cabin door opened, and the ladder was lowered. The moment his boss came into view, he strode forward as the older man came down the steps.

"It's good to see you, sir."

"And you, son. And you. Now tell me, how is Doyle?"

"Not dead yet."

His boss chuckled and slapped him on the back, sending a wave of pride through him.

"Soon, very soon."

He opened the back door for his boss, then slipped into the driver's seat as they waited for bags and staff to file into other cars.

"Well, son," his boss began, and he lifted his eyes to the rearview mirror, giving his superior his full attention. "Tell me all about your time in Cork."

A smile curved his lips as his boss, Neville Morris, settled back into his seat and smiled like a proud father at him.

CHAPTER EIGHT

DEREK

The young group of soldiers gathered near the barracks, sitting outside on this summer's eve, a roaring fire sending plumes of smoke into the night sky. One soldier sat, using an overturned bucket as a drum to accompany another singing songs of Irish patriotism.

Derek lay down in the grass, staring up at the sky as he smiled and laughed with his brothers in arms. They had been called to barracks a week ago but had yet to be sent on a mission. His team was getting restless, uneasy.

As an elite team, they were called on various missions all over the world, and Derek felt truly blessed to be part of this brotherhood, even if they were the biggest messers ever.

Derek grunted as a football bounced off his stomach and darted to his feet, tossing the ball at his best friend's head. The ball hit its mark, and Sam grinned as he tackled Derek. Derek had him on his knees a second later, and Sam tapped his arm with a boyish grin.

Running his hands through his Irish red hair, Sam punched Derek in the shoulder. "Come on, Lu, you could let me win a little. Do wonders for me ego."

Derek laughed. "Won't it be grand to win all on your own some-day, mate?"

"Nah, I'll take the easy win, mate. You're a machine."

Laughter rebounded around the group, and Derek shook his head with a grin. Derek strode over to his seat by the fire, pulled out his stash of bullets, and grabbed his penknife, the one his Da had given him when he'd enlisted.

The Irish army wasn't flush with cash; however, as his team went on special missions, they had a bit more funding than most. The pay was shite to be fair, but none of the men sitting around the campfire were in this for the money.

Derek slipped a bullet from its case and began to etch his initials into the metal. Sam noticed what he was doing and joined him. It was a ritual to them; before every mission, when given a new batch of bullets, he and Sam—who'd been fighting side by side since they'd joined up—etched their initials into each of their bullets.

It was silly, really, but as a covert team, they would never be recognized for what they did. There would be no medals of honor or songs sung in pubs about them. But firing a bullet into another person left a mark, and those bullets would bear their initials.

When the others spied what they were doing, the ruckus calmed as every soldier on Derek's team joined in on the ritual. It was a calming process for Derek, a routine to ease his mind before they were flown halfway across the world to God knew where.

"Where do ya think the brass will send us this time, Derek?"

Derek glanced sideways at Sam. "Haven't a bloody clue, mate. There are not many countries left we haven't been to."

Lips curving into a mischievous smile, Sam's eyes lit up. "No matter where we go, Derek, I got your six."

Derek made to answer when their sergeant strode out of his tent. They all stood, and Derek dropped his knife as he saluted the man. The sergeant was one of those men who had forgotten what it was like to be a soldier, his rounded belly and balding hair signs of a desk job that sent young men into war without so much as firing a gun himself.

But, hell, that was the army, wasn't it?

"Lieutenant Doyle, gather your men at zero six hundred for briefing. You will all ship out tomorrow night on a mission of great importance, one that all the special ops forces have been craving."

Anticipation flooded Derek's veins and pride that his soldiers had been chosen. There was only one mission everyone wanted—the chance to go hunt down a certain notorious drug dealer.

"Sir, yes sir."

The sergeant dismissed them, and Sam all but bounced on the balls of his feet. "Derek... do you think? Could we be the ones to go after Morris? Mate, we'll be legends!"

Derek returned his friend's grin, rubbing the bullet still in his hands between his fingers, his thumb grazing the initials he'd just etched into it. Sam was right. If they managed to take down the infamous Neville Morris, they'd be legends.

"All right, ladies," Derek barked. "Let's get some beauty sleep, for tomorrow we become legends."

He clasped Sam's shoulders as the boys all cheered. Derek couldn't wait to embark on this with his brothers.

"What do you mean it's your bullet?"

Ricky's voice dragged him from his memories. Derek peered over his shoulder at his friend, but all he saw was Sam's freckled face. He had to blink a few times to rid his eyes of his dead friend.

Clearing his throat, Derek sank on the chair as he rolled the bullet between his fingers, just like he used to do. Ash watched him with avid curiosity. Donnie had no doubt seen the memory in his head, but Derek found he couldn't say the words.

"You used to do that before a mission."

Ever's voice sent a flush of shame through his body. It was a part of him that he hadn't wanted to share with anyone—the cocky, sure-of-himself soldier who'd taken his band of brothers on a suicide mission. They'd become fucking legends, all right; Morris' cult of werewolves had obliterated the team.

"Sam and I, we started it as a joke at first, but as the years dragged on, it became like a ritual. The others soon followed suit. Some teams relaxed and played cards. Others cleaned their guns relentlessly. We etched our initials into our bullets."

Derek felt Ever walk over, and then he felt the warmth of her touch on the nape of his neck. He leaned into the comfort of it, needing it as he contemplated being the reason Ash had been shot.

"It's not, you know, the reason I got shot."

Derek's head snapped up as Donnie let out a gasp. Every single person had turned to look at Ash, who grinned sheepishly at them.

"You guys have been around a mind reader all your lives, and you're shocked at me? Listen, it's more feelings than thoughts, so stop looking at me like that. Auras change."

Derek reached out and took his daughter's hand. "I'm sorry that you felt the need to take a bullet meant for me."

"I would take a bullet meant for my family any day of the week."

"Well, she's definitely your kid, Boyband."

Derek didn't even glance at Erika, who'd popped into the room. As her gaze ran over the supes in the room, she paused, pulled her phone out of her pocket, frowned, and then shoved it away again.

When Ever glanced in her direction, the Valkyrie shrugged. "It's nothing."

Donnie came over and picked the second bullet off the table. "Are you sure it's your actual bullet? I mean, could someone have just replicated it to drive you mad?"

Derek ran his thumb over the indentations once again, shaking his head. "No, this is mine. It was my knife that etched these initials. Someone knew it would rattle me, and it fucking has. But everyone who knew about this is dead."

"Are you sure, Derek? Could one of your soldiers have survived?"

An image flashed in his mind of the broken and shredded bodies of his teammates, their blood staining the wooden floors, their insides ripped from their mangled bodies, blood dripping from mottled fur. Morris had waited until Derek woke as a wolf, then made him watch as he'd burned the bodies. He hadn't even been able to offer up a prayer and say goodbye.

"I was the only one who made it out." Derek said the words with absolute certainty, felt the power in his words. He huffed out a breath as Ever tightened her grip on the nape of his neck. She pressed her lips to his flesh, and he shivered.

"Derek, every one of us has a past we regret on some level. You lost your entire team and were changed by force. Whoever is taunting you now must know this is the best way to haunt you, or else they wouldn't do it. If this person or group is responsible for Tom's death, they wanted to hit hard and make it hurt."

Ever was right, and he knew deep down who was responsible for this. He glanced down at the bullet and wondered if this were the exact one he'd fired into Neville Morris as the monster stood over Sam's body. The only way someone would have Derek's bullet was if it had been pulled from the flesh it was shot into.

Derek had spent many a night walking the fields and roads with Caitlyn, discussing their history and the darkness that lived within them. Caitlyn knew more about him than he knew about himself, and he knew the same about her. She would understand the pain it caused him to think about his fallen brothers.

"After trying to banish the ghosts of my past alone for such a long time, it was only when I leaned on my family, my team, that I was able to fulfill my promise to my slain family. Lean on us, *mon loupe*; we will not see you face it alone."

Derek got to his feet, kissed his mate's forehead, and inclined his head toward Caitlyn. "We can't do much until dark. If Neville Morris is behind this, then I need to find out if he's in Ireland. He wouldn't come alone, and we need to know if he has an army. But dragging thousands of wolves across the world would be too noticeable. Someone would know."

"I'll get Lanie to check airports and track his movements." Ricky strode off down the hall to find his wife and get her to work her magic with computers. She may be a kick-ass vampire now, but Melanie was still a tech whizz.

"I think everyone needs to get some rest now. Come on, Derek. Come to bed." Ever held out her hand, and he took it, glancing at Ash.

"I don't really sleep," she said with a soft smile. "I'll watch over the house."

"I'll stay up with her," Donnie added, surprising them all.

The vampire had a curious look in his eyes that Derek didn't quite like. Donnie raised his eyebrows at Derek as if challenging him, but as Ash blushed and Caitlyn led her from the kitchen, Derek knew Donnie would do just as Ash had done—throw himself in front of a bullet for his daughter.

Derek let Ever drag him down the hall, helped her to bed, and then lay down next to her with his hands falling to Ever's stomach. A flurry of movements kicked not only his hand but also his heart, and he peered down at Ever.

"She's already a daddy's girl."

Derek kissed the smile on her lips. "I'm okay with that. Jesus Christ, Ever, she took two bullets for me."

"As Ricky said, she's your daughter. But she is hiding so much from us. We might never know why she's here."

Derek didn't say anything else, closing his eyes with a sudden tiredness that threatened to overwhelm him.

"Why does Loki keep sending me off to dreamland? I feel like I'm missing something important."

"Before all of the drama below," Derek said softly, running his fingers through her golden hair, "your dad knocked me unconscious and dragged me to what I can only imagine was Valhalla."

Ever sat up and faced him, her eyes wide. "Oh my God, Derek! You can't hide this stuff from me."

Derek cupped her cheek and ran his thumb over her lips. "I wasn't trying to hide it from you. Other things like our daughter getting shot got in the way. Odin wanted to make a deal with me and wasn't pleased when I refused."

Ever arched a brow. "Why do I feel like you're not telling me everything? What did you do?"

"I bit him."

Ever blinked, her face shocked, then she laughed, a deep sound that warmed his bones. "Oh, I wish I could have seen his face when you did. Odin is terrified of wolves."

"Then he should be *absolutely* terrified of me."

Ever leaned up and kissed him, and Derek angled his body so he could deepen the kiss. Ever groaned into his mouth as her hands slipped under his T-shirt, and she rose to her knees. His hands roamed down to cup her ass, and Ever reached for his belt buckle, then sat back suddenly with a hiss.

"What just happened?" Derek asked as he took in her irritated expression. He had to bite his lip as she pointed down to her stomach.

"I can't. Not while she's in there. I mean, Donnie said she's very active. What if she knows what we're doing?"

Derek burst out laughing and kissed his mate even as she swatted at him. Pulling her close, he leaned in and nipped her ear. "You know, they say sex can trigger labor."

Ever groaned and leaned her forehead against his. "I don't know how human women do this. I've only really been pregnant for a few days, and I can't stand it."

"But not every human gets to carry a child like ours."

Ever smiled, and her eyes filled with love. "That is very true."

The house suddenly began to rattle, and Derek was out of bed and running down the hall a second later, the rest of the team gathering in the living room, watching Ash try to get past Donnie.

What the hell was going on now?

"You need to let me go. You need to let me go *right now*," Ash shrieked, a look of pure terror in her eyes.

Just like when Ash had appeared, the sky outside ripped open, and a figure dressed in black suddenly stood in the middle of Caitlyn's back garden. Ash trembled and let a snarl and a curse slip from her lips. A second later, Loki appeared by her side, his own eyes wide as he glanced from the boy heading in their direction and his adopted sister's child.

"No."

That was all the master of mischief said, his tone sad as a boy with inky black hair and eyes so dark they were almost black. Derek thought the teen looked young, but the waves of power coming off him indicated this being was as old as Ever or even Loki.

The boy flicked his hand, and the patio door slid open. He ignored the rest and held out his hand to Ash, their eyes clashing.

His daughter's scent was steeped in fear, even if she sensed her wolf coming to the surface.

"Come," the boy demanded as if Ash would simply do as he asked.

The power in his words was so strong his daughter took a step forward even as she gritted out, "Fuck you."

Derek strode forward and stood in front of his daughter. "I don't know who you are or where you came from, but you will do as my daughter says and leave."

The boy smirked and leaned forward at the waist ever so

slightly. "Really, Ashlyn? Running to Daddy to try to solve your problems again?"

"Yeah, well, my dad's been dealing with psychotic wolves for decades; I needed the expert advice!"

"Ash, do you know who this is?" Derek asked.

She gritted her teeth. "Unfortunately."

He could feel the team at his back, even heard Donnie tell him to take a step back, but Derek ignored his friend's words and stepped out into the garden. The boy seemed so amused by Derek's actions that his smirk deepened. The boy's eyes darted to Loki for a moment, but then his attention went firmly back to Ash.

"I tire of these games, Ashlyn. Take my hand and let us go home."

Ash held out her hand, and Mjölnir was instantly in it, thunder clapping in the sky above. The boy grinned, and red flashed in his eyes. Derek felt his wolf rise and knew the creature in front of him was a wolf.

And his stomach plummeted to his feet at the sheer power flowing from him.

"If you hurt Zach," Ash yelled, "I'll smash your skull in, you fleabag!"

The creature rolled his eyes. "I have not hurt your little cat. I promised I would not harm him, and I keep my promises. You, on the other hand, have reneged on your word."

"Nothing in my agreement covered traveling to the past," Ash muttered.

"You have taken lessons from my father in the manipulation of words. Isn't that right?" he asked, looking at Loki.

The god paled. "How did you get free?"

"I, too, just like my Ashlyn, cannot tell you about the future. Now, Ashlyn, you have meddled far enough. We will go home."

Derek glanced at the boy and back to Ash. "My daughter is going nowhere with you."

Ever came to stand beside him, entwining his fingers with hers and leaning her head on Ash's shoulder. "Oh, Ash, I'm so sorry."

Ash smiled grimly at her mother. "Not your fault, Mom. The wolf chooses who the wolf chooses. Sometimes, the girl has no choice."

The boy folded his arms across his chest and waited, his dark eyes tinged with red.

"Who the hell *are* you?" Derek growled.

The boy simply curved his lips into a smile, revealing teeth as sharp as any wolf's.

With a pained sigh, Loki answered, "He has come to claim his mate. This is Fenrir, and he is my son."

CHAPTER
NINE

He has come to claim his mate.

Ash shuddered as the truth of Loki's words sank into her bones. She had left without a word to the slightly insane wolf that stood in front, and, of course, the psycho had forced Zach to send him after her.

"Come, Ashlyn."

She hated it when he used that tone with her, and he knew it. His eyes told her he was trying to yank the chains of her temper. He liked it when she was, as he called it, *feisty.*

"Come, Ashlyn."

And oh gods, she wanted to. Her entire body was on fire with him standing there, looking at her as if no one else in the galaxy mattered. Ash held his gaze before she let herself drink him in, the handsome, chiseled face of an angel with a pair of lips that were built for sinful things. Ash knew they'd feel hot against her skin.

She knew the outline of his jaw and the dimples in his cheeks on rare occasions when he smiled, even if it was right before he murdered someone. She knew that his eyes went red when he was angry and that when he wasn't, those eyes could glimmer as if injected by the stars themselves.

He was vicious, calculating, smart as hell, and had very little restraint. Ash tested his patience again and again. To be honest, she wasn't even surprised he'd come looking for her. Instead, she was only surprised it had taken him so long.

Her wolf prowled inside her mind whining, the little bitch wondering why Ash wasn't falling over herself to go to her mate, especially when Ash *wanted* to.

Ugh, that word. She hated it with all the venom in her veins. He was an arrogant son of a bitch who made it his life's work to get in the way of her living her life. She hated him with a passion, and now he was here, ruining things for her again.

"As I said before, fuck off. I will always tell you to leave me alone, Grey. When a girl says no, she means it."

A monstrous snarl slipped from Fenrir's lips, and he began to change. Loki let out a yelp and stumbled back as Ash rolled her eyes. Growing and growing still, the boy morphed into a monstrous gray wolf with slaver dripping from its mouth, the droplets hissing as they landed on the ground. The wolf was the size of the house, each of its paws bigger than Ash's head. And on those paws were claws as long as a saber, curled and sharp enough to rip through flesh. The drool that dripped from his lips was enough to sear the grass around them.

The legends of Fenrir described him as a monstrous wolf whose destiny was to swallow Odin whole during Ragnarök. But Ash knew different.

Derek growled, inching forward as Fenrir bared teeth as long as blades at them. Ash lowered her head as the giant wolf bayed at the moon, the sound causing her ears to ring. When Fenrir was like this, his human self was very much out of the driver's seat.

Setting Mjölnir down, Ash took a shaky step forward. Her dad grabbed her arm, and Fenrir snarled, his eyes glowing red, and Ash tried to wrench her arm from her father's grasp. Fenrir would not care that her dad was only trying to protect her. No, he'd rip Derek's arm off for daring to touch her.

"Dad, I love you, but you need to let me do this. I'm the only one who can pull him back. Trust me. *Please.*"

Her tone must have been what stopped his advancement as Ash rolled back her shoulders and walked right up to the gigantic wolf with her hands on her hips, conscious that everyone was staring at her.

Lifting her gaze, Ash glared at Fenrir and shook her head. "You just had to prove my point and go all psycho-wolf on us. Come on, Grey. Stop frightening our families with the wolf-god treatment. Do you honestly think this is making a good first impression?"

The wolf leaned in and inhaled her scent, letting out a shuddering breath. Ash reached up and ran her hand down the monstrous wolf's muzzle.

"Yeah, yeah... I smell good. I know. Now change back so we can all pretend you're a civilized person with social skills instead of the psychopath you actually are."

The wolf shivered, and the next minute Fenrir was standing in front of her, breathing hard. His eyes clashed with hers, and then his lips were on hers, and she was powerless to stop the lust that washed over her. His hands were in her hair, his nails scraping her scalp as Fenrir kissed her like he needed air.

When one of his arms snaked around her waist, and his fire-hot palm flattened against her spine, Ash snapped back into reality and yanked her lips away from Fenrir, who smiled smugly at her.

"Mine."

"Yeah, whatever. Let me go, please."

"No."

Ash let her head fall back to stare up at the sky and wondered what she had done to deserve this psychopath who'd decided she was his. Ash reached into her pocket, her fingers gripping the vial that Zach had given her just in case Fenrir decided to come after her. They'd planned for every eventuality, and Ash had plenty of tricks up her sleeve.

"Is Zach okay?"

"He's alive."

Ash rolled her eyes. "C'mon Grey, you know if you hurt him, I'll never forgive you."

"The cat is alive. I needed him to find you."

Well, that was something, she guessed.

Loki's son let his gaze wander to where Ever stood, his grin infuriating as he pointed at her bump and growled, "Mine."

Her dad snarled back, placing his hands on Ever's stomach. "Mine."

Aggression filled the air, and Ash felt the wolf in Fenrir stir again. To keep him calm, she swallowed her fear, leaned her nose into the curve of his neck, and inhaled the scent of him. His hand snaked up and cupped the back of her head.

You're hurt. I will flay whoever hurt you alive before I feast on his intestines.

Ash didn't say anything as nails scraped against her skin, causing her to shiver.

You left me.

Fenrir projected his thoughts down their bond—fear, anger, and bitterness flooded the bond Ash tried to block. Still, when he was this close, this infuriatingly smug in front of her, she was powerless to stop it. It's why she'd traveled sixteen years into the past.

Instead of using the bond, she sighed and said out loud, "I would've thought you'd be happy, Grey. I mean, I came to make sure I was actually born. Imagine how deranged you'd be if you suddenly didn't have me to calm you down anymore. You should be thanking me."

The vial was between her fingers, and between one breath and the next, Ash smashed it into his temple. Fenrir snarled, then his eyes rolled back in his head, and he crumpled to the ground. Ash caught him before his head hit the ground. Lowering his body the rest of the way, she turned to face her family.

Loki came forward and looked down at his son. "What did you do to him?"

"Zach calls it his Sleeping Beauty potion. Strong enough to knock out a berserker… or a slightly deranged wolf."

Her kinda-uncle gave her a bemused look. "How long will he be out?"

"Knowing Grey, probably not long, and he'll be pissed when he wakes. Can you take him somewhere far away from me, please?"

Loki reached out and rested his hand on Ash's shoulder, giving it a sharp squeeze. "So, this is why you hate me?"

Leaning in, Ash whispered in his ear. "No, I hate you for letting him out."

Loki blinked in surprise. "I do not know where Odin hid him away."

"You will."

"I have never seen anyone talk my son round, especially when his wolf takes over. He is stronger than he was centuries ago."

But Ash knew it was the calming influence of the mating bond that helped to rein in Fenrir and his wolf. Ever had told her a story, years ago, how before the mating bond had snapped into place for her and Dad, she'd been able to get through to the wolf even near a full moon.

Loki turned around and crouched, his hand resting on Fenrir's forehead before they vanished and Ash felt she could breathe again.

Gods, this was twisted. Her parents would see exactly what the future held for her and regret keeping her. Ever had her own destiny to fulfill, as did Ash, but when both their destinies resulted in bringing Fenrir into Ash's life, could she let them follow that path? It would be so easy to direct them elsewhere and free herself from the burden she carried.

Smoothing her hair, Ash snatched up Mjölnir and strode past her parents, straight into the living room. She ignored the shocked expressions and pale faces, went to Caitlyn's liquor cabinet, swiped a bottle of vodka, and took a huge slug from the bottle. When it was yanked from her grasp, she snarled, swiping out as Donnie caught her hand.

"Hit me if you want, but drinking is not going to block out the pain in your chest. It's not going to stop you from making the right choice or the wrong one. No one in this room will judge you, and if you know us as you claim to, then you know it's true."

Snatching back her wrist, Ash gritted her teeth. "I think I preferred you when you were freaked out by my crush."

"I think I'm more freaked out by your teen angst drama than some silly crush you had."

Ash dropped her gaze. "Can we not mention it, please?" she mumbled.

Donnie chuckled. "I think your parents might want a word about that. Your Da's already planning where to bury the body."

"I can get behind that."

Donnie nudged her chin with his knuckles, and Ash wanted to tell him something, anything, about the future as a gift, but anything she might say would be torture to know.

"I'm good with waiting for the future to unveil itself, Ash."

Donnie walked away from her, and Ash made her way to the chair beside the fire, suddenly cold. Melanie dropped down beside her, as did Kenzie. Her parents made to come to her, but Caitlyn muttered something and ushered all but Melanie and Kenzie from the room.

Ricky pressed his lips to Melanie's head as he walked by and winked at Ash before he left. Why couldn't she fall for someone less stalker and more caring?

"Well, you sure know how to bring the drama."

Ash flushed a serious shade of red, her cheeks on fire. Melanie and Kenzie laughed, and Ash's cheeks flamed even brighter.

"Ash, seriously, we're just teasing you. I mean, my ex turned out to be a drug-dealing scumbag who killed my husband, and then I killed him," Melanie said with a grin.

"And I had a crush on a sadistic monster who kept me around because I looked like Caitlyn, and then I dated a guy who was part of the drug-dealing gang that killed Melanie's husband. We all got issues, girl."

Ash smiled and shook her head. "I'm so embarrassed. I never expected him to follow me here."

"He seemed pretty intent on getting you to leave with him."

Ash lifted her gaze to Melanie's with a grin. "He'll be pissed as hell when he wakes up." Getting to her feet, Ash paced the room. "Damn, I need to hit something."

The sun was just setting, full darkness yet to descend, but Ash needed to vent her frustration in the most productive way possible. Turning to the other women, Ash quirked her brow. "Fancy sparring?"

Kenzie slowly got to her feet as she pointed to Mjölnir. "If you leave that indoors, then it's on. I held my own against Erika; let's see if I've learned anything since then."

Melanie held up her hands. "I've just gotten married. I think my husband would like to have me intact for a while yet."

Ash kicked off her shoes and went outside into the grass, and Kenzie followed her out. Ash wanted to tell Kenzie that the mess in her head got easier in time, that she learned to trust herself and others, but she didn't. As Donnie said, the future would unveil itself.

"I'll try not to hurt you too bad since you just got shot," Kenzie teased.

Ash grinned as Kenzie swung a clenched fist. She side-stepped it, grabbing Kenzie's wrist and flipping her over so that she landed on her back with a grunt. Kenzie rolled out of it and faced her, a smirk tugging at her lips.

Ash let the wolf peer through her eyes, the she-wolf already pissed at being separated from her mate. Scents became sharper, and sights became more vivid as Kenzie came forward again. Ash met the blood-kissed girl punch for punch.

Kenzie managed to hook her leg around Ash's knee and yank her forward. Ash went with it and flipped Kenzie so that Ash had her pinned. Her face inches away from Kenzie's, Ash grinned and murmured "Gotcha."

Suddenly Kenzie's features changed, her eyes flashing white as a deep voice not belonging to Kenzie said, "And who might you be?"

Ash jerked away, scrambling to her feet as she screamed for Caitlyn. Kenzie attacked a second later, the glint of a blade in her hands as the girl attacked with a strength and speed that was not her own. Ash tried to defend herself without hurting Kenzie, but Kenzie sank the blade into her shoulder, digging into the already tender bullet wound.

Ash howled in pain as magic seeped into her body from the blade, and she dropped to her knees. Kenzie smirked, lifting the blade and looking at it before she held it up and made to stab herself through the heart.

Donnie rugby-tackled Kenzie before the blade could pierce her skin, the dagger falling to the ground near Ash. The scent of her blood mingled with a magic so tainted wrinkled her nose, and she would have passed out if her dad hadn't come into focus just then.

Melanie made to reach for the dagger, unaware of the compulsion spell woven into it.

"Don't touch it," Ash yelled. "It's spelled. Full of poison." She was fairly sure the poison was now inside of her and no longer in the dagger, yet she wasn't going to risk it.

Melanie shrank back as Ash leaned against her dad's shoulder. She could feel the poison begin to travel along her veins toward her heart. The dagger was infused to kill an Asgardian, and Odin had delivered it like a Trojan horse into their sanctuary. Only someone still clinging to humanity could wield the dagger. Kenzie might be blood-kissed, but she was far more human than anyone else in this house. She was the perfect weapon.

Except Kenzie had gone after the wrong Asgardian.

"Get Ricky. I need him."

Her dad yelled for his best friend, and as the poison inched closer and closer to its mark, she groaned. Ricky raced to them, face pale as he knelt next to Ash. Lifting her amber gaze to him, she said, "Get it out of me."

"I don't understand, Ash," Ricky replied. "What can I do?" His tone was panicked, worried, but Ash didn't have time to ease his concerns. In a couple more minutes, she might be dead.

"The power in the poison is going to kill me," Ash whispered between gritted teeth. "I need you to syphon the magic out of the poison."

"I'm not sure I can do that, kid."

"Then I'm as good as dead. C'mon, Uncle Ricky, I have faith in you."

Ricky licked his lips and muttered, "I don't have a fucking clue what I'm doing."

"You do. It's like instinct. Just like you know who has the most power." Ash groaned as her blood caught fire, and her lungs struggled to retain air.

The moment Ricky closed his eyes and rested his palm on her sternum, Ash's heart raced. Sweat ran down Ricky's forehead, and he grunted out a curse word. Ash coughed, and blood coated her lips.

The magic in the poison bucked and fought against Ricky's magic, but Ricky was stronger than the poison. His eyes flew open, and he begged Derek not to kill him for what he was about to do.

Ricky pressed his lips to hers, and she felt the pull of his magic, the poison retreating from her heart with a sharpness that made her gasp. The magic rushed from her veins like a fire when the oxygen was sucked form a room.

Tearing his lips from hers, Ricky coughed and then vomited up a whole heap of black tar, the scent of it as disgusting as the taste. Melanie made to touch her husband, but he held up a hand to stop her as he retched the magic poison onto the grass.

Sitting down in the grass once it was gone, Ricky gulped in a shuddering breath. Ash's throat burned, her stomach was raw, and she was more tired now than she had ever been in her life. Ricky looked horrified by what he'd just done as Ash leaned her head on her dad's shoulder.

Battling against exhaustion, her eyes drooped, but before she let herself fall asleep, Ash grinned and whispered, "You're just as good a kisser as your son."

CHAPTER TEN

"*You, Erika, are the daughter of Livana and our friend and fierce warrior, whom I have had the honor of fighting alongside as I have done with you today. You are no mere Valkyrie; you are the daughter of the god of war, my friend, Tyr.*"

From the moment Thor had said the words, Erika's life had been flipped upside down. Even coming face-to-face with her father, seated beside Odin, the man who wanted to lay waste to the world, Erika had felt nothing more than a fleeting curiosity for the man who'd helped conceive her.

Erika could not allow herself to form an attachment to Tyr when he sided with Odin. Still, the more Erika was around Ever and watched her with Ash—and knowing that Freya wouldn't exactly win any mother of the year contests—she had begun to wonder about her own parents.

And the continuous attempts by the god of war to contact her were driving her insane. So, Erika had flashed to a café in Paris with a glorious view of the Eiffel Tower and sat outside as she shot off a text and waited, watching as dusk fell and the tower came alive in a wash of lights. Even Erika felt herself smile at the sight.

She'd been to Paris before, many years ago, had even crossed paths with Caitlyn there, though the vampire had forgotten such an inconsequential meeting and Erika respected her too much to dredge up the past for her if she could avoid it.

Erika had been glamoured to avoid detection at the time, while Caitlyn had been human, cradling a human child. Erika did not like to contemplate that a mere few months after she left the city, Caitlyn had been turned by her maker. When Erika had shown up at the station and Caitlyn hadn't recognized her, Erika was grateful. Fate had crossed their paths before, and now that Caitlyn had found a semblance of contentment, Erika was loathe to peel it away.

Her phone rang, and Erika smiled as she answered it.

"Hey, you."

"Where have you disappeared off to, general?"

Erika rolled her eyes as if her Loki could see her. "As if you don't know."

When Loki didn't respond, she was instantly worried. "What happened?"

"We've had some unexpected things happen, my love. Everyone is okay now, but I feel things are escalating far quicker than expected."

"That's it... I'm on my way."

Erika was on her feet as Loki sighed down the phone. "We can wait a few more hours for you. It is not every day that you meet your father. Send him my regards."

"I can do this anytime. I'm coming back."

"Stay. You have questions only Tyr can answer. Then you and I will discuss my proposal."

Erika rolled her eyes. "I've already told you, not yet. Not until everything is settled. Meeting Tyr is not going to change that, Loki."

"We could all be dead tomorrow, Erika. We may not have a later."

"Well aren't you a glass of sunshine dipped in sugar."

Loki sighed in that exasperated tone that Erika knew meant she was fraying his nerves. He used that tone a lot, normally when he was grumpy and Erika had to kiss the bad mood out of him.

"Hang up the phone, lover. You have company."

Erika spun round. Her eyes widened at the giant of a man standing by her table with an expression so blank that Erika took a step back from the imposing figure.

The man stood over six feet tall. His hair was the same whiskey tint as her own, his eyes equally so. He was broad and muscular, with a faint puckering of scars on his neck. Dressed in modern-day clothing, Tyr looked out of place. The dark jeans and button-down shirt that was open at the first three buttons didn't suit him at all.

His eyes and expression suddenly softened, his gaze wandering over her, and Erika felt as if she were a miracle to behold. She most certainly was not a miracle, and she blanched under his scrutiny.

"How could I not have seen it," he said, "for when I look at you, I see your mother."

His voice was like thunderclaps in her ears, and her knees threatened to buckle. Erika stumbled, and Tyr reached out to steady her. The moment his hand touched her arm, it was as if a jolt of lightning went through her veins.

"Like recognizes like."

His voice was filled with pride, but Erika was not easily floored by gods and even less swayed by a father she hardly knew. Shaking off the sensations racing through her mind, Erika motioned for Tyr to sit, watching as he rested an artificial hand on the table. Erika could not take her eyes off it.

"Modern medicine is miraculous, is it not? I struggle to

remember what it was like, wielding two hands. However, this makes it easier to blend it."

Erika jerked her eyes up. "I'm sorry, that was rude. But I was raised by Freya; she tends to not teach manners in between lessons in disembowelment."

Tyr chuckled, and Erika felt her heart stutter at the sound of it. She was uncomfortable and wanted to run away, back to the relative safety of the life she knew. Erika was used to running away from her emotions, and it was one of the reasons she had put this meeting off for so long.

Scowling, she picked at her nails. "Listen, you need to stop blowing up my phone and asking to meet me. You see me, good; now I can go back to trying to stop the end of the world."

Tyr frowned, his eyes boring into her soul. "Had I known who you were, that you were right in front of my eyes this entire time, I would have come for you, shielded you from all of this."

"Then I'm glad you didn't know because I wouldn't change anything," Erika retorted with such resounding confidence that Tyr sat back. "You may have been the sperm donor who gave me some wicked genes, but I have a family—one that I chose and who chose me for who I am. But I didn't agree to meet you to rake over the past. I have questions that only you can answer."

A muscle ticked in Tyr's jaw, and Erika glanced away at the hurt in his eyes. She wasn't here as a way of reconnecting with her father; Erika knew Tyr was honor-bound to serve Odin, even if it meant he might never see his daughter alive again.

"Ask your questions, Daughter."

Ignoring the rough timbre of his tone, Erika cleared her throat. "What was she like, my mom?"

"You do not remember her?"

Erika shook her head, picking at her nails again. "I have a vague memory of her dropping me off at Valhalla. It's hazy; I can almost remember the way she smelled, the way she sounded, but I don't know if it's more of a manipulated memory than a real one."

Tyr was silent for a moment, his eyes shutting as golden lashes fanned his cheeks. "Livy, Livana stole my heart with one glance. I heard her laughter across the great hall in Asgard, and the sound of it wrapped around my heart and never let go. Where I was a storm, she was the sunshine that broke through."

Tyr opened his eyes, and Erika was struck by the look of love and adoration in his tone. It was as if her mother were still alive, and perhaps she was, even if only in his heart. "I asked her to dance, and her friends were appalled that I would dare do so, for even though I was a god, I was afflicted. However, Livy chastised her friends and stepped into my embrace. I should never have let her go."

Erika couldn't help but smile at Tyr's words. "She sounds nothing like me. I'm... rough around the edges."

"That, unfortunately, is something you inherited from your father."

Erika snorted and shook her head. Tyr inclined his head and held out his hand on the table. Erika's gaze narrowed, and she glared at him.

"I would like to share with you a treasured memory of your mother. I cannot reach inside Fólkvangr and reunite you with your mother, but perhaps, if you see her through my eyes, you will know if your memories are true."

Erika's hand trembled as she reached out and lay it in her father's palm, shocked again at the bolt it sent into her fingers. She peered up at Tyr, and he smiled, telling her to close her eyes. Erika let her eyes drift shut and gasped.

Hair like woven silk, she beamed at me as he neared, his heart racing as he gathered her in his arms and pressed his lips to hers. He drank in her beauty, the heart-shaped face and eyes of golden brown, and marveled at how much she could love me even when he returned carrying the scent of death on my skin and blood under my nails.

There was no greater feeling, no more intoxicating sensation, than having this goddess in my arms.

Second only to the elation of war was this feeling. He assumed that had he not been born as the god of war, a being who was created to win and curate battles, he would have never known what it was he missed, had he the chance to give it all up for the love of this woman.

"I missed you, my love."

"And I you, my Livy. I counted down the hours until I could come home to you."

Livy laughed, and the sound was like a homecoming. Her eyes were bright, eager, and mischievous as if she held a secret she had yet to share with him. He stepped back and beheld her.

He had been away merely three months, but it had felt like a lifetime. Her hips had widened whilst he'd been away, her breasts rounder. Her dress was a little stretched against her stomach, and she gave him a coy smile.

Tyr gathered her into his arms and kissed her with fervor, then dropped to his knees and kissed the belly of the woman her adored and the child he would protect with his last breath.

Erika jerked back with a sharp cry that turned heads at nearby tables. It was the same voice, the same face from her memories. It was the same smile that had bade her farewell on the shores of Valhalla before her mother was gone and then dead.

"The next morning, Livy disappeared, and I spent centuries trying to uncover the truth. I know not who killed your mother, but I will keep searching until my last breath."

God, she wished Melanie were here so she could tell if Tyr was lying or not. Erika couldn't get a read on him, probably because her own emotions were all over the place. She wanted to rage at Tyr, scream at him for not trying harder to find her.

But Erika was not the same girl she'd been in Valhalla, and she no longer needed to validate her feelings.

"Thank you for sharing that with me," she said. "It can't have been easy to recall that."

Rubbing his chin, Tyr tilted his head. "It is something I see every day; I relive so I remember. Though remembering is not as hard as it was before now that I know you are alive and well."

"Until we face each other on the battlefield and possibly have to kill one another."

Tyr gave a sad smile. "He is the Allfather, and I cannot stand against him."

"Even for me?" Erika asked with a snort, shaking her head. "Thor had the balls to stand with his sister and not with a megalomaniac who wanted to hit F5 on the world. You know he offered to make me the queen of Asgard if I stepped aside and let Ever fight without her general. What did he promise you to make you side with him over your blood?"

Tyr ducked his head, shame written all over his features. Erika knew—she instantly knew—what Odin had promised him. Odin had seen the same broken heart in Tyr that Odin held within himself, and the Allfather had promised to mend Tyr's heart.

"Odin won't bring her back, Tyr. And if what you say is true, my mother wouldn't have wanted to be brought back at the expense of the universe. Would you think she would want us, father and daughter, on opposite ends of a war instead of fighting side by side? You still have time to be on the right side of history."

Erika rose, and Tyr followed her lead. For a couple of heartbeats, they just stared at each other before Erika sighed, turning to leave.

"Erika, wait."

Hesitating, Erika turned back to her father, the great god of war who looked more defeated than a man about to face a firing squad. Part of her wanted to beg him to help them, to be the god of war that she knew from stories growing up on the shores of Valhalla and not this wounded warrior who would cling to a ghost instead of helping his flesh and blood.

Tyr glanced over her shoulder, and Erika knew Loki waited for her across the street. She turned her head and grinned at Loki, who spared her a wink, an amused look on his face. The two gods nodded their heads in greeting, and then Tyr turned his attention back to her.

"Does he make you happy?"

Peeking over her shoulder for a second, Erika thought back to Loki's words, back when she had found out exactly where she'd come from.

"We were both created in chaos. We were both born to destroy. You, Erika, were like war, and I was like death. And when we clashed, darling, I loved you."

Turning back to Tyr, Erika nodded. "Yeah, surprisingly so."

"Then I won't have to break his legs for laying hands on my daughter. I may not be so compliant if he hurts you."

Erika snorted, smiling at Tyr. "If he hurts me, I'm quite capable of breaking his legs myself."

"I have no doubt of that, daughter of mine. Livy would be so proud of the warrior and then woman you have become. As am I."

Erika turned away from her father, feeling lighter than she'd felt in a long time. Striding forward, she walked to where Loki waited for her and, leaning up, pressed her lips to his in greeting.

"Well, hello to you, too."

"You know I'm kind of in love with you, right?" Erika said as she tucked Loki's hair behind his ear.

The trickster god gave her a slow smile that heated her bones. "Only kind of?"

Stepping into him, Erika wrapped her arms around his neck. She kissed Loki with a passion that left her dizzy. When they broke apart under the dazzling lights of a Parisian night, they were both breathing hard.

"If we did not have more pressing dilemmas to deal with, darling, I'd have my wicked way with you right here and now."

"Then take me home before I try to convince you it would totally be worth it."

Loki flashed them both back to his home and stepped out of her embrace as his eyes wandered to the bed. Erika turned and tracked Loki's gaze to the prone body lying in bed.

"Who the hell is that?"

Loki glanced at the floor, and Erika wondered if she'd ever seen him look so guilty.

"That, my dear, is my son, Fenrir—the wolf responsible for your father's missing hand—who crashed into Caitlyn's garden in search of his mate who had vanished into the past on him."

Erika's jaw dropped open in shock. "Shut up."

No wonder Ash hated Loki; she was mated to the most vicious wolf in all of Norse history. Boyband was going to lose his shit over this.

"And then she knocked him out with a sleeping potion."

Erika's head spun as she walked around the side of the bed. She stared at the teenager who was so still it looked like he wasn't even breathing. Erika could make out some of Loki's features in the boy's face, but her lover must be in shock, for Fenrir had been locked away, his location known only to Odin himself.

"Odin possessed Kenzie," Loki said softly.

Panic flared inside her, but as she readied herself to flash to Ever's side, Loki continued.

"We believe he meant to poison Ever. However, Kenzie stabbed Ash instead, and Ricky had to ingest the magic to save her."

"Well fuck." Erika couldn't wrap her head around everything that was going on right now.

"Eloquently put as always, general."

Erika scoffed at his remark. "Listen, I'm going to go and check on Ever and Ash if you don't need—"

A hand wrapped around her throat, and Erika felt herself being lifted off the ground as the wolf in the bed stood and snarled. Erika struggled to breathe and tried to kick her captor, but he had an iron grasp on her throat.

"Now, Fenrir, if you cannot behave in a civilized way in our house, then I must teach you some manners."

Loki flexed his fingers, and Fenrir dropped Erika. As she gulped in a breath, Fenrir grabbed his head and snarled, his eyes flashing a murderous shade of red as Loki held him unmoving in the bed. The teen looked to Erika, straining against his father's magic and power, and Erika wondered if he could breakthrough.

"Hello, Mom," the teen said with a smirk, causing Erika to swallow hard. "Where the fuck is my mate, and why is she unconscious?"

EVER LEANED FORWARD IN HER CHAIR, WONDERING WHEN ASH WOULD *wake up. The young woman looked as if she were sleeping, the rise and fall of her chest reassuring Ever that Ash was indeed okay. Derek had spent most of the night pacing the floor until Donnie pulled him away to speak to Kenzie.*

The blood-kissed girl was distraught at the thought she'd hurt Ash and could be manipulated by Odin in such a way. There was a strange debate now sounding in the kitchen as Kenzie tried to persuade Caitlyn to change her.

Ever had closed the door to the bedroom a short time later, not wanting her daughter disturbed. Ash looked so young, lying in bed as Ever squeezed her hand.

"Come on, Ash. Time to wake up now."

And yet, Ash didn't so much as twitch in response.

Donnie reassured both Ever and Derek that Ash was simply using her sleep to recover from the effects of the poison and that her mind, her mind was very active. When Ever had asked Donnie to divulge what was inside her daughter's mind, Donnie had given her one of his charming smiles.

"I told you before that unless it's life or death, I will keep the secrets of those not strong enough to shield their thoughts from me. Ash is family, and I will not betray her trust."

Donnie had left shortly after, and Ever had felt so lost, so unable to help the girl who'd left her friends and family to travel back in time to stop Ever from making the biggest mistake of her life.

The door to the bedroom opened, and Erika stepped inside. Her whiskey-colored eyes darted to the bed and, with a sheepish grin and the faint imprint of fingertips around her neck, Erika said, "Please don't kill me for this, but I know how to get her to wake up."

Hope sparked inside Ever's chest, then suddenly dropped to the pit of her stomach as Erika stepped aside and Loki's son strode into the room, his eyes firmly fixed on Ash.

The baby in her stomach began to move in a frenzy, and Fenrir glanced at Ever with the most wolfish grin she had seen in her entire life. Her heart raced so fast she felt dizzy, and she placed a hand on her stomach to try and calm the child inside her.

When Ever lifted her gaze to clash with Fenrir again, she sucked in a breath as the young man walked over to her seat. He reached out and placed his palm on the top of her rounded belly and said in a commanding tone, "Rest."

The movement stopped, and Fenrir winked before turning his attention back to the prone figure in the bed. He brushed Ash's hair from her face, and Ever saw a muscle in her daughter's cheek twitch.

"Ashlyn."

Ever watched as her daughter's fist clenched, and Fenrir continued.

"Wake up, Ashlyn. Wake up little red. The big bad wolf is here, and he is rather pissed off at you. Now, stop being a goddamn martyr, Ashlyn, and wake the hell up."

And then Ash growled.

CHAPTER ELEVEN

ASH

A branch snapped behind her as she ran as fast as she could, her bare feet stinging. Zach was hurt, and she needed to get him some help; the fact that she was being chased didn't erase that fact. The scent of her own blood filled her nose and made her easier to track, but with no powers, Ash was simply a human.

The woods were eerily quiet as if they knew of the monster that had been unleashed and now, despite the various creatures that roamed through this magical forest, they were afraid of the one that chased her. And rightly so.

Ash stumbled over a tree root and rolled, ignoring the pain that bloomed in her shoulder. With a hiss, she got to her feet again and held out her hand, urging, pleading for her trusty Mjölnir, but the hammer of the gods failed to come to her aid.

Ash let loose a growl of frustration as she came to a diverged path, one going to her right and one path leading to the left. The path to her left led only to darkness, but the path that was illuminated by moonlight meant she'd be easy to track and easily seen. If she wanted to get help for Zach, she needed to be brave.

She heard her name on the wind as the darkened forest beckoned her forward, and without another thought, Ash bolted down the pitch-black pathway as fast as she could. Her eyes scanned all around her, yet she could not see a single thing and had to trust herself not to stumble or to be able to stop herself before running into danger.

Well, more danger.

Gods, her dad had been right. She should have left well enough alone, should have stopped the curiosity that had sparked in her veins when the team had discussed venturing into the forest in search of the mystical creature. Something primal in her had driven her, and Ash had convinced her partner and best friend to come along.

"Curiosity killed the cat, Ash," Zach had teased as he shoved supplies into his backpack.

"Then at least one of us will be alive to tell the tale, Z," Ash had teased back, thinking they were both indestructible.

She'd been so wrong. Dead wrong.

Her hood slipped off her head as she ran and ran for what seemed like days, and she still had not been able to find her way out of the forest. Skipping to a stop, she blew out a shaky breath. A deep, masculine chuckle sent shivers up her spine, and her wolf tilted her head in interest.

Ash felt the hairs on her neck stand to attention as a firm hand cupped the back of her neck, and Ash froze. Even in the dark, she sensed him watching her, knew he stood beside her, felt every one of her nerve endings ignite as he leaned in and brushed his nose against the nape of her neck. His scent overwhelmed her, the smell of wolf and magic and the air after rain had fallen.

"Little wolf, little wolf. Little red hood. I do love a good chase."

Ash felt panic surge through her body, and the urge to fight coursed through her. Reaching down to the waistband of her cargo pants, Ash gripped a dagger, slowly edging it out of it sheath until she felt the kiss of the blade against her stomach.

"Do you know who I am, little wolf? Do you know what I am?"

"Don't know, don't care. You hurt my friend, and now I'm going to repay the favor."

Ash jerked the blade up and struck, driving the dagger into the monster's neck. He let out a hiss as Ash stumbled away, the darkness of the forest suddenly lifting. Ash had to blink at the sudden brightness that flooded them. Her eyes took a moment to refocus, her vision blurry as she stepped back and glanced over her shoulder for an escape before turning her attention back to the monster that had hunted her.

Her wolf howled so loud pain laced through her mind as Ash's mouth dropped open. Standing in front of her was a boy so gorgeous he could only be of the gods. His inky-black hair was cut raggedly as if he'd used a blade to cut the ends that had gotten too long, and his eyes were so dark they resembled the night sky. He watched her from behind hooded lids, with lashes so long and dark they brushed his cheeks. And gods, when he smirked, those high cheekbones and full, sinful lips made Ash want to crawl out of her skin for him.

He was broad in shoulders and muscular, his tee straining against his chest as he yanked the blade from his neck and tossed it back to her. Ash caught the blade at the hilt, then braced herself for a fight.

The monster smiled as he stepped closer, and for every step he advanced, Ash retreated one step. The boy's grin deepened, and Ash felt her wolf flex her powers. Ash was powerless to stop the inevitable.

Ash gasped as the wolf's mating bond snapped into place, connecting her mind to his. The magic of it was like someone had whipped her mind, and Ash growled, resenting her mind linking with the monster's. Her parents were going to kill her.

"Mine," the boy growled.

Ash snorted. "I don't think so. I need to have a word with my wolf and convince her to make better choices. So, why don't you stay there, and I'll go straighten things out."

"What is your name, little wolf?"

Ash knew the mating bond would tell him all he needed to know, as it would Ash, but it would be a cold day in Hel before she messed with the magic of the bond and set the thing firmly into place. She needed to break it because she would rather die than be forced into this.

"What is your name, little wolf?"

Ash growled and readied herself to run, but a second later, the monster was in front of her, his hand wrapped tightly around her neck. For a second, the boy licked his lips as his eyes wandered down to her own lips. For a brief moment of madness, Ash wanted him to kiss her, needed him to kiss her. It was all-consuming and terrifying, but she didn't care.

"What is your name, little wolf? I will not ask you again."

Gritting her teeth against the command in his tone, Ash found herself saying, "Ashlyn. Ash. My friends call me Ash."

"Hello, my Ashlyn. My name is Fenrir, and I have been waiting for you for an eternity."

"Ashlyn."

Ash stepped back as the memory faded around the edges, ripping her to the brink of consciousness.

"Wake up, Ashlyn. Wake up little red. The big bad wolf is here, and he is rather pissed off at you. Now, stop bring a goddamn martyr, Ashlyn, and wake the hell up."

Ash growled as she felt herself being jostled, and without even cracking her eyes open, she knew that Fenrir had cradled her in his arms, her head resting in the curve between his shoulder and his neck. His scent overwhelmed her, like it had when she'd first come face to face with him.

"Ashlyn, stop being so stubborn and wake up. Your mother is worried about you."

"Fuck off, Grey," she muttered. He chuckled, his grip on her tightening as Ash slowly opened her eyes, the wolf very present as she lifted her gaze to her mother's.

"Hey, Mom."

Relief washed over Ever as she squeezed Ash's hand. "You gave us quite the scare. I need to tell your father that you're awake."

"Maybe it's best not to tell him that Aunt Erika let the psychopath into Caitlyn's house to try and wake me up, yeah?"

Ever got to her feet slowly, using Erika to help steady her as she leaned in to press a kiss to Ash's forehead. "All that will matter is that you are okay. We will give you a few minutes."

Ever and Erika left her alone with Fenrir, who watched her silently. Ash tried to slip out of his grasp, but it was solid as iron.

"Don't," he said.

"When will you learn that ordering me about doesn't make you any more appealing?"

"I think you find me appealing enough. Nice trick with the sleeping potion, by the way. Quite devious. I liked it."

Ash rolled her eyes. "Only you would be pleased that I acted in violence toward you. That's not healthy, Grey."

Fenrir chuckled, and Ash sighed as she gave in to her need to feel his skin against hers. Closing her eyes, Ash ran her fingers through his hair, felt it through the bond as Fenrir went deathly still. When her nails scraped over his scalp, Fenrir gasped, and Ash delighted in the fact that she had some sway over his emotions as well.

"Come home with me, Ashlyn."

"I can't. Not yet."

Fenrir sighed, and Ash shifted off his lap and stood facing away from him. She couldn't go back yet because she hadn't been safely born just yet, and there was still a chance she might not have fixed the crack in time that would be fractured if she were not born.

"Do you know what it felt like when you left? Chaos in my mind. Madness crept back into my thoughts, and the wolf took control. I almost disemboweled your cat because he was the reason you had been taken from me. The only thing that stopped me was that only he knew how to send me to you or bring you back."

Ash dropped her gaze to the floor. "Look, I didn't mean to hurt you, but the chaos and madness would have been way worse if I wasn't born. I still have a job to do, and I can't do it with you here, Grey. You need to go back. When I come back, we'll talk."

A hand on her arm spun her around, and Ash gritted her teeth as Fenrir gripped her chin. "I do this, and you stop avoiding me. I show you that I can be reasonable, and you agree to us. We are mated, Ashlyn. You need to learn to deal with it. Stop looking for magic scrolls and means to break the bond. Swear to me that you will stop, and I will return to the future."

Giving Fenrir her most coy smile, Ash countered, "You leave now, and I will *consider* stopping looking for a way to break the bond. I will agree to go on a date with you and try and get to know you. That's as much I can promise right now."

"Deal."

Fenrir pressed his lips to hers, and as he felt the power of the deal being bound as he cupped her face in his hands. Ash let him tug on her bottom lip, his tongue tasting her lips before he pulled back. Ash touched her hands to her lips without meaning to.

Fenrir backed away from her, removing a familiar and comforting piece of glass from his pocket, a shard of the Bifrost, and a bit of home. He used the shard to cut his palm, and with one more blistering look, Fenrir was gone. Ash felt as if a piece of her soul had gone with him.

Taking a moment to gather her thoughts, Ash was about to leave the bedroom when a short rap of knuckles sounded before the door cracked open, and Ricky ducked his head inside.

"You alone?"

Ash grinned and gestured to the room. "Yup. I managed to convince the psycho to go home. You can come in."

Ricky opened the door and stepped inside, Melanie coming in behind him, her hand resting on the small of Ricky's back as if to reassure him that everything was okay.

Ricky scrubbed a hand down his face, and Ash smiled. It was

such a familiar gesture, one that Zach did all the time when he was trying to think of the right thing to say.

Ricky studied her for a minute before curiosity got the better of him. "What put the smile in your eyes?"

Ash snorted as she sat down on the bed. "Zach does the same thing all the time. I tease him a lot because we all know the stories of Ricky Moore, the reckless rookie who became one of P.I.T.'s best agents. We joke all the time that I somehow inherited your reckless streak, and he inherited my dad's logic and reasoning."

Ricky gave her a beaming grin that was achingly familiar, but then his eyes darkened. "How did you know I could do that?"

Ash shrugged her shoulders. "I didn't. You've only just begun to understand the magical changes becoming immortal has given you. I hoped that the need to save me would outweigh any fears you had. I'd be dead now if it weren't for you."

Ricky opened his mouth to speak, then clamped it shut. He glanced at Melanie, and she rolled her eyes with a smile before she turned to look at Ash.

"He's spent the last couple of hours apologizing to me and Ever and avoiding Derek because he had to kiss you to get the magic out. I think my husband is a little uneasy about how it happened."

Ash shrugged her shoulders. "There's nothing to be uneasy about, Uncle Ricky. And my dad won't care how you did it, just that you saved my life."

"I was," Ricky began, his voice low and tinged with sadness. "I was compelled by a succubus once and forced to hurt people I cared about. I don't think I can deal with being like this if my magic makes me do stuff like that. I can't be like that. I won't."

Ash's heart threatened to break for her uncle, and while she didn't want to divulge too much about the future, she felt that since Ricky had saved her life, the fates would be okay with her sharing one small detail.

"New magic," Ash began, loosening the grip on her wolf and watching her fingers elongate into claws before firmly putting a leash around the wolf and watching her fingers became normal once more, "is the hardest to control. There has not been a physic vampire created in over two hundred years, and Caitlyn killed the last one for Cain. The new powers in you don't care about finesse or you being uneasy, they just want to feed. In time, you'll be able to reach out without touching to feed."

Ricky's shoulders sagged in relief as Ash glanced up at Melanie. "Just like your own powers will grow as Donnie's do. One day, Melanie Newton-Moore, you will be able to not only taste lies, but also make someone tell you the truth."

Melanie's eyes widened as her mouth formed an O, and Ricky nudged his wife with a smile.

Ash rubbed her temples as she heard raised voices down the hall. Ricky excused himself, and Melanie turned to follow but stopped and turned back to Ash.

"When you talk, you make it sound like we win. That we defeat Odin, and we all live our lives. What aren't you telling us?"

Ash knew to be careful with her words, had learned at a young age to do so. "The more belief you have that you will succeed increases the chances that when I return home, the future will be as it is meant to be."

Melanie inclined her head and paused as if she knew Ash had something else to say to her. Ash chewed on her bottom lip as Donnie stepped into the room and caught her eye. Ricky must have told him what she'd said, and now he was intrigued as to where his powers could go.

Melanie raised her brows as if impatient, and Ash smiled as she bit the bullet. "When he asks if he can call you Mom in a few years, don't hesitate before you answer. It stays with him that you hesitated. He thinks you only said yes because he wanted it and not because you think of him as a son."

Blinking in surprise, Melanie muttered her thanks before she slipped from the room, patting Donnie on the arm as she passed. Ash made to join her, eager to see what was causing all the arguments in the living room, but Donnie blocked her way.

Folding her arms across her chest, she said, "What happened to 'I'm good with waiting for the future to unveil itself, Ash'?"

Donnie grinned. "Touché. But I've always wondered where my powers could go."

"Powers mature over time, Donnie, and now that you are mated and Caitlyn is one of the oldest of her line, the power trickles down the line... When you turn—"

Ash bit out a curse and clamped her mouth shut, singing a 90s rap song over and over in her mind to keep Donnie out of her head before she wagged a finger at him.

"Sneaky vampire. Almost had me saying things I shouldn't. Now, shall we go calm Kenzie down before your mate gets too upset?"

"Ash... wait."

Ash brushed past Donnie and made her way through the kitchen and into the living room. Everyone was arguing as Caitlyn and Kenzie screamed at each other, Derek and Loki were having words, and Ricky and Melanie were trying to make peace. Ash stood in the doorway and growled loud enough to quieten the room, Kenzie immediately dropping her gaze to the floor.

"I did not come all the way from the future to watch you all self-implode. Get your acts together for fuck's sake. Now, I'm going to hunt for an arsonist who likes to lull people to sleep with a lullaby of smoke and death. Who's gonna be a goddamn adult and help me?"

∾

Standing outside the cottage that had kept its historical features gave the arsonist a sense of nostalgia that prickled on his conscience, even when he thought he'd erased that part of himself over a century ago.

The framed windows and thatched roof would burn within minutes, taking much of the usual pleasure of burning the house to cinders from him, yet he did not feel that this would bring him much joy.

He'd sat inside this house, eaten at its table, and shared a laugh and a joke beside the fireplace. He'd once been so welcome here that he could simply knock and shout a greeting before crossing the threshold, never to be turned away when he needed a hot meal or a roof over his head.

Those people no longer dwelled here, but the bricks and mortar held the essence of those long gone.

With a hint of remorse, he allowed the heat to rise to his palms as he placed a hand on the door that was once always open to him. The door was engulfed in flames a second later, and he turned his gaze away from the memories of his past.

Derek Doyle was lucky that his niece was not home this evening, or she'd be another body to bury. Or had he planned it so... because burning down the childhood home of Derek Doyle hurt him more than it should have.

CHAPTER TWELVE

DEREK

Derek couldn't help but feel chastised by his daughter... and also a little envious of her. She was dealing with enough of her own drama, however, without dealing with his team's emotional baggage. Yet here she was, calling them out while focusing on the job at hand.

She was definitely his kid.

Ash rolled her eyes when no one bothered to answer her, then strode over to Kenzie and folded her hands across her chest. Kenzie tapped her foot nervously before taking a sharp breath and snapping her head up to meet Ash's gaze.

Derek watched as Kenzie held Ash's gaze for longer than she should have before glancing down. Ash cleared her throat, and Kenzie looked up again.

"You done beating yourself up? Good. Grandfather got in your head and made you stab me instead of Mom because he doesn't have a clue who I am. Good. Donnie stopped you from hurting yourself. Good. You and me? Good. And no, Caitlyn won't be turning you into a vampire, so stop whining, put on that badass hunter face of yours, and let's go hunt some criminals."

Kenzie was so shocked by Ash's cold tone that she staggered back as if pushed. Caitlyn steadied her with her hand. With a snarl, she took a step forward before realizing what she was doing, and Ash laughed.

"Come on, killer. You want to throw a punch at me, go for it. You'll spend the next few weeks healing a broken fist."

Ash turned and walked out into the night air, slamming the sliding door shut behind her so hard the glass shook. Caitlyn squeezed Kenzie's shoulder and made to go after Ash.

"Cait, don't. Give the kid a few minutes. She needs a few minutes to herself."

Everyone glanced at Donnie, who held up his hands. "Hey, stop glaring at me. This was definitely a life-or-death situation, because the next person to get in her face is getting smacked with that hammer."

Ever winced, and Derek dropped down to his knees. "You okay?"

She smiled at him through the pain. "All good. She's just being overactive."

"I think you should go somewhere safe until she arrives. I get the feeling she's gonna make an entrance."

Ever reached up and patted his cheek, and he felt the love she had for him down the mating bond. It was the reason why Derek hadn't tried to fight Fenrir when he'd claimed Ash. If the mating bond were strong, even though he might not like it, Derek would only hurt his daughter by arguing with her and her mate.

Ever closed her eyes and leaned back in the chair, Derek's hand pressed to her stomach as she smiled. Derek grabbed a throw from over the back of the couch and placed it over Ever as she slept.

Getting to his feet, Derek turned and decided to use Ash's

direct approach. He pointed to Ricky, who swallowed hard. "You, me, kitchen. Now."

Ricky opened his mouth to argue but turned on his heels and went to the kitchen. Derek walked in as Ricky pulled two beers from the fridge and slid him one, opening his own and taking a gulp before he could even look at Derek.

"Listen, D—"

Before his best friend could finish, Derek had stalked around the counter and put his hands on Ricky's shoulders. "Thank you for saving my daughter's life."

"Dude, you can't be thanking me for shit like that, especially when I had to kiss her to do it. She says I'm not like *them,* that I just can't control it right now, but I feel sick thinking about it— more so than when I upchucked the poison onto the lawn."

Derek stepped back and lifted his own beer to his lips. When he'd finished and Ricky was still looking at him like he expected Derek to deck him, Derek set the bottle down. "When you tried to save her life by touching her, did the magic compel you to put your lips on hers?"

Ricky bobbed his head stiffly.

Derek smiled. "Then we have no issues, Ricky. You saved her life. I don't care how you did it. I'd expect you to do it again, for any of us, if you needed to."

"You're just jealous that I kissed Donnie and not you, right? Don't go courting death just because you want a kiss, D. I mean, come here right now, and no one needs to know."

Derek barked out a laugh as Ricky grinned. If his friend was making jokes, Derek knew he'd be all right. Glancing outside, he saw Ash leaning against the fence and watched Loki walk cautiously toward her. Derek nodded to Ricky and slipped out through the kitchen door.

He wasn't fool enough to think neither Ash nor Loki knew he'd come out into the garden, but he only lingered off to the side in case Ash needed him.

"My son is quite besotted with you."

"Your son is a psychopath who is obsessed, not besotted."

Silence hung heavy in the air; Derek scented the tinge of sadness in his daughter's tone. Loki leaned over the fence, and it seemed as if neither would speak again until Ash began to speak softly.

"Part of me wants to tell you not to look for him, even though I know you've been searching for centuries. Part of me wants to lie and tell you that finding him will set into motion far greater consequences than you can imagine. But I can't do it. The future is what it is, and Grey might be a thorn in my side, but even I cannot change fate."

Loki wrapped an arm around her for a second before dropping his arm and turning to face Ash. "Why do you call him Grey?"

Derek leaned against the wall as Ash rolled her eyes. "He always calls me Ashlyn, never Ash, no matter how many times I ask him to. So, after he showed me his wolf for the first time, the huge, gray monster that terrified me, I've called him Grey to piss him off. Doesn't seem to faze him, but I'm in too deep now to take it back."

Derek's phone rang, interrupting the moment, and he yanked out the device and answered it without looking at the screen. "Doyle."

"Oh my God, Derek, the house is on fire. Grandmother's house is on fire."

Derek's heart plummeted to his stomach as his niece cried on the phone. "Chloe, get away from the house right now."

"Derek, you need to get here right now. The fire brigade is on the way, but it's gone, Derek. The house is gone."

The line disconnected, and Derek bolted around the side of the house, fishing in his pocket for his car keys when he remembered he didn't have his car with him. Ricky's car was parked sideways in the drive and, as if his partner knew what was happening, he appeared in the doorway and tossed his keys into the air.

Derek was in the car and driving in a moment, ignoring Ricky's pleas to wait for him. He peeled the car out of the drive and shot through the streets of Cork at speeds not legal in any country. Derek's childhood home was situated just outside Blarney, on a tiny slip of country road. He could see the plumes of smoke in the distance, his heart breaking that the only link to his human life was now up in flames.

When he arrived, he skidded to a halt and leapt from the car, leaving the door open as he crossed the road and raced toward Chloe, who was standing next to a member of the garda. The uniform stood back as Derek reached his niece.

"You okay?" he asked as he tucked her to his chest, his eyes glued to the house.

Chloe nodded. "I wasn't inside when it went up. Justin and I have been taking some time, and I used the spare key to get in. We'd decided to meet up tonight but got into another fight, and I stormed off early. Half an hour earlier and I'd have been inside."

"It's okay, munchkin. Once you're safe, that's all that matters."

Chloe laughed despite the fear leaking from her pores. "You know it freaks people out that you call me munchkin, especially when I look older than you."

"Tough. You'll always be my little niece. But now I need you to go home to your ass of a husband and stay there. Someone is coming for me, and I can't worry about him catching you instead."

Chloe looked at him with her million-dollar stare that made hardened criminals quake in their boots. "Don't go dancing with death, Derek. You are not superman."

Derek flashed her a grin as he motioned for a uniform to come over. Leaning in to Chloe, he whispered in her ear. "I don't intend to die just yet. I have a mate and a soon-to-be daughter on the way. I'm not going anywhere."

Chloe was still grinning madly at him as the uniform escorted her away, leaving Derek to survey the damage done to his childhood home. The embers had begun to die down, and the gallons of water doused on the house flooded the road and sloshed up against his boots.

Detective Pierce came up to Derek and inclined his head. "Same magic as before, Agent Doyle. Our resident fire mage sensed the same signature, although he said it's nothing he's ever felt before. The fire's almost out now, so we'll be leaving soon."

Derek thanked the detective and stared at the house as the flashing lights disappeared into the night and left him alone with the dying embers of his childhood. Closing his eyes, he could almost hear Sylvia and Mark's laughter as they raced each other around the garden. He could smell his mother's stew cooking on the stove and the crisp smell of his father's cigars. He remembered sitting on the front steps after getting his heart broken for the first time. He remembered his father shouting at him when he came in drunk for the first time at fifteen.

Then Derek was struck by a memory so hard it felt like a punch in the gut.

He'd been standing outside the house now for the better part of an hour, terrified to walk in and tell his family he'd enlisted in the army. Derek had never been one for school, he just didn't see the point of it— especially when the only outcome for him other than service would be to follow in his father's footsteps, and his father had already chosen to train Mark in the business.

The rain pelted down hard as Derek stood outside, his clothes clinging to his body and water dripping down his face. He hadn't the heart to walk in that door and get chewed out by his Ma again for enlisting in the army of his own free will when he'd likely be called up anyway.

The door to the cottage opened, and his mother stood in the doorway and called his name. Derek tried to shake the water from his eyes as his mother ordered him in that tone of hers and scolded him for standing outside like a misbehaved pup.

Derek went inside and let his mother usher him toward the open fire. She sat in her armchair and waited until he'd warmed himself a little, then she said, "You've done it then, eh?"

"I have, yeah."

"When do you go?"

"Tomorrow, Ma. They say they require me tomorrow, so I will go."

His mother regarded him for a moment before she tsked. "Then go get yourself out of those wet clothes, Derek Doyle. I'd say it will be a long while before you have another decent hot bath. Or a hearty meal, I would think. Leave that to me. Tell your sister that I want her when you pass her room."

Derek had nodded and called on his sister, who'd refused to talk to him until the moment he'd tossed his bag over his shoulder, dressed in his army uniform, and headed off at the young age of sixteen, when she'd told him not to die on her.

His ma had stayed quiet and stoic, even as his Da sent him off with a grunt before heading back inside. Derek strode away from the house that was home, up the winding road until his family was a blur in the distance. Still, he was certain he could hear his ma weeping, the sound of it carrying along the road with him as he went.

Derek's eyes snapped open, his heart aching like it had been shot with an arrow. While he kept some mementos of his past in his current home, he had kept most here, in this house filled with ghosts. Now that the ghosts were not bound inside, he'd have to carry them with him, all the days of his life.

Derek's phone rang, the sound breaking the silence of the night. "Doyle," he answered with a gravely tone.

"Hello, pup."

The voice on the other end of the line did nothing to dissuade Derek that burning down this house hadn't unleashed his ghosts, the voice being the reason why his father had drunk himself to an early grave and his mother had thought her son dead.

"I had a feeling this was you, old man. Can't fight your own damn battles, you have to send thugs and broken little boys after me," Derek growled.

Neville Morris chuckled. "Still have the fight in you, pup, good to know. Now, it's time for a reckoning. Come meet me."

"If you wanted a reckoning, Morris, then you should have faced me like a proper werewolf, teeth and claws, and not killed someone who was a better man than you could ever be."

"And because you told countless people in interviews that Sergeant Thomas Delaney was the man responsible for who you became, I had to remind you who your real creator was, dear boy. It was my bite that made you, and I was damn well not going to let a mangy bear lay claim to my work."

Derek snorted. "You killed Sarge because you were jealous? Your bite may have changed me, but Sarge is the one responsible for keeping me alive. Burning down houses and murdering innocent people for having the misfortune of sharing my team's initials proves just how pathetic you are."

There was a pause, and Derek heard a car drive slowly toward him, the lights suddenly flaring so he had to shield his eyes from the beam. The engine running, one of its doors opened, yet no one stepped out.

"Playing games, Morris? Trying to intimidate me? I have faced down gods and not even trembled. What makes you think I'm the same pitiful wolf that was chained in your compound and forced to fight for your entertainment? I will rip off your head without even breaking a fucking sweat."

A growl rumbled in his ear as Morris swore, and Derek allowed himself a cocky smile.

"Get in the car, Doyle or my associate will be forced to

encourage you. I wonder how much burning it would take before you howl for mercy."

"I'd die first."

"We'll see, pup. We'll see. Now drop the phone and get in the car. See you soon."

Morris hung up. Derek tossed his phone into the front seat of Ricky's car, bracing himself to fight whatever crony Morris had sent to bring him in. Derek was spoiling for a fight, his wolf already agitated as the figure got out of the car and came forward.

The beams were meant to disorientate him, keep him from seeing his assailant's features. Still, even so, the other man seemed to hesitate before stepping forward.

"Ask yourself if Morris' mission is worth it. Are you willing to die because some old man asks it of you?"

"Isn't that what young men do in war, mate? We die because old men tell us to."

Derek shook his head, not believing his ears as a once — familiar, lilting tone hit him like a sledgehammer. They were words he'd said over a century ago, one night over a campfire, as one of the newer lads asked why they had to fight. Derek was sure his mind was playing tricks on him, the voice he heard was a ghost; that couldn't be possible.

"I must say, you look good for an old man, Lu. Sure, weren't you always a handsome bastard?"

Derek couldn't move, couldn't utter a word as, like an apparition, his biggest regret and person he had missed and bled for, stood in front of him. A shock of red hair and freckles, Sam's cheeky smile tugged on his lips as if they were still soldiers messing around by a campfire.

"You're dead," Derek mumbled, stepping toward the man who'd somehow been reborn from the darkness.

The man did a little twirl. "Nah, Lu. I *was* dead, just like you, but I came back as something bigger and badder than a wolf."

Fire engulfed the palm of his right hand, and Derek's stomach churned as he realized that his ghost had been the one to kill Sarge. Morris had known nothing in the present could hurt Derek more than the loss of Sarge, and he'd sent Derek's best friend to do it.

"Sam... how is this possible?"

The ghost that was Sam grinned, dousing the flames in his hand. "I rose from the fookin' ashes, mate."

Sam sucker-punched him, hitting him square in the jaw, and the last thing Derek saw before his head bounced off the tarmac was a murderous glint in his former best friend's eyes, the flames dancing in the dark.

CHAPTER THIRTEEN

EVER

E ver and Erika lay on their stomachs in the dunes, trying to sneak a peek at the gathering of immortals taking place just over the rise. Ever was itching to get closer to see for herself what was happening; however, Freya had inexplicitly banned them from coming closer. Even now, they skirted around disobeying a direct order, but as Erika had pointed out, Freya had only banned them from setting foot on the beach below them, she never mentioned the dunes.

Freya reclined in a chair made from bamboo at the head of the table, her golden hair braided like that of a warrior, her sword resting across her lap even as she supped her mead. Her eyes were cold and distant as she scanned the assembled crowd. Even though Ever and Erika had both seen gods before, to see so many out in the open still made both girls stare in awe.

Ever glanced at Erika, and her best friend and future general was staring at one immortal god in particular—her adopted brother. Loki lounged in his own chair at the foot of the table, a golden goblet so encrusted with jewels the sun glinted off it as Loki lifted it to his lips. Ever rolled her eyes, hoping that her friend would get over this little crush she had on her brother before it got weird. Loki of Asgard was the type of man who was never short a bedfellow, and Erika would end up with a broken heart should she even contemplate waiting for him to notice her.

Ever nudged her, and Erika's cheeks heated as she dragged her eyes away to peer at the other immortals gathered on the sands of Valhalla.

Ever's brother Thor and his wife, Lady Sif, stood off to the side with Tyr, the god of war, his body tense. Her uncle and Freya's twin, Freyr, leaned forward in his seat as he said, "Odin has begun to kill those who may be strong enough to oppose him. He has also doubled his efforts to find anything Ragnarök related."

Tyr shook his head. "I cannot stand by and listen to this treason. I will not inform the Allfather of this, but I want no part of it."

The god vanished a second later as Erika muttered asshole under her breath.

Ever watched as her family pondered how best to solve the growing problem that was Odin. She wasn't sure when her relationship with her father had changed; he had always showered her with love and affection, a direct contrast from Freya. But recently, since Frigg had passed on to Fólkvangr, something had been triggered in Odin. Now, all of her family were trying to determine who could best handle Odin and his quest to usher in the end of days.

"He has been searching for the scrolls of fate," Freya sighed. "obsessed with bringing Frigg back. He summoned Hel to Asgard, and when she advised him that not even she could break the rules to bring Frigg back from death, he cursed her back to Hel to remain there for a half-dozen centuries before she could stand foot in Midgard once more."

Loki glanced down at his goblet as he tried not to betray his emotions. His children were always a touchy subject, and he only let his true feelings slip through when he was intoxicated.

"We must think long and hard before we publicly stand against Father," Thor boomed, "for we, too, could end up banished to the far corners of the nine realms for centuries."

Ever shook her head. Thor did not have a quiet bone in his body.

"He has become obsessed with remaining the most powerful god in Asgard," Sif added. "Odin cornered me one day and asked if I planned to have children with Thor. There was a darkness in his eyes that made me feel fear for the first time in an age."

Thor rested a hand on Sif's shoulder, and they smiled sadly at one another as if they now knew children were not in their cards until after Odin had recovered from his madness.

"Then he will come after Ever," Freya said. "Odin may control Asgard, but she is the one to inherit the rule of Valhalla. She will control the armies, according to the fates, when and if Ragnarök is ushered in. Odin will want control over the Valkyries and the dead who wait to be brought forward in the final battle."

Freya's voice was a little tense as she took a sip of her own mead. Loki glanced toward where Ever and Erika hid in the dunes, and Ever thought for a moment that her brother would give them away. Motioning with her head, Ever crept along the sand. After a few minutes and a curse, Erika followed her out.

Dashing through the forest, they burst into Ever's little hut and flopped down on their beds. Erika rolled over on her side to face Ever and frowned. "Thor wants to have children?"

"Is that not what adults do to create a being in their image?" Ever asked, wondering of the two, whether she was more like a maddening Odin or cold Freya.

"Well, I never plan on letting myself be tied to another by a child. There will only ever be one of me, and that is quite enough for the nine realms."

Ever let loose a whoop of laughter and smirked. "Not even if it was the child of a certain brother whom you find rather enticing?"

Erika snarled and tossed her pillow at Ever. "Hardly! Loki's children are as feared as he, and I don't particularly fancy giving birth to monsters now, do you?"

Ever made to retort, but her friend was not finished. "But that is not to say," Erika continued in a low tone, her eyes narrowing, "that we would not have much fun. I imagine him to be a relentless lover."

Pulling a pillow over her head, Ever groaned into the fabric as Erika chuckled softly. Ever found herself smiling, too, keeping her own fears and expectations to herself because she could not wait for the day when someone loved her enough to create life.

Ever's eyes fluttered open slowly, and she sucked in a breath. The mating bond was suddenly shut down, so quickly nausea rolled in her stomach. Blinking her eyes a few times to clear the fog of sleep, Ever focused on the face of her best friend and the deep form of concentration marring her beautiful features.

"Where's Derek?"

Erika said nothing as Caitlyn came in and handed her a mug of sweet-smelling tea. Ever cracked an eyebrow, and Caitlyn smiled softly. "During my final few weeks of pregnancy with Jessamine, whenever I was exhausted or feeling queasy, Bass would brew me this tea. It helped with the nausea."

Sadness in her heart, Ever gave Caitlyn a small smile. "Thank you. But I need to know where Derek is. I know something's wrong; I can feel it through the bond."

Erika shifted in her seat and sighed. "Boyband got a call from Chloe to say his family home was on fire. Derek took off by himself, and now he isn't answering his phone."

Ever closed her eyes and pushed her own power into their bond, flinging the door open for the briefest of moments before Derek slammed it shut again. However, in that fleeting moment, Ever brushed against fear, sadness, shock, and panic.

Snapping her eyes open again, Ever staggered to her feet, growling as Erika reached out to help her. "Erika, get my sword. My mate is in trouble, and I need to get to him."

"Ever, you aren't exactly in fighting form. And if you get hurt, then Ash gets hurt."

Placing her hands on her hips, Ever took a step toward Erika. "I'm going. Either you come with me, or I'm getting in a car and driving myself to Derek. Something is wrong, and he needs our help. If I'm right, then I cannot let Ash grow up not knowing her father. Now, get in a goddamn car, everyone, or I'm going to make someone bleed."

Ash chuckled, and Ever turned to look at her. Hammer in hand, Ash headed for the door, but not before she magically changed from her everyday clothes to her Asgardian uniform, her red cloak billowing as she walked.

Erika handed Ever her sword and led her out to the cars waiting outside. Every single member of the team was going with them, all piling into two cars: Caitlyn, Ash, Erika, Ever, and Loki in one, and Donnie, Kenzie, Ricky, and Melanie in the other. As Caitlyn slipped into the driver's seat in front of Ever, Ever's heart began to beat like a drum.

Glancing in the rearview mirror, Caitlyn's gunmetal eyes held hers as she said, "Derek will be okay. He will fight to get back to his family."

They pulled out of the drive, and Ever felt a ripple of magic against her skin as they exited the property and headed down the hill.

Ash reached over and patted her hand. "Ricky and Caitlyn strengthened the wards on the house when the arsonist was targeting P.I.T. It stings a little when you aren't expecting it."

Ever felt a slight twinge in her side but ignored it as Caitlyn suddenly barked out a curse in her native tongue and skidded the car to a halt.

"Do not leave this car, Ever," Loki ordered. "No matter what happens, you do not leave this car. The cars are warded and cannot be entered by anyone meaning to cause harm to anyone in the team or our families. Heed our warning and *do not* get out of this car." With that, Loki vanished and suddenly reappeared outside, standing with his back to her.

Caitlyn and Erika jumped out next as Ash squeezed Ever's hand and flashed away but did not reappear on the road like everyone else. Donnie rushed past the car, the vampire rolling up his sleeves. Melanie strode over to stand beside Caitlyn as Ricky's hands flared with blue flames.

Ever leaned forward to see what was going on, but her friends and family were blocking her view. Reaching for the handle, Ever pushed the car door open slightly as lightning streaked through the sky, cracking it like glass and shattering the night.

Ever swung her legs out of the car, and the moment her feet hit the road, a hand grabbed her arm. "You never could follow the rules," a familiar voice hissed. "I blame the general for your poor lack of self-preservation."

"I was taught never to let others fight my battles for me. No matter what, letting others die for me is never how I intend to rule."

Freya's eyes flared with pride. "And that is what makes you mine and not his. Valkyrie," she shouted, "protect your queen and future queen."

Freya helped Ever out of the car, and the Valkyries formed a barrier around her. There was Danae, once a prideful girl who'd wanted to be in charge, wielding an ax. Rebekah, a raven-haired warrior with palmed daggers and death in her eyes, stood next to her. Finally, Almira, the bookish girl who lacked the blood-lust to be Valkyrie. The usually subdued girl lifted her chin and snarled, a sword gripped so hard in her left hand that Ever could see the whites of her knuckles.

Many of her kin were dead, slain by Odin and his berserkers during his reign of madness. No more would die if Ever could help it.

Ever headed for the assembled crowd, and Erika turned to roll her eyes at her friend. "I guess asking you to go back to the car would be a waste of perfectly good oxygen, right?"

"We are Valkyrie; we do not back down from any fight."

Ever felt a sharp tug on the mating bond and gasped. "Derek."

Ricky rescinded the flames and came over, a silent question in his eyes.

"Go," Ever said. "Go find my mate and bring him back to me."

"You got it." Calling for Melanie, Ricky hesitated for a second before Caitlyn pushed Melanie toward Ricky, telling the vampire to go with her husband and be safe.

Ever was certain not a single one took a breath as Ricky and Melanie reversed up the road and took the long way round. With the gap in her field of view, Ever was now able to see what had caused them all to leap from their cars and prepare for battle.

Odin stood in the middle of the road, his white hair fluttering in the wind, his eye focused on their group. Ever let her gaze drift to the patch covering the eye that she had taken from him. His staff was primed as lightning crackled from the sky, striking the staff and sending power crackling across her father's skin.

"Come out and face me, Daughter. Or have you gone soft spending time with inferior creatures?"

Ever stepped forward, letting Erika block her body from full view. "I do not spend time with inferior creatures, Odin; I spend time with warriors more worthy of the halls of Asgard than you are right now. These *inferior creatures* are the family my mate and I have chosen as our own."

The sky cracked again with a double burst of lightning, and Ever smiled slyly, even as she took in the army of berserkers gathering behind Odin. Hundreds of the rabid beasts crested the hill, and Ever feared they would not be enough to stop Odin this night, but she did not let an ounce of that fear into her voice or demeanor.

"You stand alone, Father, apart from the creatures who follow any who promise them death and blood. What of your gods and goddesses? Have they all abandoned you to your madness?"

Odin's jaw ticked before he collected himself and banged his staff on the ground beneath his feet. The earth shuddered, groaning before—like lightning shattering the skies—a crevasse streaked along the road and split the team in two.

Caitlyn and Donnie reached across the gaping hole, and Donnie lifted Caitlyn's hand to his lips as if saying a silent farewell should they not survive. Caitlyn turned to incline her head to Kenzie, who stood closest to Ever and Donnie, and the blood-kissed girl tilted her scythe to Caitlyn.

Loki stepped forward as if to try and speak to Odin when the god swiped out with his hand and a cut sliced down Loki's cheek. Loki didn't so much as flinch. Instead, the god of mischief tapped into his hidden heritage, his lips turning blue, his breath frost as he flexed his fingers and shot ice at the ground.

They were all poised to fight to end Odin's reign of terror. They were all prepared to die. And Ever could not stand by and watch them die for a cause that was not theirs. Before she had time to contemplate any further, however, Odin raised his staff, and the first round of berserkers charged forward.

Donnie went in hard right away, taking the first berserker down with a shoulder tackle straight out of a rugby handbook. As soon as the berserker hit the ground, Donnie snapped his neck with bare hands and was on to the next one.

Caitlyn moved with an assassin's grace, her motions mesmerizing as she stabbed and slashed her way forward, blood streaking her face and clothing. Kenzie moved just like Caitlyn, her scythe calling those she felled to death from one breath to the next.

Loki only had to touch a berserker, and the rage monster was instantly cast in ice. Then Loki kicked each frozen statue, and they crumbled in a frenzy of ice and blood. It was terrifying to behold, but Ever felt a surge of pride that her brother, the once carless god, now fought like a man possessed because he had someone to fight for.

"Go help Loki, Erika."

"I do not leave your side."

"That's an order," Ever ground out as another twinge gripped her stomach.

By the gods, not now. Please, not now.

Freya came to stand beside Erika. "General, you stay where your place is, beside your queen. It is time I faced the demons of my past."

Freya unleashed her wings with a battle cry, the feathers composed of white and gold, and Ever marveled at their beauty as her mother surged forward and began cutting through berserker after berserker, their blood staining the country road. One knocked her with a clenched fist, but Donnie caught her foot before she crashed into a telephone pole and flung her back into the fray.

Odin raised his staff. More berserkers roared, joining in the battle. Ever knew they were sorely outnumbered and in desperate need of reinforcements. Her hands on her stomach, Ever glanced around at her sisters. "Valkyries, you must go into battle."

"We protect the heirs, my queen. Freya ordered us to."

Erika clamped her hand down on Danae's arm. "And your queen has asked you to go into battle. I will protect the queen and the heir. Go forth, my sisters, and let the berserkers see who are the *most* bloodthirsty creatures in all the nine realms!"

Erika's last words were a call to arms, and her kin responded with a battle cry as they charged away, leaving Erika and Ever standing to the side. A figure flashed in front of them, and Erika put a hand protectively in front of Ever, her best friend's body tense.

"Do not force me to take the other hand, Tyr," she said.

"You would maim your own father for following orders like you are doing?"

"I would cut off my own hand before letting any harm come to my queen."

Without any more posing or pageantry, Erika kicked out and Tyr stumbled back, his eyes widening before he reached for his own sword.

"Odin killed my mother, and you fight for him. She would be disgusted with you."

Ever gasped at the revelation as Tyr staggered and then winked out of view, but the distraction had been enough. Ever felt Odin's presence at her back just before she felt the callouses of his palm cupping her neck.

Terror like she had never felt before electrified Ever as her hands fell to her stomach even as Erika yelled, and she offered up a prayer to the fates that, even if she were to fall, her daughter would be safe.

"Foolish child. There was no other way for this to end. I have lost my son, my protégé has chosen to side with you, and you are more like your mother than I had ever wanted you to be. Today, you die your final death, Kyria, and I will mourn you only a heartbeat."

Odin shoved her forward, and as another bout of searing pain coursed through her, Ever fell to the ground, eyes wide as her sword skittered across the pavement and out of reach. Her father lifted his staff, gathering lightning from the sky as he raised it, poised to strike, and Ever felt the chill of death creeping into her heart.

CHAPTER
FOURTEEN

RICKY

What was it with his team and running off into danger without backup?

Ricky growled the thought to himself as Melanie reached over and patted him on the thigh, sirens wailing and lights flashing as he drove through the streets of Cork like a man demented. He should never have let Derek go off by himself. That lone-wolf bullshit grated on Ricky's nerves.

Had Derek not learned from all the shit they'd gotten themselves into that dashing off by themselves got them nowhere? Caitlyn had run off to Paris to face Cain alone, and in the end, they'd faced him together. Melanie had stormed off because she was angry at something dickish he'd said, and she'd ended up on her second life. Even Donnie had walked out to try and sever his tie to Caitlyn, and he'd had to regrow a hand.

And Derek. Derek was beginning to be a pro at getting himself kidnapped.

Now, Derek could be up to his neck in trouble with only Ricky to watch his six, and *his* mind kept wandering back to the battle that was no doubt taking place behind them. Ricky had been torn about leaving to find Derek, wanting to stay and fight with the rest of the team.

Ricky thought back to all the times he and Derek had watched each other's backs. Even when he'd questioned Sarge's reasoning for partnering the two seemingly opposite personalities together, Sarge had been adamant that Ricky and Derek were meant to be partners.

Ricky slammed the files down on his desk as anger flooded his veins. Who did the goddamn furball think he was ordering him about all the goddamn time? It was bad enough that he forced Ricky to wither behind a desk when all the action was going on, but it had been Ricky who'd cracked the case, Ricky who'd figured out where the children were being kept before being trafficked to Europe.

And now, when the team was out kicking in doors and saving the night, Ricky was stuck doing bloody paperwork like some rookie who couldn't be trusted in the field because he wasn't a wolf or a vampire or a shifter. Like being a warlock was as bad as being human on a supernatural task force.

He'd joined the force when he was eighteen, much to his Da's ire, and was top of his graduating class in Templemore. Ricky had worked the beat and then gone undercover again and again. He made a name for himself through hard work, blood, sweat, and some tears. He'd done that. Ricky had not used magic much on the job because he wanted to prove to his father that magic did not maketh the man.

He practiced at a weapons range nightly, versed himself in all the lore and history, and fought his way through the academy to be chosen for P.I.T. He'd been delirious when he was chosen to work alongside the legendary agents whom he'd studied and strived to be.

But they had him riding a goddamn desk.

Ricky had not clawed his way to becoming an agent in the Paranormal Investigations Team to sit behind a desk doing paperwork. Slamming a fist down on the desk, Ricky blanched as Sergeant Thomas Delany strode in and arched his brow.

"Feeling frustrated, Moore?"

Ricky busied himself with the papers on his desk. "Not at all, Sarge. I was merely excited that the case was solved. I was celebrating."

Sarge chuckled at his dry tone, and when Ricky expected the man to leave him to it, the bear dragged a chair over and sat down at Ricky's desk. Reaching over, Sarge took a stack of papers and flicked through them.

"You did good work on this case, Agent Moore. Sometimes, good work means staying back and ensuring that every stitch of evidence is so damn tight there's no chance the monsters get free on a technicality. It's not always about riding in to save the day."

"It would help if I actually got to ride in and save the day sometimes," Ricky muttered, and Sarge barked out a laugh.

"You and Derek are so alike it's not even funny. I don't know why I did this to myself."

Ricky snorted as he shook his head. "Derek and I have nothing in common. He's good police, but he's too by-the-book—he can't see the gray areas, and that's where some of us live. I get the feeling that Derek only tolerates me because he has to."

It was the truth because even though he'd been on the team for six months now, Ricky had yet to feel as if he were part of it. Caitlyn and Derek were cut from the same cloth, and Donnie, while friendlier than the other two, wasn't exactly inviting him out for a beer after work.

Maybe he wasn't cut out for the team.

He must have said the words out loud because Sarge answered him. "You are part of this team, Ricky. When Derek first started on the team, I made him stay behind to do paperwork. I taught him that it wasn't always about kicking down doors because being a cop was more than that. Derek is teaching you as I taught him. Think about that."

And Ricky had, staying until well after three in the morning to finish up. As he made to leave for the night, he placed the paperwork neatly on the table. He did the same for the next three cases without complaint. He gritted his teeth and did what was asked of him. He continued to prove to them that he deserved to be here.

Ricky trained even though he wasn't one for the grind of working out. It was repetitive and boring, but he sparred with Donnie and bided his time. He did his time riding a desk and learned from those around him.

When it neared exactly one year since Ricky had joined P.I.T. and the team was headed out on a raid, Ricky automatically put his head down and began to shift through the paperwork even though he was itching to go.

Ricky had thought everyone had already left, but then Derek Doyle had stuck his head around the door to their squad room and, with a wolfish grin, said, "Moore, you coming or what?"

Ricky had been out of the chair so fast you'd think his ass had splinters. Since the night Derek had been shot by silver and Ricky had put a bullet between the unsub's eyes, Ricky had been Derek's partner, their bond cemented in the fact Ricky hadn't hesitated when faced with someone who wanted to end Derek.

Now, Derek could be dying. Yet, here he was again, riding a metaphorical desk.

"Derek will be fine. He's too stubborn to die."

Ricky stole a glance at his beautiful wife and drank her in. He wanted to pinch himself every damn day at how lucky he'd been to find her, even though it had taken him a minute to realize everything he wanted had been in front of his eyes all along.

"You got there in the end. We both did."

Ricky snorted as he felt a ripple of love down the vampire bond that pulsed between them now. Ricky might not be a typical sort of vampire, his Hunger far from normal, but he was glad Melanie had tried her hardest to keep him alive even if he had transitioned a little wrong.

It was an adjustment, trying to focus his mind and magic when he had no guidebook for what he was. Melanie had Caitlyn and Donnie to teach her how to be a vampire, but Ricky couldn't ask them about this... this growing well inside him that wanted to take and take all the time. It made him wonder why

Cain had Caitlyn kill the last psychic vampire for him and what, exactly, Caitlyn knew about his kind.

Melanie ran her hand up and down his thigh. Under normal circumstances, Ricky might have teased his wife a little and proposed they pull into some dark lane and do something illegal just to make her smile. But she was worried about her sire, her friends, and so was he.

"They'll be fine, Lanie. They have to be."

"Okay."

Ricky drove over a bump in the road. The car swerved to the right, causing Melanie to gasp. He flashed her a sheepish grin, knowing she was a little scared of cars since they'd ended up in the River Lee, and he had died ...ish.

As they entered Blarney, Ricky felt the fire that had consumed the house at the exact moment he spotted tendrils of smoke in the air. Licking his lips, he could taste the embers of it as he spied his car with its door still open and the lights flickering as if they were about to die.

Pulling the car to an abrupt halt, Ricky burst from the vehicle, gun already drawn as he scanned the abandoned road. There was no sign of Derek.

Melanie ducked out of the car and began typing on her phone. "The tracker in his phone says he's here, Ricky."

Melanie walked over to Ricky's car and crouched. When she stood again, she dangled Derek's phone from her fingers and frowned. Derek had to have left the phone behind on purpose, his attacker knowing that everyone's phone had a tracker embedded in it for such occasions as this.

Ricky should have put the bloody tracker *in* his partner.

"Goddamn it, D, you couldn't make this easy for us, could you?"

Ricky holstered his gun and desperately looked around for clues, but there were none to be found. It was as if Derek had vanished into thin air. The last time Derek's past had come back to bite the werewolf, Derek had had to face old demons; Ricky was certain Neville Morris was behind this disappearance, too.

And Morris wanted Derek dead.

"Can you find him like you found me? When Donnelly kidnapped me?"

Ricky turned to his beautiful, smart wife and grinned. "Not in exactly the same way, but maybe a little different."

Shrugging off his jacket, Ricky dropped to the ground and crossed his legs. Rolling his shoulders, he exhaled a breath. Ricky had spent the last week worrying so much about his new powers that he'd forgotten he was a born warlock and would always carry that blood in his veins. It was the same blood in his son's, and one day soon, Ricky would have to teach him.

Beckoning Melanie forward, he held out his palm. She placed it into his outstretched hand. Gripping it tightly, he opened his eyes, smiled, and winked. "Love you."

"I know," she said with a roll of her eyes.

Smothering a grin, Ricky closed his eyes again and reached inside himself for the magic that was his, the one that was written into his DNA, and it sparked to life like the embers of a fire. His body heated, and he cast his power and his mind out into the night, searching for his partner.

His magic brushed against something dark, primal, and then Ricky felt a sharp punch blast through his mind. The next thing he knew, he was smacking his head off the concrete.

"Son of a bitch!" he screamed in frustration, righting himself and running a hand over the back of his head. It came away wet, stained in his own blood.

"Did it work?"

"No, I think the stubborn bastard pushed me out."

"You two are as bad as one another. Are you gonna stop?"

Ricky got to his feet and shook his now-tender head, one that was beginning to pound. "Hell no. If Derek isn't going to let me help him, then I find the killer."

Melanie tilted her head as he crossed the distance and quickly pressed his lips to hers. He could feel her smile against his lips, the curve of her mouth so inviting, but Ricky and Melanie had hundreds of years to be husband and wife.

"No matter what happens to me, you don't come near me. I'd never forgive myself if I hurt you."

With that, he dashed forward into Derek's smoldering childhood home. He ignored Melanie calling his name as he stumbled across debris and inhaled the scent of the fire. A part of his magic that had always been in him flared, and Ricky sent a wave of magic out in search of an essence that would only come from the person who'd used their magic to set this place ablaze.

Ricky slowed his pace through the remnants of the house, and suddenly he was drawn to the fireplace in the living room. Everything else had been burned to ash, all but a framed picture that lay flat on the fireplace. Ricky traced the back with his fingertips and felt something...

Turning the picture over, Ricky saw it was an old picture of Derek, no more than twenty or so, standing and grinning in an army uniform, a light in his eyes. This was Derek when he was human, a clean-cut soldier boy, and there was a reason why this photo still stood.

Closing his eyes, Ricky concentrated on the last person who had touched this frame, and he felt anger, resentment, and, surprisingly, sorrow. He knew the man who'd last touched the frame was their arsonist. "Where are you?" Ricky muttered, and as if compelled by the words, Ricky heard the rumble of an engine, scented the smoke on the driver's skin, and found himself linked with the arsonist's essence.

The Shandon bells rang in Ricky's ears even though he was nowhere near the north side of the city. The driver looked into the mirror and grinned at him. Ricky all but knew he was face-to-face with the monster who'd killed Sarge and taken his partner.

"I feel the fire in you, warlock. Like calls to like."

"I'm not like you."

"We'll see. I can't wait to meet the man who Lu replaced me with."

The link that bound them together flared, and fire engulfed Ricky's body. He staggered away from the link, but not before he caught sight of where the car was going. As soon as the link was broken, his own magic snapped out to combat the other fire —wielder's magic, and he let out a roar as his flesh singed. Ricky pushed with all his power and grunted in pain as the magic crackled against his skin before finally dying out.

Dropping to his knees, Ricky squeezed his eyes shut and tried to rein in the voice inside his head that was telling him to panic. Calming himself, he put the lid back on his magic, slowly got to his feet, and staggered out of the house, his strength depleted.

Melanie came forward, her eyes wide at his burnt clothing and skin. Ricky held up a hand as his Hunger clawed at him, the feeling worse than having his flesh burnt.

"Ricky…"

"Stay back, Lanie. I don't think I can control myself."

But his wife didn't listen to him. Instead, she came right up to him and wrapped a hand around his throat. Brushing her nose against the curve of his neck, Ricky felt the barest hint of fang and shivered.

"Mine."

It was what Melanie had said to him when he'd seen her as a vampire the first time, and Ricky remembered that he'd felt claimed and needed, and it had woken something inside him. She was his, and he was hers.

"Mine," he growled back as he wrapped a hand in her flame-red hair and dragged her lips to his. He kissed her like he was starved for her, and he was. He kept a hold on his Hunger right up until the little minx scored his tongue, and then he was all for stripping her in the middle of the road.

His Hunger crawled inside him, taking a little sip of Melanie's power, and Ricky staggered back before he could take more. His eyes were fixed on her lips as she licked at the blood, and Melanie gave him a smug grin.

"See, I told you you were stronger. Nice to see you still have that fire inside ya, babe."

Ricky chuckled as he shook his head and drew her in for a quick hug before releasing her. "Not my exact words, wife, but near enough."

With a smile the size of Texas, she patted his cheek and glanced down at his clothes. Melanie walked around to the back of Ricky's car, rummaged a bit, and tossed him a clean T-shirt. Once he'd changed from the ruined tee, Ricky grabbed his jacket off the ground and slipped his arms back into the sleeves.

"What happened?" Melanie asked as she fixed the collar on his jacket before she brushed a strand off his face.

"I got inside the arsonist's head. He wasn't very welcoming. But I heard the Shandon bells ring out in the distance as he pulled into a building. There was a picture inside the house of Derek—back when he was human. I've never seen D like that. I think he went to the old army barracks where Derek would have been a soldier."

Melanie placed a hand over his heart, one that still beat even though he was dead, and she nodded her head. "Then let's go save the day, babe. Neither of us was made for riding a desk."

Ricky chuckled as he pressed his lips quickly to Melanie's. "I don't deserve you. I really don't."

"Yeah you do. And so do I. Now, stop being a sentimental fool and get in the car. We need to go save the big bad wolf."

～

NEVILLE MORRIS SAT IN A CHAIR AS SAM DRAGGED DEREK IN BY THE *scruff of the neck. Leaning forward, he watched as Sam clasped chains, the exact ones Derek had been held by when he was nothing more than a pup, around the wolf's ankles.*

Sam leaned Derek against a pillar. For a moment, Morris wondered if the boy had lost his nerve now that he was faced with the man himself. Doyle had that effect on people; he'd been an alpha before Morris' bite had changed him, a born leader who'd died trying to protect his men. Morris respected that. Of course, Sam would never know Derek had fought bloody and clawed until his last human breath to save him. Morris needed Sam to believe Morris had saved him to ensure his loyalty.

Morris felt Derek's wolf stir and pushed out with his power to try and shut the wolf down, but nothing happened. Derek was an alpha and no longer kowtowed to him.

Derek Doyle was more than Morris could have ever imagined when a white-haired man had appeared to him and told him a strike team was coming for them. The man had smelled a little of terror as his wolves snuck out of the shadows before he disappeared.

Morris felt someone looking at him and lifted his gaze to behold the amber eyes of a wolf who snarled as he tried to shake himself free. It took all of Morris' control not to lower his gaze as his own wolf whimpered.

"Hello, pup."

CHAPTER FIFTEEN

DEREK

"Lu, I've got a bad feeling about this."

Derek glanced over at Sam, who'd paled as they crept along the compound located north of Phnom Penh, the capital city of Cambodia, just shy of the Mekong River. It was nestled under cover of a thick forest, shielded from the natives by a wall and armed guards.

Derek was suspicious at the lack of soldiers guarding the drug lord's lair, but he swallowed down his own fears as he turned to grin at Sam. "You know better than to listen to your gut, Sam. Last time you felt uneasy, it was just a bad reaction to McCourt's cooking."

Sam frowned but flashed a cheeky grin a minute later. "Whatever you say, Lu."

Derek held up a fist, and his team halted. A guard walked past them, unable to see them hidden under the foliage, but it didn't take long until he rounded the corner out of view.

Derek whistled softly and O'Brien and Byrne darted forward, tossing a rope up and over the wall, then scaling it and disappearing on the other side. Derek nodded to Sam, and they took off running toward the rope. Climbing up and over the wall, they dropped to the *ground. Derek tapped Byrne on the shoulder, the soldier moving forward, his rifle ready.*

Derek went next and felt Sam tap his shoulder. They moved like the well-oiled machine they were, the drills they'd run over and over again, making this like second nature to them. As they crossed a court-yard, the scuffle of movement alerted Byrne, and he called them to halt.

Backs against the concrete of the main building, Derek could not believe his eyes as a dog—no, a wolf the size of a pony—strode by as a young woman talked to the creature. The creature huffed out a breath, and when Derek saw the size of its teeth, every instinct in him called for a retreat.

"Jaysus, Lu... what in God's name was that?"

"Nothing I want to dwell on, Sam. Let's do what we came here to do and get the hell out."

Derek stepped into the lead and planted a foot forward. The moment he did, the entire courtyard lit up, and they were trapped out in the open. The creature they'd seen was back, along with a dozen more of the terrifying things. Derek locked eyes with one, and for a moment, he felt as if there was an intelligence behind the animal's eyes.

"Retreat! Go!" Derek shouted. "Charlie Team to Base—we need immediate backup. We are overrun," he barked into his radio, but he got nothing but static back.

That's when Derek knew this was the night he would die.

Byrne aimed with his rifle, and one of the creatures snarled. Before Derek could stop him, a black monster swiped at Byrne with a paw, and the soldier's intestines spilled out into the courtyard.

Byrne's eyes were wide as his head smacked off the ground, thank-fully dead before he hit the ground. O'Brien gagged and dropped his rifle, pulling his handgun from its holster. He emptied the clip into the largest wolf, but all it did was piss him off. O'Brien's screams punched a hole in Derek's chest as the angered wolf opened its mouth, leapt, and, with monstrous fangs, worried and tossed O'Brien about like a chew toy. Bones crunched and snapped, and as his blood leaked from his wounds, the life drained from his eyes.

Then the wolf began to feast on the dead soldier's flesh.

Shots rang out from the wall, and Derek urged Sam backward and into a house, calling for the team to stand down. Barring the door, Derek listened as Sam began to recite the Our Father in Irish, but Derek knew God had abandoned this place long ago.

Drawing back the curtains, Derek was unable to stop himself from watching as Dylan, Murph, and Kelly were snatched from the wall and then ripped into pieces without a second thought. But his stomach rebelled as Sam muttered his name, and Derek realized they were not alone.

Stepping from the shadow was a man whose eyes were a burnt amber shade that was not human. Derek never believed that there could be anything other in this world, but now he was going to die from his naivety.

"Lu, what are we gonna do?"

Derek yanked his gun from his hip and desperately fired into the monster until his clip was empty. And the monster just continued to smile.

Without warning, the monster lunged and grabbed Sam around the neck. The bastard moved quicker than Derek had ever seen before, and Derek heard himself scream for his friend as claws slashed against Sam's throat. Blood gushed from the wound. Sam clutched at his throat, but there was no stopping the bleeding.

The sound of Sam's body hitting the ground snapped something in Derek. Dropping his gun, Derek punched the fiend with his fists, and even though it felt like his knuckles were breaking, he kept on fighting until he ran out of steam.

Claws slashed at his chest, and Derek jerked back and slid down the wall as Sam's eyes watched him even in death. The monster crouched and pressed his hand into the wound at Derek's chest, and he sucked in a shaky breath.

The monster licked at the blood and tilted his head. "Interesting."

A refined American accent was all Derek heard as his heart began to stutter, and the monster started to change in front of him. Soon, a wolf stood in front of him, and Derek himself began to recite the Lord's Prayer.

He heard himself call for Sam as the wolf opened its mouth and bit into his throat.

Derek knew Morris was trying to call his wolf forward, but it had been decades since any other wolf could influence his own. Calling to the other half of himself, Derek cracked open his eyes, letting his wolf snarl as the man struggled to get free.

"Hello, pup."

But Derek had not been a pup for a long time, and Morris was about to see just who was the alpha. Derek held his stare and held it some more. Sweat dripped down Morris' face and then, so slightly that he would have missed it if Derek hadn't been watching him like the prey he was, Morris subtly ducked his eyes to the ground.

Derek gave Morris a wolfish grin. "I am no longer a pup, Morris. I am alpha, and you are nothing."

When Morris snarled, Derek growled and snapped. "Look at me, Neville."

Neville's gaze snapped to his before the older man bit out a curse and stood up so fast his chair crashed to the ground. As Morris tried to rein in his wolf, Derek took in his surroundings. His stomach lurched as he recognized the barracks where he had trained his men.

"Hasn't changed a bit, has it, Lu? Still smells like burnt toast and scrambled eggs."

Sam came into view and grinned, reminding Derek of the cheeky, fun-loving man full of contagious light that made his eyes brighten even on a dark day, the man who had been his best friend. The one he had mourned the most, and the one who Ricky reminded him of.

But that young man had been replaced by a cold killer who'd

been alive this whole time Derek had been mourning him. Sam sat down across from him, and flames sparked to life in his palms, then danced up his arms. Sam's hair began to flame, and Derek could feel the waves of heat from his skin.

"What the hell happened to you, Sam? I saw you die. I watched that son of a bitch rip your throat out. I mourned you every goddamn day, and you come back now, murder people I care for, and burn down a house that was once your home as well? Or have you forgotten that my mam put a roof over your head?"

Just like many years ago, when Derek had emptied bullets into Morris, the shots Derek fired at Sam didn't penetrate the skin. Instead, Sam smiled, flicking sparks at Derek, the embers landing on his jeans and scorching through the fabric, burning his flesh.

Derek didn't so much as flinch. Folding his arms across his chest, Derek stared as Sam looked completely captivated by the flames, mesmerized even.

"The old man died without fear, Lu. And he told me you would kill me for what I did."

"He was right. I will."

"Don't you want to know how I came to be, Lu? How I became Other, just like you?"

Derek snorted, already tired of listening to him drone on. Sam sent a blaze of fire down Derek's side, and while the wall of flames was almost suffocating, Derek forbid his wolf howling or killing.

Patience. Soon, he told his wolf, and he felt the urge to rip flesh with his teeth well up inside him. Sam was oblivious to the inner turmoil inside Derek, who kept an eye on Morris as well. Morris was watching their interaction with interest, as if he'd waited for this moment all his life, to remind Derek of what he'd lost that night.

"I'd always been fascinated by fire, ye see. Couldn't explain it, really, but now I know why. It called to me like a siren song, and when I died, the dormant gene in me awakened."

Sam glanced at Morris over Derek's shoulder and then back to Derek with a grin, as if they were soldiers once more around a campfire and playing cards. "They burned our bodies the next night," he continued. "My body burned to ash, and then I came back to life with my body aflame, the fire healing my wounds and flooding my veins. Morris was as surprised as I was to see me walk out of the fire bare-ass naked and with the ability to wield fire."

Sam stretched out his legs before he continued. "I'm a fookin' phoenix, Lu. A mythical creature who cannot die. If Morris hadn't of burned me body, then I'd have stayed dead, but instead, I can't die now. We tried it. Over and over again. But my body always turns to dust, and I am reborn stronger than before."

Eyes wide like a child, Derek realized Sam was waiting to see his reaction, like he needed him to be impressed. Instead, Derek shrugged his shoulders. "I'm a werewolf mated to a Valkyrie queen, the daughter of Odin himself. My best friend is something so unique there is no other like him. I call a truth-seeker, a mind reader, and the queen of vampires, my family. My daughter carries the blessing of Thor, and you expect me to be impressed by your parlor tricks?"

Sam blinked in surprise before lunging forward and placing a searing palm on Derek's throat at the exact point where Morris had bitten him over a century ago. Pain laced through Derek as his flesh bubbled and burned. But while Sam was distracted with burning him, Derek snagged the keys to his cuffs from his pocket, thanking his lucky stars that Ricky had taught him how to pick a pocket for fun one day.

"That's enough, Sam."

Sam released Derek with a hiss and stood up, his face so full of rage that Derek chuckled.

"What's so funny, Lu? I could use a laugh."

Derek lifted his brows and, though he would never admit it, channeled Erika, snickering, "I might be a wolf, but Morris made you his little bitch. He can never say that of me. Can you, Neville?"

Sam lurched at Derek again, halting when Morris barked another order and told him to go cool down. The furious phoenix stormed off toward the back of the barracks as Morris took his chair again, having righted the fallen furniture.

"You claim to be surrounded by all these creatures, Derek, but you were a lone wolf when Sam came upon you. All alone."

Derek bared his teeth. "My team will figure it out. They always do. Answer me one question, Morris, before you die. Why now? Why come for me now?"

Morris leaned back in his chair, resting his clasped hands in his lap. "I was meant to kill you that day you arrived at my compound. We were warned by a man so utterly terrified of wolves the scent of his fear slipped through his mask of indifference. He appeared to me again, weeks ago, and told me that tonight was the night I would kill you."

"Let me guess—white beard, patch over his eye?"

Morris said nothing, which spoke volumes. Derek now knew Odin had been playing with his fate since before he'd even crossed paths with Ever in this lifetime... and suddenly, he realized his family was in danger. Derek squashed down the panic that flared in his chest; he knew his team would protect his mate and child. He knew it bone deep.

"That man," Derek said, "is my father-in-law, and I suspect he's using you to keep me from my mate, his daughter. You've spent your entire life using others as pawns, Neville. How does it feel to be one for a change?"

Morris' jaw tightened as the idiot tried to rein in his anger, but hiding it from Derek was impossible. Derek had spent decades studying Morris, every line, every tell, every movement of his body. The wolf had honed his skills so well that Derek knew how Morris was going to move before the man himself did. It was a skill that had kept him alive, but it was also one that had haunted him when he began to work for the Paranormal Investigations Team.

His mind wandered back to his walks with Caitlyn, those therapy sessions that healed them both in their own ways when Derek had admitted that because he was so good at getting into monsters' heads, he was afraid of himself. Caitlyn, who, even more so than Derek, had been created by a monster, understood him more than anyone when they talked about killing the monsters that haunted them.

Derek had been the one to ask the question: How do you destroy a monster without becoming one yourself? And it was Caitlyn who'd answered. Derek had never been so in awe of someone's strength of character than he was by Caitlyn as she'd said, "You need to remember that there is still good in the world, and to ensure that, sometimes good people have to do terrible things."

So here he was, a good person ready to do terrible things to protect the good in his life. It didn't matter what Morris had done to him. It only mattered that Derek ended it and finally put to rest the demons of his past. He could mourn the loss of Sam—*his* Sam, not whatever Morris had turned him into—once he and his family were safe once more.

Derek racked his brain for information on how to kill or subdue a phoenix, but he came up blank. So, for now, he would taunt Morris into making a mistake.

"The great Neville Morris, who once led the greatest pack of murderers, rapists, and deranged monsters in the world, now stands here alone with just a phoenix at his disposal. What happened, Neville? Did all your disciples get tired of bowing to a wolf with no real power? Did they start to grow restless at having to share their women and fight with each other?"

Morris growled, his lips curling into a sneer as Derek aimed true, and his words hit like bullets. Jerking out of his chair, Morris smacked Derek across the face. Derek swept his shackled feet out at the same time, sending Morris crumpling to the ground. The older wolf scrambled back as Derek reached for him, the scent of Morris' fear urging him on.

Derek spat blood on the ground. "Resorting to a bitch slap, Morris? That's beneath you... Then again, maybe it's not."

Morris pulled out a gun and pointed it at Derek, trying to ignore the slight tremble in his hand as he aimed for the spot between Derek's eyes. Derek calmly sat himself back down, tucking his legs behind him as he worked the keys into the locks.

"Did you think it would remind me of where I came from, having the chain from your basement brought over? All it makes me want to do is rip you limb from limb."

Morris snapped his fingers, and Sam came forward, causing Derek to smirk. Ignoring it, Morris removed the clip from the gun and deposited three silver bullets into Sam's hand. The grin that spread over Sam's features made Derek's wolf stand to attention.

The locks on his ankles finally snapped open, but Derek could do little but watch as heat flared in Sam's palm, and the bullets melted. His heart kicked like a drum in his chest as Sam dragged him to his feet and, right where Morris had bitten him, where the skin was still marred from Sam's burn, his once best friend clamped a handful of molten silver over the wound. Derek couldn't help but hiss as the silver fused into his skin, and he knew there would be no healing this.

Sam hadn't noticed his legs were free yet as Derek ground hit teeth together so hard he thought they'd crack. Leaning in, Sam whispered in Derek's ear.

"You were always such a handsome bastard, Lu. It's almost a shame to do this to ye. Almost."

And then Sam intensified the heat, and Derek's legs threatened to buckle as he wrapped the chain around his knuckles and waited, just like the predator he was, to strike out at his unsuspecting prey.

CHAPTER SIXTEEN

DEREK

Nothing could explain the agony that ripped through Derek's entire body, sweat coating him as his bones snapped, his knees buckled, the chains at his ankles creaking under the strain. He was both hot and cold at the same time, but it was the way his bones cracked and broke before reforming that made tears streak down his cheeks.

He had been fighting the change, unwilling to accept that he'd become a monster like the ones who'd killed his men. Voices echoed around him, whispers sounding like someone was beating a drum in his ear. They watched him now like they had done since he'd woken in the basement, unable to hold back an inhuman growl.

Derek had refused to eat; the raw, bloody meat they tossed at him made his stomach lurch even if some part of him was starving and wanted to sink its teeth into the meat.

It disgusted him.

His wrists snapped and he yowled in pain, ignoring the sniggering as his hands lengthened into claws, his teeth to fangs, and then cracked as they changed to human once more.

The door to his cell opened, and Derek's eyes darted to the immense wave of power stifling the air as Neville Morris crouched in front of him. Derek held his gaze, something primal in him telling him not to drop his eyes as Morris reached out to grab his shin. The rough gesture burned his already sensitive skin.

Morris jerked his gaze away as he growled, "I am your alpha now, soldier. Do not dare look me in the eye. You will learn that in this pack, you are so low in the pecking order that a submissive female ranks higher than you."

Derek, wanting to end this miserable life and have Morris kill him for real this time, wrenched his head back to hold the gaze of the man in front of him with a snarl.

Amber flashed in the man's eyes as Morris' lips curled into a snarl, and Derek could almost swear the man was struggling not to look away. Morris clocked him so hard he felt his teeth rattle as he hit the ground and lay there for a moment, his head against the cool cement, hoping for a reprieve.

But Derek got none.

"The full moon will force the change in him, sir. We should leave him to this torment for the next few days."

Morris glanced at the other wolf, inclining his head as he rose. "If he makes it to the full moon, you mean. It would be such a shame to give him the gift of the bite only for him to die on us. I'm sure he'd be very entertaining in the arena."

Morris turned his attention to Derek, pulling so much power from the men in the room that Derek felt Morris tug on his waning strength as well.

"Get up."

The command had Derek trying to rise, his ankles feeling like delicate china as he struggled to stand. The fragile bones in his ankles suddenly fractured, and Derek crumpled to the ground even as the command in Morris' words compelled his body to do as asked.

"I am alpha, pup, and you will obey me. No more resisting. No more of this disobedience. Change."

The growl that came out of Derek was terrifying even to him as he begged his body not to comply, but it was ingrained in Derek to follow orders, just as it was to give them. He'd tried begging Morris to end his life, but that hadn't worked. The man had laughed at him, and so had the other monsters in this room.

"Change."

The command was stronger this time, but Derek still resisted. Through the agony, he heard one of the wolves speak. "He shouldn't be able to resist this early, boss. The wolf in him could be an alpha himself."

"Shut up."

Derek wasn't sure why that made a difference as he had no desire to be an alpha like Morris. He didn't even want to be alive. He craved death and even tried to ask God for solace, but Derek already knew the divine had abandoned him.

He felt another wave of power as Morris drew more on the pack bonds. With a power that was not his own, he commanded Derek to change once again.

The blast of power was too much for Derek, and his body gave in to the command. His jaw broke and reformed, his hands became mottled with fur and tipped with claws, his teeth became fangs, and his eyes hazed. His body kept on breaking and being remade.

Hours, days, weeks. Derek wasn't sure how long had passed before the pain subsided and he stood on four shaky legs, his paws tender and claws clicking on the cement floor. His senses were so sharp, so inhuman, that he whimpered as Morris reached out and grabbed him by the scruff of the neck.

"The change is complete. You are now Lycan. Obey, and it will make eternity better for you."

Without thinking, Derek lunged for Morris, but one of the other wolves had snapped a chain around his neck and yanked Derek back just before his massive teeth sank into Morris' bones. Derek hit the wall hard, the wolf snarling as he slowly rose to his feet.

"Leave him like this; let him change back himself. If he doesn't change back in 48, we'll force him back to his human skin."

The wolf holding the chain affixed it to the wall, and they all strode out, locking Derek in the dark with only the brightness of his eyes to illuminate the black.

Alone, Derek lay down, resting his nose on his paws. He felt a tremendous emptiness as he thought of his family, his slain soldiers, and the fact that he could find no way out of this life. Outside, wolves howled in unison, a pack united after the successful defense of their home. Their song froze Derek's heart, and he clamped his eyes shut and again prayed to a God he no longer believed in.

Derek wanted to scream at the unbearable scent of burning flesh, the pain of it reminding him of his first change. However, Derek had long since learned how to block out pain and torture, and all he cared about now was finally, after over a century, putting the ghosts of his past behind him.

The chain still wrapped tightly around his knuckles, Derek pushed off the pillar and punched Sam square in the jaw. The phoenix staggered back, the flames vanishing from his palm as his eyes widened in shock. That surprise lasted five seconds before Sam went ablaze, his entire body a raging inferno.

Grinning, he took a step toward Derek, but Derek moved faster than he ever had before and darted around Sam, going for the monster who'd orchestrated all of this bullshit. As Morris tried to use Sam as a shield, Derek lengthened the chain in his hands and, in one quick movement, had the chain wrapped around Morris' throat. The older wolf went rigid in his grasp, and Sam readied a ball of fire, aiming it right for Derek.

"Ah, ah, Sam," Derek chided. "Wouldn't want to miss and get the boss now, would you?"

Sam peered at Morris, who nodded, before he let the flames die out. Derek took a few steps back, dragging Morris with him as he snarled into the old man's ear.

"Not very pleasant, is it? Being chained against your will. I think I've figured it out. I think I'd always figured it out."

"You're rambling, pup. Spit it out or kill me. Prove to everyone just what kind of monster you are—one that I created. One who hunts down monsters because he thinks like them. Because he *is* one. I felt it, don't you know—through the bonds of the pack—whenever you ripped a heart from a wolf and feasted on it, I felt the elation, the triumph. You are a monster just like me, Derek Doyle; you just don't admit it."

Derek tightened his grip on the chain, squeezing Morris' airway uncomfortably. "I never denied that I was a monster, Morris. I was just better at keeping it at bay. I learned that you can still be a monster and live a life that means something. I learned that you can let the worst parts of you be seen and still have people call you a hero. That no matter what kind of monster you claim to be, there is always an eviler monster out there."

Derek chuckled, a bitter sound that coated his next words. "And I also learned that it takes a monster to catch a monster. That the darkness in me is what makes me such a good cop. We cannot change our pasts, but how you use it to fuel yourself in the here-and-now is what makes you... or, in your case, breaks you."

"I am still an alpha, pup, and you will obey me!" Morris roared.

Derek kicked the backs of Morris' knees, and the wolf went down so hard that when his knees hit the ground, Derek heard a bone snap.

"You were never a true alpha. You were simply a leech who used the fear you'd instilled in your wolves to allow you to feed on the power of the pack bond, on *their* strength, to fuel your ambitions. I can scent you now, Morris, and I've known teenage wolves with more alpha in their bones than you have right now."

"If you kill me, they will come. My pack will come, and you will still lose," Morris hissed, desperate words from a desperate man.

Derek yanked the chain hard, dragging Morris' gaze up to his. "If that were the case, wolves would be here right now. You would never have left with only your pet phoenix. I think you ran with your tail between your legs to try and take out the person who started the chain of events that led to others questioning your position as alpha."

Sam sneered at being called a pet. Derek knew he'd have to face the other man once he'd finished with Morris, but that would have to wait for now. Thunder rumbled overhead, and Derek glanced at the window. Morris used the distraction and lunged upright, digging his fingers into the searing wounds at Derek's throat.

Derek ground his teeth together and loosened his grip on the chain just a little. Feeling the slack, Morris tried to run away, but he didn't get farther than a few feet before Derek tugged the chains again. But a few feet was far enough. Sam reached out and grabbed the chains, melting the links and freeing his boss.

Now Morris was standing between Sam and Derek, closer to Derek than he would like, Derek thought. Derek had always been so afraid of this man, this sorry excuse for a wolf, that he'd been ashamed of himself, of what he'd become, for decades. It had stopped him from living for such a long time that Derek realized—*sometimes, you cannot fight fate, you can only ensure you don't let it consume you.*

"My father told me years ago, back when I was a pup, that you have to be one with your wolf or it will control you. At first, I used to panic when I changed because everything was so overwhelming, but you were with me, stayed with me, until it became second nature. Full moons are still my favorite time because I get to spend them with you."

His daughter's words rang in his head like an affirmation,

and Derek embraced them, finally accepting that he was exactly where—and what—he was supposed to be. The loss, the suffering that he'd lived through had been so Derek would know how precious the life he had now was... and he wouldn't trade it for anything in the world.

Something silver flashed in front of him, and Derek sidestepped as Morris slashed at him with a blade made of silver. Morris came at Derek with a fury, using the knife to strike at his arm, slicing the skin and releasing the lingering scent of copper into the air.

"If you hadn't forced me to let you leave, none of this would be happening. You just *had* to fight, Doyle. I should never have indulged my curiosity to see how you would turn out, to see why he wanted to kill you so badly. When you fled, they started to question. You ruined everything."

Morris lashed out again with a growl, his movement missing Derek's abdomen by mere inches. "They began to forget. The legend of the pup that managed to get out diminished over time, and then there you were, on the bloody telly being interviewed about catching a child trafficker. You told them all about the man who made you into everything you were, and that Thomas Delaney was that man."

Derek smirked at Morris, which only seemed to anger him even more.

"*I* made you, Doyle. *I* fucking made you, not that bear, and that's why Sam took him, because you had to realize I'm responsible for the man you've become, not some team of misfits."

Shaking his head, Derek scoffed at the jealousy in Morris' tone. He wondered how he'd ever been so terrified of this man.

"Sarge was twice the man you could ever be. He made me, not you. You might have been the one to bite me, but Sarge was the alpha I respected, the one I followed without question. Sam understands, because he once did it for me, followed me without question because there was a trust between brothers in arms. Sarge had my respect and my claws. You've never had either, and you never will."

Derek could have sworn he saw Sam flinch at his words, but then Morris was coming for him, slashing wildly, frantically, blindly hoping one of his attempts would cause harm. Derek lunged forward, his shoulder connecting with Morris's stomach as he took the other wolf to the ground. They rolled until Derek pinned Morris and, with a balled-up fist, punched the false alpha so hard it knocked a tooth loose.

Grabbing the collar of his shirt, Derek pulled him up until their noses touched. "You are and always were a sorry excuse for a wolf. A man who broke those in his command for his own personal gain. Do you have any last words before I kill you?"

Fear, the scent of it, leaked from every pore on Morris' body as Derek called upon his wolf, let the power he'd tamped down for so many years pulse through his veins. As his eyes blazed amber, he didn't bother waiting for Morris to answer.

Clamping an arm around Morris' neck, he gave it a sharp twist. Bone snapped loudly in the silence of the barracks, and Morris' blank stare held his own as Derek let him fall to the ground and left him to die.

He waited to feel a sense of relief, of closure, of remorse for killing Morris, yet Derek felt nothing at all. It didn't matter if Morris was alive or dead, because Morris had never mattered.

Clapping dragged Derek away from his thoughts and back to the bigger threat in the room. Sam put his hands together in a sarcastic manner that had Derek's wolf bristling. Facing his former best friend, Derek watched as Sam leaned against the pillar that he'd tied Derek to earlier.

"I'm impressed, Lu. I mean, you were always a little ruthless, willing to do just about anything for the mission. I used to admire that about ye—that single-minded focus to get the job done. I fookin' hero-worshipped ye."

Derek shook his head, holding out his hands. "I never asked that of you, Sam. You were my brother. But I think the lieutenant I was and the soldier you were, they both died that night in Cambodia, and the people who came back aren't the soldiers who had been like family. You're not the same Sam who sat at my mother's kitchen table and ate our food, then braided my sister's hair."

Sam said nothing as he blinked, his lips closed firmly as Derek continued. "I'm not the same Derek who walked into the barracks on that morning in May, shy and reserved and desperately in need of a friend. And you're not the same Sam who strode on up to me with a stupid grin on your face and said, "Cheer up, mate, it's not like we're heading into war or anything."

Sam's lips twitched as Derek took a step forward, patting the spot where his heart rested beneath skin and bone. "The Sam I loved with all my heart died right beside me in Cambodia as I tried to save him. The Sam who was my brother, who helped me through the nightmares, would not have been so cruel as to kill a man for simply being a mentor."

"Shut up." Sam tossed the words at Derek, but they held no force.

"The Sam I knew would not have been so calculating and callous as to kill innocent people as surrogates for my family. Just like you and me and O'Brien and Byrne and Dylan, Murph, and Kelly were a family."

When Sam offered no response to the names of their fellow unit, Derek inched forward again. "You knew I was alive this entire time, Sam, and you never once came to my aid. I'm guessing you witnessed the abuse and the torture, and not once did you have my six."

"The first time I knew you were alive was when I saw you rip out some poor sap's heart and eat it. I was so fookin' happy, Lu, that Morris stopped me from running to you. He told me you'd changed, and he was right. The Lu I followed into death would not have taken pleasure in a kill."

"And neither would the Sam I knew."

Derek saw the switch in his gaze as Sam grinned, his eyes dancing with flames as he said. "Then fook the past, Lu. Let's just kill each other and see which one of us ends up in hell."

CHAPTER
SEVENTEEN

E ver had died many times, yet this time she feared the blow
Odin was about to strike more than any other almost-
death strike she had borne. Her eyes darted around, looking for
Ash, but her daughter was nowhere near. Ever feared the reason
why Ash had been fading in the future, ripped away from those
she loved, was because Ever was going to die right here and
now. It broke her heart that if that were the truth, then the
world would not get to tremble at the feet of the woman she
would become. That the world would be a far darker place
without Ash's light in it.

As Odin gathered his power to kill her, he glanced down at
her and sneered. "Your champion is not coming to aid you. I
sent an old foe to rid me of the nuisance. Did you know it was I
who warned Neville Morris about the attack on his compound?
Had I known this iteration of your mate would be an *Úlfheðinn,*
then maybe I would not have had him killed by a wolf."

Úlfheðnar were warriors who turned into savage wolves
when the song of battle called to them. Before the bargain had
been struck, the first Derrick had been a slain *Úlfheðinn* bound

to Valhalla upon his death, the magic of the realm making him flesh and blood once more in preparation for the final battle. And Ever had fallen for her champion.

Perhaps the blood of his ancestors had always been in Derek's veins, for she knew he was no ordinary wolf. If she knew her mate, he would be fighting like hell to get back to her this very moment. And even though he'd shut down the mate bond between them, she knew he was still alive because she could feel the faint pulse of it deep inside her.

Erika dove for Odin, her twin blades screaming for blood, forcing Odin to let Ever go. Ever scrambled to stay on her feet. She was helpless to watch as Odin whirled and snared Erika by the throat. The goddess of war grinned a feral sort of grin as she plunged a blade through his patch into the socket Ever had long ago relieved of its eye.

Her father let loose a roar of astounded fury as he dropped Erika, and she rolled to crouch before Ever, shielding her from her furious father. Odin smirked as he took one step forward and then another. The battle still raged before them, but Ever tried to focus on protecting herself and Ash from Odin.

Erika stole a glance over her shoulder, and Ever saw something flash into her eyes that made Ever's heart pound. "My sword will always be yours, my queen," she said quickly. "Until my last breath, and most likely after."

"Erika, no." Ever breathed the words as her lungs seized and her general, her friend, and her sister grinned.

"May we meet again, systir. Tell your brother I love him, okay?"

Then she was gone, a bundle of fury and rage, her swords cutting and slicing through those who'd come to aid Odin, and even as she bled, even as her flesh was shredded and torn, Erika did not stop fighting. She flared her wings and soared into the sky, looking every inch the goddess of war she was, yet also like an avenging angel who'd come to drag Odin to Hel.

Ever picked up her sword, dropping it a second later as pain rippled through her abdomen. Donnie must have felt her pain, because he doubled back, picking up one of the berserker's axes on the way, and began to strike them down just like a Viking warrior would have done.

He snagged a second ax and worked to keep those who tried to get to her at bay. Ever had never felt so powerless in all her life. She should be out there, fighting alongside them, but she could barely lift her sword. When the pain in her stomach came again with a ferocity that threatened to drive her to her knees, Donnie glanced at her.

"You okay?"

"I think my daughter has decided to make an appearance."

"Well, fuck."

Ever would have laughed at his fearful expression, but just then, she heard Erika cry out, heard Loki call her name as Odin aimed his spear at Erika's heart. Time seemed to freeze as Erika jerked her head up and smirked as Odin poised the spear to strike.

Then suddenly Erika flew backward through the air, away from Odin, as Tyr flashed into view and took the blow meant for his daughter. The spear pierced Tyr's flesh, a bolt of lightning pouring from the weapon as it no doubt incinerated the god's heart. Odin let loose a howl of frustration as he yanked the blade from Tyr's chest.

Erika's father dropped to the ground, the earth shaking as another one of the prophecies of Ragnarök came to fruition—the death of the old gods.

Erika cried out, a mixture of rage and grief as she dragged herself over to where Tyr lay dead. She placed her fingers over his eyes and closed them, muttering, "May we meet again, Father."

"*Enough,*" Odin screamed into the night, and everyone turned to watch as light shimmered around Odin. He lifted his hand

and summoned the lightning, a Godbolt that would kill anyone with the blood of the gods in them.

"I *will* kill you, Ever, and then I will make sure that when the world is reborn, Midgard remains a shell of what it once was. Perhaps I will let your wolf live to wander the earth alone until it drives him crazy."

Odin flexed his fingers, and Ever licked her lips. "Donnie, move. You don't need to die for me. Think of Caitlyn, what your death would do to her."

Donnie flashed her a grin. "My Cait has survived worse. She'd survive this."

Ever wasn't so sure, but the vampire would not move, and his bulk was too much for Ever to move, especially since she could barely breathe now without gasping in pain.

"Odin!"

Ever heard Freya's voice of steel before she saw her, and Odin simply smiled as she flew to where he was. He ran his eyes over her mother, then dismissed her with a wave of his hand. But Freya would not be moved.

"Do not kill her. If you kill her, then you kill your grandchild."

For a moment, Odin looked surprised as hell, but then the cold mask slipped into place again. "It matters not," he said, "I diluted my bloodline when I lay with you, and we created her. Any child of hers would only dilute the bloodline further. She must die."

Thunder rumbled so loudly that Ever had to cover her ears as streaks of blue flashed across the sky, and Odin questioned, "Thor? Son?"

Suddenly, Ash flashed into view and swung Mjölnir at Odin as she grinned. "Hey, Grandpa!"

The mighty hammer hit him square in the chest and knocked him back about fifty feet, wiping the surprised look off his face. He hit the ground hard, the already fractured concrete crumbling further, and quickly scrambled to his feet as if the ground itself could drag him down to Hel.

The berserkers charged Ash, and she tossed Mjölnir toward them, sending the creatures flying as if they were pins knocked down by a bowling ball. As if it were a boomerang, the mystical hammer sailed back through the air into her grasp, and sparks of blue shimmered across Ash's skin.

Odin recovered from his shock and fired the Godbolt at Ash, who ducked right and rolled before driving her hammer into the ground. The concrete rose at the force of her hammer, and, as if the rug had been pulled out from underneath him, Odin stumbled just as he unleashed another Godbolt, sending it shooting sideways.

Donnie ducked in front of Ever, taking the Godbolt in the shoulder and dropping his axes as he went down hard. His chest rose and fell once as he groaned, his eyes rolling back in his head, before they closed.

Ever couldn't breathe; she had no way to know if he were alive or not since vampires were already dead—even if she checked for a pulse, none would be there. She had to believe Donnie would live, for Ash knew him in the future, but a Godbolt to the shoulder could have killed him.

Ash stalked toward Odin, the older God watching her with slight intrigue as they stood inches away from one another, glaring.

"You smell just like your mutt of a father. You look like him, too."

"Thanks, Grandpa. I think that's the nicest thing you've ever said to me."

Odin sneered as he gathered another bolt of lightning.

"I wouldn't do that if I were you," Ash growled.

"Why is that, little girl?"

"Because I can wield not only thunder like Thor, but also

lightning like you." To prove her point, Ash held up Mjölnir. Lightning crackled in the sky, gathering in her trusty hammer.

Ever had been right all along—Ash had been hiding a lot from them, *especially* the extent of her powers. Ever watched as Ash glanced behind Odin and laughed as she tilted her head.

"And besides," Ash added, "trying to hurt me will only piss *him* off, so I'd run off before you make him angry."

Odin chuckled as he stroked his beard. "You are interesting, like a bug I want to crush. No one can hurt me, child, for I am a god."

"Are you sure? Can you be certain, old man? Because I've seen him angry, and he's looking at you like dinner has been served."

Odin sent a bolt of lightning at Ash, and it hit her square in the chest. She staggered, returned one of her own that knocked Odin back a step, and then let her wolf into her eyes.

"Abomination," Odin hissed.

Looking behind him, Ash smiled and sang, "Who's afraid of the big bad wolf?"

Odin barked out a laugh as Ever, watching her daughter face off against her father, got to her feet.

"I have nothing to fear of you, little wolf," Odin replied. "You are barely settled into your power. I am the father of worlds; you are nothing."

Resting Mjölnir on her shoulder, Ash rolled her eyes. "Oh, it's not me you should be afraid of. There are bigger and more psychotic wolves who are itching to take a bite out of you. I suggest you flee, Allfather, before my mate decides to make another of your dreaded prophesies come to fruition."

Odin laughed again as if he could not sense the predator stalking him, the death towering over him, red eyes blazing.

"You are but a child; what silly boy had the distaste to claim you as his mate?"

Ash flipped her hair off her shoulder. "He's sort of famous.

I'm sure you've heard of him. Bound for centuries by gods who feared him."

"No, that is not possible. He is hidden."

"Not anymore. Grey, come say hi."

The snarl that ripped from the monstrous wolf's mouth had Odin whirling round, and Fenrir opened his mouth wide enough to have swallowed the god then and there. Odin disappeared as Fenrir snapped his mouth shut, a very wolfish grin on his face as he inclined his head at Ash.

"Yeah, yeah, I agreed, didn't I? Now go back before Z yanks you back."

The gray wolf's eyes danced with amusement before he up and vanished.

The berserkers that remained turned and darted off into the night once Odin disappeared, retreating until the next battle. Ash jogged over to Ever and helped steady her as Caitlyn dropped to her knees and placed a hand over her mate's forehead.

"He still lives. *Mon Dieu*, he still lives."

The relief in her voice was enough to bring tears to Ever's eyes, but then she groaned as another wave of pain erupted in her abdomen. Her knees buckled, and if Freya had not caught her, Ever would have fallen.

"We need to get you to a hospital."

Ever nodded her head as she panted lightly, breathing through the pain. An eerie calm filled the night around them, and suddenly unease ran its fingers down Ever's spine.

"*Caitlyn!*"

Erika's scream ripped through the silence. Caitlyn got to her feet and took off toward Erika, who was pulling dead berserkers off Kenzie. The young woman lay motionless on the ground, her eyes wide, blood dripping from the corners of her mouth. Her hand was gripping her scythe even as Caitlyn arrived and dragged the last berserker off her.

Much like Donnie, Kenzie had been struck by the Godbolt, but Kenzie was mostly human. Her body had been paralyzed by the power Odin had sent into her. Blue slivers coursed over her body from the wound at her shoulder.

"Someone get Ricky… he has to syphon the magic. He has to save her."

They all knew Ricky was too far away to save her. He wouldn't make it in time, even if they could contact him. However, the Godbolt should have killed her immediately, so something inside of Kenzie was stopping it.

Kenzie blinked a few times and managed to blurt out, "I don't want to die."

Ever, with Freya's help, staggered over to where Kenzie lay, her heart breaking as Caitlyn wept for the girl. Ever glanced at Freya, who nodded her head.

"She has the blood. It is faint, but it is there. She is a worthy warrior. She fought bravely beside us and would be welcomed by all of your systirs."

"She saved my life with that scythe of hers," said Danae, the hardnosed Valkyrie. Fisting a hand over her heart, she added, "I would welcome her into our family."

"Help me down."

Freya helped Ever to her knees, and she placed a hand on Caitlyn's shoulders. "I heard a rumor once that you were the descendant of Van Helsing. Is that true?"

"Why does that matter?" Caitlyn ground out.

"It matters," Ever bit out as she breathed through another contraction. "It matters because when Skadi tired of being a hitwoman for the Vanir, she traveled to Midgard and took an oath to only hunt creatures of evil and blessed those of her bloodline to be warriors, hunters. She fell in love and married a man called Abraham Van Helsing."

Caitlyn gasped as she realized what that meant for her own legacy.

"Kenzie has Skadi's blood in her veins and has proven to be a warrior of worth. I can try and make her Valkyrie. With some help."

"Do it. I cannot lose her," Caitlyn said, her voice breaking.

Ever reached for her mother's hand. "Help me?"

Freya took Ever's hand, the power in Freya's veins reaching for Ever's own, and then as Ever lay a hand over Kenzie's heart, she let her instincts take over. Magic of mother, daughter, and granddaughter reached into Kenzie's soul and tugged on the slight thread that was Valkyrie.

All of her sisters gathered around as Kenzie arched her back and cried out, the Godbolt flaring before it vanished and Ever claimed Kenzie as one of her own, much like she had done with Derek after Donnelly had tried to kill him.

As quickly as it happened, Ever sank back, letting go of Freya's hand, unable to stifle a scream of her own as Kenzie sat upright with a gasp. Caitlyn embraced her as Ever bit down so hard on her bottom lip she tasted blood.

A sensation clenched at Ever as wetness coated her legs, her waters breaking. Something tickled her nose. As she lifted her fingers to her nostrils, they came away bloody. Ash flickered in front of her. Ever thought it was a trick of her eyes, but when she glanced at her legs, blood dripped down them.

"Help me," she whispered as she tried to reach for someone, anyone who could help her.

A jolt of pain had her screaming out, and everyone turned to look at her. She screamed for Ash, who was staring at her hands in disbelief, fear in her eyes as she looked up at Ever.

Loki rushed forward, having lingered around the edges of the end of the battle, scooped her up in his arms, and the next thing Ever knew, they were standing in the middle of the emergency room. Freya flashed into view next with Erika appearing a second later.

The entire hospital froze as soon as they appeared, taking in the blood and wounds as Loki declared, "I am Loki of Asgard, and my sister is dying. Someone help us."

Maybe it was the anguish in his tone or the fact that he had given them his name, but a doctor rushed over, and then Ever was being laid on a gurney and rushed down a hall. Erika fought with one of the doctors, growling and snarling as she pushed her way forward.

Ever closed her eyes, and when she woke again, she lay staring at an ice-white ceiling while people around her were shouting over one another. She strained to hear what they were saying.

"There's too much blood."

"She's hemorrhaging."

"The baby is in distress."

"Prep for an emergency C-section."

"Erika," she managed to croak, "I need Derek."

Erika's tearstained face came into view. "I have the Valkyrie out searching for him, Ever. But I'm here."

Wetting her lips, Ever held her best friend's gaze. "Help him with her, if I don't. Be his friend."

"Shut up with talk like that. You'll be grand."

Ever made to say more when she suddenly felt pulled under by the darkness. Erika was dragged from her view, and all she heard was Erika begging them to save her as someone yelled, "She's crashing!"

And then an alarm drowned everything out.

CHAPTER EIGHTEEN

D erek dodged just as Sam shot a blaze of fire in his direction, hitting the wall with a grunt as pain bloomed in his shoulder. Derek had been running around the barracks, trying to avoid getting burned any more than he already was by Sam's fire. Thankfully, he was quick, but he was no match for a being made of fire.

His only hope was to tire Sam out and then make his move. That was the plan, but Sam didn't seem to be tiring at all. The phoenix seemed to be enjoying stalking him all around the bloody barracks.

The door to the barracks flung open, and Ricky and Melanie burst in. Both had their guns out as Ricky scanned the room. Relief flooded them both as soon as they laid eyes on Derek. Melanie flashed him a grin as Ricky seemingly ignored Sam.

"I'm supposed to be the reckless one, D. You're one supposed to be saving *my* ass, not the other way 'round."

Derek chuckled. "My bad."

Sam watched the exchange with interest, his eyes wandering over Ricky with a grin. "Hello, replacement best friend."

Ricky rolled his eyes. "I'm no one's replacement. I'm the new-and-improved upgraded model with heated hands and a wicked sense of humor. I also come fully equipped with sarcastic comments, roguish good looks, and unwavering loyalty. I also have a thing for redheads, but you seem a bit unhinged for my taste, mate. Too bad."

Derek found himself suppressing a smile as Melanie took a step toward Derek, shrieking as Sam shot a stream of flames in her direction. He glanced from Derek to Ricky and back again.

"Does the warlock know of your murderous past, Lu? Does your new bestie know how you rose to this alpha status of yours through blood and fang? He's got a kid, right? Does he trust you with his kid?"

"You bet your ass I do, motherfucker!"

Derek held up his hand and stepped toward Sam. "This isn't about them, Sam. Come and fight me without the fire, and we can settle this one on one. Fairly."

"Life isn't fair, Lu. We should have known back then that guys like us don't make it our alive."

"But we did, Sam. We made it out."

Sam shook his ginger hair into his eyes. "Nah, Lu, we're still in Cambodia, fighting our way out. Hundred years later, and we're still fighting."

Derek didn't know what to say to him, this Sam who he didn't know at all. Sensing Derek's trepidation, Sam turned on Ricky and tapped the side of his head.

"Neat little trick of yours, getting into my head like that. Last I checked, though, warlocks were still just a step above humans. Should I kill you first and break Lu's heart? Or should I see if your pretty little vampire burns as bright as her hair?"

Apparently, Sam didn't know Ricky was far more than a normal warlock. That could be used to their advantage. Ricky moved into a more strikable position, settling away from

Melanie and Derek as Sam called his fire forward, the orange flames dancing in his palms.

Ricky rolled his shoulders and flexed his hands to let his own blue flames crawl along his skin. Derek could see that neither man would back down, and there was a possibility that these two could burn the entire barracks down with a flick of their wrists.

Sam flicked his fingers first, and then Ricky countered, the flames hitting one another and blazing upward, scorching a hole in the roof, pieces of the roof falling to the ground as Sam and Ricky met in the middle. Derek had to shield himself from the intense heat that began to suffocate the room.

Melanie raced to Derek, her eyes falling to his neck where the skin still blistered from the silver. "Oh, Derek."

Derek nudged her chin with his knuckles. "It's okay, Melanie. Might stop Erika calling me Boyband now, though. Every cloud and all that."

Melanie looked from his mangled neck to her husband, who was giving as good as he got against Sam. Derek wasn't sure what could stop a phoenix, for even if Sam were killed, would he not just rise again? They needed to find a permanent way to stop him.

"Why isn't he just siphoning the magic? C'mon, Ricky, just end it."

Derek realized that Ricky was holding back. It was as if he wanted to disarm Sam, but didn't want to kill him in case Derek thought he could save him. Ricky would risk life and limb for him, and Derek would sure as hell do the same for Ricky.

"Sam! It's me that you want, not Ricky. Come on, you and me—let's go."

Sam spun around and shot a fireball at Derek, who dropped to the ground and rolled into a crouch, shouting, "Ricky, do it!"

Sam turned as Ricky grabbed his arms and snarled, hunger

in Ricky's eyes as he grinned. "I guess redheads *are* my favorite flavor. Yummy."

Then Ricky pressed his lips to Sam's, the fire dimming and dimming until Sam staggered away. Ricky let him, power making him sway as if drunk.

Melanie walked over to her husband. "We have *got* to have a conversation about you making out with strange men."

"I told you I had a thing for redheads," Ricky said with a groan.

Derek could feel the flames and power rebuilding slowly in Sam as if he had a well of magic in his veins. Derek grabbed him and whirled him around.

"Go on, Lu, kill me. End it now, and when you do, I'll fookin' haunt you for another hundred years. Kept your partner's powers quiet. I know a few bounty hunters who would love to mount his head on a wall."

Derek growled as Melanie called his name and pointed. Loki stood nearby, his eyes heavy, and Derek reached through the mate bond to find just a fraction of it remaining.

"What happened?" Derek demanded as he all-but dragged Sam with him.

"There was a battle. Odin was pushed back. There were casualties, injuries. Ever went into labor. The human doctors are operating as we speak."

Panic and anguish welled in his chest as he looked from Sam to Loki. "Any idea how to kill a phoenix?"

Loki gave Derek a smile that screamed murder. "Robert Frost once said that, for destruction, ice is also great. If you have to say goodbye, I'd do it now."

Derek glanced at Sam, ignoring the overload of emotions as he shook his head. "I grieved a long time ago for my friend. This is not him."

Pushing Sam toward Loki, the god looked at Derek's neck before clamping a hand around Sam's throat. Ice crept over

Sam's flesh, and the phoenix screamed, trying to thrash against the ice that set into place all over his body. When Sam was fully encased in ice, Loki removed his hand and squeezed it shut.

The ice cracked, and then for a split second, there was only silence. Then the ice shattered into a million different pieces of frozen Sam. Loki summoned the shards, then blew on them, scattering the particles like ashes in the wind. Again, Derek tried to feel remorse but felt nothing.

He just wanted to get to his mate and child.

Shouting at Melanie to get a picture of Morris' body, Derek let Loki grasp his arm. In the blink of an eye, Derek stood inside the family room of the hospital. He knew the place inside out, having delivered bad news to many a family there.

Freya paced the room, giving him a brief nod when she sensed his presence. Was Ever alone all this time while he had rushed off to face his past? He would never forgive himself if something happened to her while he wasn't there to protect her.

"Erika has not left her side. Ever has not been alone."

The door to the room opened, and a doctor stepped inside. "Mr. Doyle?"

"Is my mate okay?"

His voice was a growl, but he didn't care. Neither did the doctor. "Your mate suffered a tremendous amount of blood loss. In her condition, we had to perform an emergency C-section. Your daughter is perfectly healthy, and her aunt is guarding her. We need to look her over, but her aunt has repeatedly threatened my nurses."

Loki chuckled behind him, and Derek made a mental note to thank Erika at some point.

"And my mate?" he asked, unsure if he wanted to hear the answer.

The man gave Derek a tentative smile. "She should be coming out of surgery in the next hour. We stabilized her, but the next 48 are critical. It's up to her now. We've done all we can."

Freya sucked in a shuddering breath as Derek nodded his head. "Can I see my daughter?"

"Of course."

Derek followed the doctor out and down the hall, but he would have known where to go without him as he heard Erika's voice booming down the hallway.

"Try and take her again, and I swear by the old gods and the new that you will lose a hand."

Derek stood at the end of the hall, watching as Erika bared her teeth, a small bundle in one arm and a dagger in the other.

The doctor gave him a tired smile and pointed to his neck. "You should get that looked at."

"Silver in the wound, Doc," Derek said. "There's no fixing that."

Derek strode forward as one of the nurses made to take Ash from Erika's arms again. The Valkyrie kicked out with a little force, and the nurse cried out.

"Erika."

The goddess snapped her head toward Derek, and he had never seen the fierce warrior look so... shattered. He walked toward his mate's best friend and held out his hands. Erika handed him the little girl, and Derek looked down.

She was perfect, this little combination of him and Ever who squirmed and settled as soon as Derek rested her against his heart. He placed his free hand on Erika's shoulder. "Thank you for protecting them both. We are lucky to have you."

Erika flushed, her eyes skimming over his neck as she wiped away her tears. "Don't get all mushy on me now, Boyband. I'm tired and worried and grieving, and if you're nice to me, I might cry."

Derek squeezed her shoulder. "Who did we lose?"

"Tyr, my father. He sacrificed himself to save me."

Derek leaned in and ran his nose along Ash's skin, marking her with his scent as the baby slept in his arms. "I'm sorry for your loss, Erika."

The Valkyrie shrugged. "I barely knew him. We only just met. It feels wrong to grieve for the idea of him."

"Grief isn't wrong just because it doesn't make sense. Just because you didn't know him well doesn't mean you still can't mourn his loss."

Erika blinked, swallowing hard before she regained her composure. "Stop being nice to me, Boyband. It's weird."

Derek smiled as the doctor motioned for Derek to come into one of the rooms, nudging Erika along with him. He reluctantly let Ash out of his arms and into a little cot where the doctor checked her over thoroughly. Once he told Derek that his daughter was fine, he excused himself.

Derek pulled off his T-shirt, scooped Ash up, and held her to his skin as he paced the floor listening to Erika fill him in on what had happened. He worried for Donnie, his hardheaded friend who was too stubborn to die, and Kenzie, who would either survive her change or not.

Loki wandered in soon after, just as they wheeled Ever into the room. The doctors and nurses fussed about, setting up heart monitors and machines Derek had no names for. After all of that, they pulled up the arms on the side of the bed. They all waited until the nurses had Ever settled before anyone dared speak again.

Erika huffed out a breath. "Gods, she looks so fragile," she said, and Loki wrapped his arm around her, pressing his lips to her cheek.

A tentative knock sounded on the door, and there was a brief pause before grown-up Ash hesitantly popped her head inside. "Can I come in?"

Derek flashed her a warm grin. "You don't even have to ask, Ash. I bet your mom could do with hearing your voice."

Ash came in as the door closed softly behind her, giving him a small hug and tapping her little self on the nose. Then Ash walked around to the side of Ever's bed, pushed down the arm, and climbed in next to her mom. Curling up at her side, Ash rested her head on Ever's shoulder.

"I lied, Mom," Ash said softly, and Derek listened intently as his daughter expressed her truth. "I lied when I said that it was only Erika and Caitlyn who trained me. I said it to hurt you because I was hurt and thought you didn't want me. But I learned twice as much from you as I did from them."

Little Ash stirred, and Derek hushed her back to a contented slumber. Loki leaned in and whispered to Erika, who glared at him before finally letting herself be led from the room, leaving Derek alone with all his girls.

"I learned to be strong but not hard. I learned that even when the world is dark, it's okay to let a little bit of light in. You taught me to follow my heart and my gut, and that it's okay to be afraid."

"Ash," Derek said softly, but Ash just shook her head as she continued to speak.

"And I'm afraid, Mom. Afraid to go home in case you're not in it. That I changed the wrong things by coming back. That there is no point in going back to a world where you're not there. I won't be me in a world without you in it."

Derek rose and moved to stand at his daughter's side as Ash sobbed into Ever's shoulder. Holding her newborn self in the crook of his arm, he rested the other on Ash's head and ran his fingers through her hair. "It's okay, Ash. It's going to be okay."

Ash cried herself to sleep, refusing to detach herself from Ever's side. Derek dimmed the lights, feeding baby Ash when the nurses advised him to, changing her when needed. The hours bled from one to another, and still, Ever did not wake.

At some stage during the day, Freya appeared in the room with fresh clothes for him and Ash, as well as some clothes for the baby. She folded a blanket over the back of the chair and told Derek he needed to eat before he fell holding the baby.

The Valkyrie then quickly vanished after Derek offered his thanks. Day broke and grown Ash woke, excusing herself to freshen up as she grabbed the clean clothes and ducked out, leaving Derek to pace and worry as Ever's heartbeat beeped on the monitor,

He tried to stay calm for everyone else as he constantly tried to reach Ever through the mate bond, but it was still dormant, a low hum inside his head that would get no louder.

The door opened a few seconds later, and Derek turned, expecting to see Ash and a little surprised to see Ricky walk in carrying enough food to feed an army. The other man grinned at him and proceeded to arrange the food on the side table.

"Before you go all growly and broody at me," Ricky said in a low tone that had Derek smiling, "I bet you haven't slept or eaten a damn thing since before you rushed off to get yourself kidnapped again. Caitlyn can't be here to use that stare of hers to make you obey her, and Melanie is with Kenzie, so you got stuck with me playing mother hen."

Ricky piled food onto a plate and then turned and pointed to it. "Eat."

Derek arched a brow and inclined his head to the sleeping baby in his arms.

"Now that sounds like an invitation," Ricky beamed. Holding out his hands, he said, "Gimmie. My turn. And for the sake of every mere mortal in this hospital, put on your damn T-shirt."

Derek chuckled as Ricky took Ash from him and began to sing softly to her. Derek obeyed his friend, knowing that with the full moon so close, a hungry wolf was a volatile one. He obediently ate his fill of food, and then, when Ash came back, Derek ordered her to eat as well.

"I missed out on all this with Zach," Ricky admitted, a small, sad smile on his face. "I didn't get to hold him when he was this tiny. I think about that a lot."

Ash took a bite of her sandwich, chewed on it, and then said very matter of factly, "Z doesn't care about that. Do you know that every Mother's Day you make sure he remembers Sadie? That you let his uncle teach him about being a cat even though you guys do not get on? He got angry once when he realized Sadie had kept him away from you for so long, and you told him that Sadie was right to do what she did because you weren't good enough to be his father yet, that you had to learn from Derek and Sarge how to be a father."

Ricky stared at the little girl in his arms even as her older self said, "Five years of not knowing, Uncle Ricky, when Zach barely even remembers it, doesn't matter. It's soccer games and school projects. It's showing up to parent-teacher meetings or family days by yourself or asking to move the science fair to nighttime so Melanie can go. It's being the first person he calls when we need bail money."

Eyes widening, Ricky stuttered over his words as he said. "I'm sorry, what?"

Derek chuckled, and Ash grinned, biting into her sandwich with a shrug. Letting his eyes wander over to Ever, still and unmoving, his heart felt a little heavier.

C'mon, Ever, wake up. Someone can't wait to meet you, Derek said down the bond, but his mate still slept.

Donnie

DONNIE WASN'T SURE WHERE HE WAS. HE WASN'T ENTIRELY CERTAIN IF he was even alive or had been given his final death. All he knew was that the bolt he took in the shoulder to stop Ever from being hit had been worth it.

Sitting upright, he saw that he was in an ancient palace of some sort. The markings on the walls were in a language he didn't understand, but as his gaze settled on an elaborate painting of someone he recognized, Donnie began to wonder if he were simply dreaming.

The tapestry on the wall depicted Thor, Ever's brother, storming into battle as lightning struck his hammer. Blood smeared Thor's face, and bodies lay at his feet. There was wording etched into the solid-gold frame. Donnie traced his fingers over the runes.

A shuffling of feet made him freeze, yet the woman who stalked past him either ignored him or couldn't see him. Petite in stature, the woman had two-toned brown hair, with a braid of red platted into the side. She carried a sword and a blank expression as she moved, sparing only a glance at the tapestry. Donnie caught a brief flash of emotion in her eyes at the sight before she continued down the hall.

Donnie cautiously moved along the wall, intrigued to see where the woman went. His footsteps made no sound as he glanced around the corner before stepping into a room right out of one of his beloved Marvel movies.

The tiled floor was mosaiced with images of battles and warriors, what Donnie assumed were the Vanir and Aesir, though it was purely a guess. The open windows let the bright sunshine through, illuminating the depictions and halting Donnie in his tracks.

There was no protection here from the sun, although, since he was sure he was dreaming, Donnie reached out a tentative hand and felt the warm rays on his skin for the first time in over twenty years.

It felt like a gift and a curse at that moment, because he had forgotten how it had felt to walk in the sun—hadn't thought much on it, really. But now, even if this was a dream, it felt as real as when he'd been human, and he was reluctant to take his hand away.

The woman stood in front of Odin and bowed at the waist like a soldier. Donnie wondered if the stiffness in her movement was because this woman did not want to bow to a king intent on destroying the world.

Odin sat upon a throne of bone and gold, his staff resting across his lap, his chin resting in the palm of his hand, with a bored expression on his face. But his eyes. His eyes held a hint of fear that had removed the cockiness from his expression.

"My husband is dead, and his sister lies dying. Tyr is dead, having sacrificed himself to save his daughter. You have murdered gods and allies, Odin. You are running out of people willing to do your bidding."

Her voice was strong and did not waiver, even when Odin arched a brow and sent a wave of power across the room. The woman staggered but held fast. Donnie looked at the woman again as Odin spoke.

"Your husband chose his side when he sided with his sister over his father. He chose his side when he gave his power to that sister's child. How does it feel, Lady Sif, for Thor to choose a half-breed mongrel over his own sons?"

So, this was Thor's wife...

"My husband would have chosen, at the moment, whoever was worthy. He was not a tactician, my husband, but he had a good heart. If he chose his niece to wield Mjölnir, then I respect his decision."

Odin laughed, shaking his head. "I oft wonder if the fates try to upend me. I have lost my sons and my beloved. My son's legacy is tainted now by a girl who thinks herself a god. She must die, however, for I fear that the allies she will amass could be the true end of it all."

"What do you care," Sif asked, her fingers twitching as if itching to grab a weapon, "if you plan to kill her regardless?"

"Ragnarök is not so simple to set in motion. There are many steps one must take to ensure not only that I survive but that those who would impede me are safely out of the way when the time comes."

"And is that why you have kept the Hróðvitnir's location a secret? Is Loki's son not the one fated to defeat you in your final battle?"

Donnie heard the threat in her voice just as clear as Odin did. The old god smirked. "Why, Lady Sif, do you dare threaten me? I doubt you wish to leave your children orphans so soon after losing their beloved father. There are only three people who know where the fame-wolf is; Tyr, the fates, and myself. Unless you know where it is that I have hidden the wolf?"

Face a mask, Lady Sif answered Odin stiffly. "Not at all, Allfather. I was merely thinking out loud."

"If you wish to keep your head, I suggest you leave me be. I have had enough of family for one day."

Odin turned his head away, dismissing Lady Sif with the gesture, and Donnie could swear the warrior woman gritted her teeth as she stalked out of the throne room, with Donnie compelled to follow her.

She stormed through the palace, nodding her head to guards as she passed. But then she halted, glancing sideways before slipping inside a room, leaving the door ajar as if she knew Donnie was following her. Then she began rifling through drawers and cupboards.

"I'm not sure who you are or why I know you are here," she said, still rummaging, "but the fates told me that Tyr had something you need. So, I do the fates' bidding."

Donnie said nothing as Sif dropped down to the ground and slid under the bed. She blew out a frustrated breath and glanced around the room once more. As Donnie followed suit, his eyes landed on the picture frame at the same time as hers.

A thick box frame held a photograph of a woman who was no doubt Erika's mother—their features were very similar. Sif let out a sigh as she glanced in Donnie's general direction. "Tyr loved Liviana. Spent centuries searching for his child. When he realized Odin knew all along where his Erika was, Tyr lost faith like many of us did, and we came together to try and stop him."

Lady Sif smashed the frame off the cupboard and reached inside the back. When she held out her hand, a small, round compass lay in her palm, and Donnie felt compelled to take it from her. Sif lay the compass on the bed alongside the photo, which she cleaned of glass before she headed for the door.

"Tyr told us that this compass is a way to find what you and your Valkyrie queen need to finish this war. For now. Ragnarök is not something I wish to endure, if at all possible. I wish you well, night walker."

Then Lady Sif was gone from the room, leaving Donnie alone. He slipped the picture in the back pocket of his pants first, careful not to damage it for his friend. Then he palmed the compass, and a jolt of magic shot from it and into him.

Donnie came awake with a gasp, sitting upright and gulping air as if he needed to breathe. He could feel the pull of the magic call to him from his palm, and when he uncurled his fingers, the compass was real and solid in his hand.

A throat cleared, and Donnie snapped his eyes to those gunmetal grays he loved so much. He had almost died and lost her. She had nearly lost him.

Setting the compass down on the bedside table, Donnie was out of the bed and hauling her to him before she could protest. He took her mouth with a roughness that surprised him, needing to remind himself that he was alive.

Caitlyn met his need with one of her own, her fingers tracing over his scalp and dragging her fingernails over the bristles of his head just like she liked to. He growled, turning and tossing her on the bed. A slow, sexy smile crept over her lips as he pulled her leggings down, then her black lace panties, and, after shoving down his pants, claimed her body as his with one powerful thrust.

Mine, she purred into his mind as he lost himself to her.

Mine, he growled back.

They rode the pleasure until they both were panting and found release. Then Donnie curled his woman to his chest as she ran her delicate fingers over his sternum.

"Well, it seems redundant to ask if you are okay considering what just happened."

"I'm good. What happened after I got knocked out?"

Donnie listened as Caitlyn told him about Derek killing Neville Morris and his best friend from a century ago who had been a phoenix. Told him all about Kenzie and her own brush with death. His heart broke for Derek as Caitlyn explained that Ever still had not awoken and Derek had yet to leave her, caring for his newborn faithfully without considering he needed to look after himself.

"We need to see him."

"Then you must shower first. You have been asleep for three days and nights, and we both need to wash that off."

Of course, they showered together, and Donnie was unable to stop himself from taking his mate against the cool tiles of their shower. When Caitlyn moaned his name, a slow, deliberate smile crept over his lips.

After, they walked hand in hand to the kitchen. Donnie kept running his fingers over the compass in his pocket as he glanced outside and watched Caitlyn's niece in awe. Kenzie was sparring with a hulking Valkyrie, the one called Danae, her movements deadly and powerful. Kenzie had been both of those things before, but now, wings of darkest midnight hung from her shoulder blades, the edges of the feathers a blood red that fitted the blood-kissed human.

"You drag your wings like that, little Valkyrie, and someone will cut them off for you," Danae shouted at Kenzie. The former assassin gave her new warrior sister her middle finger.

Spying them watching her, Kenzie lifted her hand in a wave and then ducked just in time to avoid a large meat cleaver that Danae swung at her.

They drove in relative silence to the hospital, Donnie with one hand on the wheel and one hand still in Caitlyn's. She glanced outside into the night, and Donnie could sense she had something on her mind as she stole glances at him when she thought he wasn't watching her.

"We will need to remodel the house to accommodate Kenzie's wings."

"I'm pretty sure she can magic them away. But we can do that if you want."

Caitlyn was silent again as they parked at the hospital, and

Donnie angled his body to face her. "Tell me what's bothering you."

She didn't say anything for a while, simply picked at the skin on her fingernails. Finally, she spoke. "The last child I held in my arms was Zach. But the last baby I held in my arms was my sweet Jessamine."

"Okay, let's go home." Donnie started the car and put it in reverse, halting only when Caitlyn let out an aggravated sigh that he was used to by now.

"I am quite afraid that I will set my eyes on Ashlyn and be unable to see anyone but my daughter."

Donnie shook his head, cupping the back of her neck. "Ash loves you. Hero-worships you. I've seen some of her memories, and never once does she feel anything other than love for you. Jealous, sometimes, of how you and Zach are, but never in a bad way."

"Ash mentioned the same to me. I do not care for Melanie any more or less than Kenzie."

Donnie pressed his lips to the nape of her neck. "No. You, my beautiful, smart, fierce mate, have the biggest heart. I saw you, Caitlyn Hardi, when you tried to pretend you could not feel, and I know that those whom you claim as your own are loved equally. Except for me. I'm special."

Caitlyn chuckled softly, the tension leaving her body as they left the car and made their way inside the hospital, Donnie placing a possessive hand on the small of Caitlyn's back. Donnie gave a slight knock on a hospital door after following his nose to where his friends and teammates were.

Caitlyn pushed open the door, stepping inside as Donnie followed her. His eyes fell to the prone body lying in bed, a sleeping Ash curled up alongside her mother. Erika sat in Loki's lap, her head on his shoulder. Ricky and Melanie sat on the floor with their backs against the wall, fingers entwined. Derek paced the floor with his baby girl in his arms, a bottle at her lips as he lifted his gaze to Donnie's.

Donnie ignored the others in the room as he brushed past them, placing his hand on top of Ever's forehead and closing his eyes.

Ever stood on a beach, her hair whipping in the wind as waves crashed the shore, water lapping at her toes. She wore a warrior's suit of armor, a sword at her hip as her blue eyes scanned the ocean.

Donnie stepped up beside her, folded his arms over his chest, and said, "Don't you think you have slept enough?"

"I am not ready yet. My body needs to heal before I can wake up."

Donnie smiled. "I get that. But when you do wake up, I have a lot to tell you."

Ever glanced up at him, a small smile playing on her lips. "And you won't tell me, will you—not until I wake?"

"Call it an incentive."

A soft laugh carried with the wind as Ever said, "Everyone is well?"

"They will be when they know you are simply healing."

"I had not known that you could walk in someone's dreams."

Donnie shrugged. "Neither did I. I guess your Ash was right when she said our powers grow."

"Go back and reassure them that I am resting."

"When will you wake?" Donnie asked.

Ever glanced at the sand and replied, "Soon."

Donnie turned to leave her in the sand when she called his name.

"You fought with the might of a Viking and protected my daughter. I will not forget. Tell my mate that I love him, and his voice comforts me."

Donnie lifted his hand from Ever's forehead and staggered, blinking a few times to make sure he was indeed in the real world. Turning to Derek, who looked at him with wolf-amber eyes, Donnie smiled. "She dreams. She sleeps to heal her body. She assures me she will wake soon, that she loves you, and that your voice gives her comfort."

Derek sighed in relief as Caitlyn stepped in front of Derek and, her tone nervous, asked if she could hold Ash. Derek handed his daughter over without hesitation, and Donnie watched as his mate fell in love with the little girl much as she had with Zach—instantly and without reservation.

Donnie grunted as Derek drew him into his arms, the other man hugging him so hard his ribs might have broken if he'd been human.

"Erika told me how you stood in front of Ever and took the bolt meant to kill her. You would have sacrificed your life for them, and I can never repay you."

Donnie stepped back, setting his hands on either side of Derek's shoulders. "We are family, Derek. I would lay down my life for anyone in this room. It was nothing."

"It wasn't nothing, Donnie. It wasn't nothing."

Emotion choked Derek's tone as Donnie removed his hands. Melanie drew herself off the floor and wrapped her arms around his waist. "I didn't know you could put yourself in someone's dreams."

"Neither did I 'til, like, five minutes ago. I only meant to listen to her thoughts."

When Melanie went back to her husband, Donnie walked past Ricky, bumping fists with him as he crouched to be on level with Erika. Taking the photo out of his pocket, he handed it to the Valkyrie, who eyed him with suspicion.

"I'm not sure how, but when I was knocked out, I paid a visit to Asgard, and it seems Tyr was working as a double agent, helping a group of gods trying to find a way to stop Odin. I got a weird-ass compass that's supposed to take me somewhere, courtesy of your dad. He had it hidden in the frame around this picture, and Lady Sif left it out for me to take."

Donnie rose as Erika turned the photo over and gasped, leaving her to her gift. Walking over to Caitlyn, he wrapped his arms around her, looking over her shoulder at the sleeping baby.

"Donnie."

Unwrapping his arms from Caitlyn, he turned back to Erika.

"Thank you," she said quietly. "I don't remember what she looked like. I never knew her."

"Don't worry. I know what it's like never to know what your mother looks like. I saw a picture once in my aunt's home, but I could never pluck up the courage to ask for it."

Ash lifted her head from her mother's shoulder, a grin the size of Texas on her lips. "You know, hearing that you helped save my life doesn't do anything to stop me from thinking you're hot."

Donnie shot Derek a bemused look as if to say. *That's your kid* as the room laughed. They fell into easy conversations, with Ricky fussing over Derek and forcing him to eat, despite the growl that rumbled in Derek's chest.

Then the silence came, and no one knew what to say. Derek glanced at Caitlyn, and when she gave her eldest friend a slight bob of her head, he pulled down the arm of the bed, climbed into the bed beside his mate, and lay his hand over her stomach.

Ash reached out and rested her hand on Derek's arm. Finally, after three days, the wolf closed his eyes and slept, a sign that he felt protected by those gathered in the room and trusted them to keep him and his family safe.

As the hands on the clock ticked by, night to day and back to night again, Ever still slept.

Derek

DEREK STOOD IN THE CEMETERY AS SHOTS WERE FIRED INTO THE air, his heart pounding with every load of the rifle, the scent of gunpowder wrinkling his nose as the shots rang out into the night sky. He was on edge, being away from Ash, but the baby was surrounded by her older self, Freya, and the Valkyrie.

Still didn't make this night any easier.

The crowds that had gathered put Derek and his wolf on high alert, scanning the gathering for threats to him or any of the mourners. But considering the entire police force had come out to St. James Cemetery to pay their respects to Sarge, he didn't have much to worry about.

He felt a hand lightly pat his knee, and Derek glanced at Caitlyn through hooded eyes. "Breathe, *mon loupe*, it will be over soon enough."

Derek had dreaded this day, when they all had to say goodbye to a good man who died for no real reason but petty jealousy. His guilt had been pushed aside as he'd dealt with being a dad whose mate was still unconscious, but it was back in full force today.

Sarge's funeral took place a week after his daughter's birth, and the team had carried Sarge to his final resting place in honor of the man who'd carried them on his shoulders for years. Each member of the team shouldered his coffin: Derek, Caitlyn, Donnie, Ricky, Melanie, Kenzie, and Erika.

Erika had taken over from Derek in carrying the coffin as he ordered the team to lower the coffin. As they did, the entire force that had gathered stood and saluted the man whose integrity called to anyone who wore the badge. Derek suppressed a smile as he wondered what Sarge would think of all this fuss, of the sight of the entire team in their dress blues, hats in all.

The tricolor was draped over Sarge's coffin as Derek got to his feet and marched over to where a uniform soldier folded the flag and handed it to Derek with a salute. Derek returned the salute, strode over to where Anna sat, and held out the flag to her.

"No, Derek," Anna gasped, eyes wide. "This should go to one of you, his family."

"It is, Anna. Sarge would have married you given half a chance. Please. He would want you to have it."

Anna reluctantly took the flag, and Derek saluted her, the witch's eyes leaking tears that made Derek wish he could weep openly for the friend he'd lost.

The service ended quickly after that, the crowd slowly dispersing, leaving Derek and his team alone to say some private goodbyes. He stood off to the side, having said all he needed to say to Sarge when he'd stood before the gathered mourners to deliver Sarge's eulogy.

"Agent Doyle."

Derek had scented the man before he spoke and knew it was the human police commissioner who called him. He'd seen the commissioner attending the funeral along with a handful of politicians and members of the council. When Derek had looked around the cemetery during the funeral, he'd seen Samhain Chace exchanging a look with this man before her eyes clashed with Derek's, their argument two days ago still vivid in his mind.

"You are the reason my daughter lies in that bed."

"You'll find it was her biological father who triggered her labor and put her in that bed, not me. And I would ask you to keep your voice down. Your granddaughter is sleeping."

Samhain glared at the young woman sleeping beside Ever, then back to the baby in his arms as she scowled. "Don't you dare chastise me, wolf. I had to find out about Ever's condition from Richard Moore's mother. Do you know how embarrassing that is?"

Derek snarled as Ash fussed in his arms. "Conrad knew. It's not my fault your husband chose not to tell you. Now, get out before I forget my manners, Samhain."

Samhain had stormed from the room, slamming the door and waking Ash, who cried for a full hour straight before Ricky waltzed in and stole Ash from his arms, his singing putting a stop to her crying an instant later.

"Agent Doyle."

Derek shook himself from his thoughts and turned to the man who'd called his name. Shorter than Derek, the commissioner had dark, thinning hair and intelligent eyes that were hidden behind thick-rimmed glasses. He was thin and Irish-pale, with a dusting of freckles on his cheeks.

"Sir, my apologies. It has been a long few weeks."

The other man inclined his head. "No need for apologies. I am sorry for your loss. I knew Tom well, and he was a great man."

Derek said nothing as the man motioned for Derek to walk with him.

"I spoke with Tom only last month when he handed in his retirement papers. He was pretty clear that when he retired, you, Agent Doyle, would take over as sergeant of the team."

Derek kept his mouth shut as the man continued. "We at headquarters feel that a bigger Paranormal Investigations Team is needed, as did Tom, and we want you to take over command. You will be promoted to captain and, as requested by Tom, promotions for the rest of the team are already working up the chain of command, waiting to be signed off on."

Opening his mouth, an answer on the tip of his tongue, the commissioner held up a hand. "Don't give me an answer now when you have so much on your plate. We can meet in a few weeks. We want to invest in a training facility and recruit young supernaturals who would be the future of the team. Think it over, and we'll talk again soon."

The commissioner shook Derek's hand, and as he walked away, Caitlyn came to stand beside him. "What was that about?"

Facing his oldest friend, Derek shrugged, the collar of his shirt itching the burns on his throat. The scars would be permanent—the silver ensuring that they'd be a constant reminder of Sam.

"Sarge put in his papers, but not before requesting promotions for all of us. The commissioner wants me to lead the need to expand P.I.T."

"And will you do it?"

Derek shrugged again. "Considering my daughter and Zach seem to become agents, I don't have a choice, do I?"

"Do any of us?"

The rest of the team joined them, and then they walked away together. Ricky opened the back door of his car and tossed his hat inside, scratching his head. "I forgot how itchy that bloody thing was."

Donnie grinned, lifting his own and running a hand over his bristles. "Too much hair, mate, that's your problem. I have a razor that'd work wonders on it."

Melanie punched Donnie hard in the shoulder. "I like his hair just the way it is, Brother."

"Yeah, she likes to grab it when—" Melanie clamped a hand over Ricky's mouth. Even though he couldn't see it, Derek knew Ricky was grinning like an idiot.

"Derek?" Caitlyn's voice was soft and soothing as if she expected him to lose his shit. They'd all been treating him with kid gloves since Ash had been born, and Derek had waited for it to hit him, himself.

"We will go straight to the hospital, *oui?*"

Night after night, day after day, Derek had no shortage of visitors at the hospital. His team was always there to catch him should he fall. He couldn't believe how lucky he was to have them.

"I have somewhere I need to go first. Can you let me know if there's any change?

"Do you wish for someone to go with you?"

He let his lips curve slightly. "No, but thank you."

They all went their separate ways, Derek confident his family was in safe hands until he could be reunited with them. He drove to Kennedy Pier, where he was greeted with a nod as he stepped onto the ferry that would take him across the sea to the remote prison.

Spike Island had once been a travel destination, bringing in millions of tourists each year to visit the old grounds. Still, when it became apparent that regular prisons would not hold supernatural criminals, Spike Island had been reclaimed to house the worst criminals in Ireland. The waters around Spike were patrolled by sea shifters, from sharks to dolphins, seals to otters.

The strongest wards had been embedded in the soil. Not a soul could escape the island, and any who tried would be shot dead by eagle-eyed snipers.

The ferry pulled into Spike, and Derek disembarked, advising the ferryman he wouldn't be long. Derek made his way across the courtyard, wary that he could feel eyes on his from all around.

The warden greeted him and informed him that the man he'd come to see was waiting for him. He unlocked a steel door and ushered Derek inside, where a young man stood with his back to Derek, looking out of a window slit into the night. His reddish-brown hair was longer now, the ends of it touching his shoulders.

The man turned slightly, his murky eyes studying Derek as he shuffled, the chains on his ankles and wrists clinking loudly as he moved. His eyes widened at the scars on Derek's neck.

"Looks like you've been having fun, Doyle."

Derek took in the raspy tone and gaunt look in his eyes and snorted. "As have you, Christopher."

Christopher Gomez had come for Derek, blaming him for killing his father and sending his mother into a depression that left Gomez an orphan. He'd held Derek captive and shot both him and Ricky, but his team had apprehended him.

"I do not see a bag of dripping blood. Another broken promise."

"I promise you one day I will kill him. And bring you his head in a bag."

Derek had promised the other wolf he would kill Morris and bring him proof. It wouldn't make it up to Christopher for the losses of his parents, but it might bring him some comfort.

Leaning against the wall, Derek pulled his phone from his pocket, leafed through the pictures, and slid the phone across the table.

"I snapped his neck. Felt the life drain from his body. I had one of my most trusted agents burn his body. He is nothing more than ashes on the wind; a horror story those of us who survived will tell others. He can harm no one anymore."

Christopher shuffled over to the phone and gazed down at the picture. Derek told him to swipe, and the wolf did. Finding a video clip, he pressed play, and Derek could see the satisfaction in Gomez's eyes as he watched Ricky burn Morris' body.

The other wolf watched the video twice more before pushing the phone away. Glancing at Derek's neck, Gomez pointed. "A parting gift?" he asked.

"Yeah, but not from Morris."

Derek closed another door to his past as he walked from the room, thanked the warden, and hopped back on the ferry back to Cork. He drove back to the hospital and made his way to the place where his mate and child were.

Lights flickered overhead, and the hairs on the back of his neck rose. Quickening his pace, Derek rushed inside the room. Everyone had changed except for him, a table had been brought in, and they were just setting food on the table when Ash smiled, handing him some clothes and telling him to change.

When he returned, Ash patted the chair beside her. Derek

pressed his lips to her forehead as he toyed with his food. A growl made him smile, and he looked up to see as she glared at him and then back to the food. Derek mechanically ate as ordered, remembering how only a few days ago, he'd run as a wolf under the moon with his daughter.

The moon was high, her call a siren song as Derek shook out his fur and lifted his muzzle to howl in appreciation as the scent of his daughter greeted him. Fresh from her own change, she ran her nose along his cheek, her paws dancing in impatience, waiting for Derek to lead the charge.

With another howl, he bolted off through the forest with Ash's steady gait by his side, and Derek felt a new wave of happiness that he'd never felt in his entire life. They ran and ran until their legs grew weary, and then Derek hunted for a rabbit, bringing it back to share with Ash.

After they'd licked the blood from their paws, Derek sat staring up at the moon as Ash leaned into him, panting contentedly as howls from other packs called out to them.

With a wolfish grin, her tongue lolling, Ash lifted her nose in the air and joined in the song of her brethren. Derek thought the sound of it was the closest thing to magic he would hear in his lifetime.

He joined in with the calls until he could not differentiate between the many offerings to the moon. He was simply a wolf. For the first time ever, both wolf and man were in harmony.

Ash glanced at him then, her amber eyes brightening as if she knew what he was thinking about. She set down her fork and chewed on her bottom lip. He could scent her worry.

"When do you go back?"

His voice was tight, even though he tried to sound reassuring, knowing that his daughter had her future to return to and could not stay here forever, no matter how much he wanted her to.

"I'm supposed to go back tomorrow, but I can't really. Not

until I know Mom's okay. I can't go back not knowing if she'll be there or not."

"And your Grey?"

Ash squirmed in her seat, as uncomfortable talking about Grey with him as he was talking about his daughter mating, especially since that mate was Loki's son and slightly psychotic, according to Ash.

"A few more days won't hurt. When Mom wakes up, I'll go back. I told him so. He'll be grand."

Melanie coughed at the sour-tasting lie and arched her brows at Ash, who shrugged, returning to her food and ending the conversation.

Derek knew he should be encouraging Ash to return to the future, yet a selfish part of him wanted to keep her close, dreaded having to say goodbye, even if she was with him anyways.

Ever, though, had missed her chance to say goodbye to Sarge, and it would break her heart to think that Ash had also gone home before she could say goodbye. He glanced toward his mate as he pushed the thought into her head.

Wake up, sleepyhead. We need you.

Still, all Derek got was silence.

The lights in the room flickered, Melanie yawning as the sun began to rise in the sky. She was still young enough that the sun dragged her to sleep, so she rested her head on Ricky's shoulder, the tinted windows blocking the sun's rays from being dangerous.

The lights flickered once again, and the machines beeped. Then alarms started to blare all over the hospital. Derek got to his feet, taking Ash from Caitlyn as he walked to the window and gazed outside.

The sun looked frozen in time, neither rising nor falling, and Derek scented magic in the air. The team came to stand next to him, their own eyes wandering over the view, when suddenly the sun vanished into thin air, bringing night slamming back into place.

Bloodred rain fell in torrents outside, hitting the ground with a hiss. Screams rang out as cars crashed, and not a single soul knew what to do.

Derek held his daughter close to his chest as Loki pointed toward a figure atop a horse with eight legs and a coat of silver grey, his staff a beacon in the night sky as he lifted it high.

The sky cracked open, and the foundations of the hospital shook so hard that Derek feared the ground would swallow them whole. Odin reared up on his eight-legged horse and pointed to the City of Cork.

An army of berserkers marched over the hill and filtered down into the darkened city. Odin gathered lightning in his staff and sent it toward a mast, striking it and plunging the city into further darkness. All electricity was snuffed out in the hospital.

Ash let out a wail as Derek tried to shush her, caught between wanting to defend the city and needing to care for his child. He was torn between duty and family, and he didn't know what to do.

"If there were ever a time for someone to shout *Avengers assemble*, this would be it."

Derek ignored Ricky's attempt to ease the tension as winged warriors took to the sky in a wave of feathers and fury. Kenzie shucked off her jacket, pushed open the window, and climbed out on the ledge. She glanced at Caitlyn as if seeking permission. When Caitlyn nodded, Kenzie pushed off the ledge, flaring her pitch-black wings to join the other Valkyrie, her scythe glinting in the moonlight.

Ash raced over to the window and held out her hand. Mjölnir sailed through the air, and when it landed in her grasp, Ash ordered everyone to stand back as she rotated her arm a few times and then let the hammer carry her forward, out the window and through the air. Derek could only watch as she dropped into the parking lot and fought against the berserkers.

Erika kissed Loki quickly before she followed the others and was airborne a second later, barking orders to the Valkyrie as they plunged into the fray from above. Derek watched until he could only make out the glint of metal in the darkness.

Screams and panic rang out in alarm throughout the world as the Valkyrie rode out into battle witout their Queen to save the realm of Midgard that she loved so dearly. Lights flickered inside the hospital as the scent of fear hit Derek's nose. Windows shattered in the floors below and Ricky darted out into the corridor with Melanie hot on his heels

Everyone else was focused on the impending doom that was raining down on them, eyes filled with terror reflected in the glass as Derek held his little girl a little tighter. The time of Gods was among them, and Derek was not certain if the city could survive an ansualt like the one unfolding on the streets before him.

Everyone was so focused on watching the world begin to fall apart, not a single soul noticed as Ever Chace moved one finger, then another. Underneath her blankets, a toe twitched and not a single person noticed when Ever's pulse began to speed up.

A nurse raced into the room, asking what was going on, and Loki answered her straightaway, no hint of amusement in the god of mischief's voice.

"It's the end of the world, love. It's the end of the fucking world."

ALSO BY SUSAN HARRIS

THE EVER CHACE CHRONICLES

Skin & Bones, book 1

Collateral Damage, book 2

Smoke & Mirrors, book 3

Night of the Hunter, book 4

Never Back Down, book 5

Shortcut to the Grave, book 6

Arsonist's Lullaby, book 7

Of Gods And Monsters, book 8

DEFY THE STARS

A Tale of Two Houses, book 1

Until Death Do Us Part, book 2

In Defiance of the Stars, book 3

Shattered Memories

THE SANGUINE CROWN

Chaos Theory, book 1

Butterfly Effect, book 2

Wicked Game, book 3

Burn Notice, book 4

Fight Song, book 5 (coming January 2022)

CHARACTER PLAYLIST

Derek:

Hozier—Arsonist's Lullabye
Stormzy—Still Disappointed
The Hunna—Cover You (feat. Travis Barker)
Charlotte Lawrence—Joke's On You
ADONA—Hit Me With Your Best Shot
Matchbox Twenty—If You're Gone
The Cranberries—Zombie—Acoustic Version
Cage The Elephant—Goodbye
I Prevail—Hurricane
Nothing But Thieves—Is Everybody Going Crazy?
The Hoof—We Play to Win
Belako—Maskenfreiheit
Apocalyptica—Live or Die (feat. Joakim Brodén)
Don Diablo—Bad
The Weeknd—Until I Bleed Out
Fleurie—Soldier
Marilyn Manson—Killing Strangers
2WEI—Toxic
Ran-D—Zombie
2WEI—Survivor
2WEI—In the End
Hayley Williams—My Friend
Tusks—Toronto
Halflives—Rockstar Everyday
Silverstein—Madness

Ever:

Elbow—Empires
Tom Grennan—This is the Place
Hayley Williams—Leave It Alone
Cold War Kids—Who's Gonna Love Me Now
All Time Low—Sleeping In
Lady Gaga—Stupid Love
Dermot Kennedy—Resolution
SVRCINA—Astronomical
Tommee Profitt—Wake Me Up
Jackson Guthy—Giants
SHAED—Trampoline
Plested—Beautiful & Brutal
Claire Guerreso—How It Goes
Biffy Clyro—End Of
Off Bloom—Love To Hate It
Hayley Williams—Roses/Lotus/Violet/Iris
Coco Bans—Pray
Matt Emery—I Put a Flame in Your Heart (Vessels Remix)
aYia—Ruins
2WEI—Insomnia
Lindsey Ray—Here Right Now
VG LUCAS—Time's Running Out
Fleet Foxes—If You Need To, Keep Time On Me
Silverstein—Infinite
Boston Manor—Halo

Ash:

Hayley Williams—Simmer
Halsey—I HATE EVERYBODY
All Time Low—Some Kind Of Disaster
Ozzy Osbourne—Dreamer

AWOLNATION—The Best
Mabel—Boyfriend
PVRIS—Dead Weight
Doja Cat—Boss Bitch
Ellie Goulding—Worry About Me (feat. blackbear)
Matchbox Twenty—She's so Mean
Shakira—She Wolf
David Guetta—She Wolf (Falling to Pieces) [feat. Sia]
Circa Waves—Call Your Name
Stereophonics—Just Looking
The Weeknd—Missed You—Bonus Track
Twenty One Pilots—Level of Concern
All Time Low—Monsters (feat. blackbear)
You Me At Six—Save It For The Bedroom
Anavae—Human

Ricky:

Eminem—Those Kinda Nights (feat. Ed Sheeran)
Circa Waves—Be Your Drug
Slipknot—Nero Forte
Sick Love—Bad Girl
Matchbox Twenty—Unwell
The Pretty Reckless—Zombie
Imagine Dragons—Real Life
Stereophonics—Pick A Part That's New
Goody Grace—Scumbag—Acoustic
Simple Creatures—Special

Melanie:

Larkins—Hit and Run
Halsey—You should be sad—Acoustic
Gold Brother—Before You Do It Again

The Weeknd—In Your Eyes
Noah And The Whale—Blue Skies

Erika:

Halsey—3am
Tinie Tempah—Pass Out
Tones And I—Bad Child
Ubi—Read Em' And Weep
Regina Price—Meant to Be
Dimitri Vegas & Like Mike—Mortal Kombat Anthem
—Club Mix

Donnie:

Dropkick Murphys—Smash Shit Up
Oh The Larceny—Check It Out
Victory—Feeling Good
The Filthy Souls—Here I Am
Stereophonics—The Bartender And The Thief
Speak, Brother—Lions Roar

Caitlyn:

The Coronas—Haunted
Sam Fender—Back To Black—BBC Radio 1 Live Session
Ki:Theory—Suspicious Minds
Shinedown—How Did You Love—Acoustic
Jenn Grant—Green Grows the Lilac-
Au/Ra—Ideas
Winona Oak—Lonely Hearts Club
Christian Löffler—Haul (feat. Mohna)

ACKNOWLEDGEMENTS

Rebecca, Courtney & Marya,
Thank you all for the support and belief in my books.
I'm very blessed to be a #CTP author

Marya,
Arsonist's Lullaby has the most epic cover! I swear it looks like a
action movie poster and I love it! Thank you for always putting
up with me!

Melanie Newton,
There are very little words that I could write to sum up how
much I value our friendship. Thank you for listening to me get
lost in new worlds and story ideas and being such a massive
support to me.
I really don't think I would be living my dream if it wasn't for all
that you do for me.

Jamie,
My trusty beta reader!
Thanks for all that you do x

My Parents,
I love you both so very much.

LJ and Taylor,
I love you both to Infinity and beyond x

My circle is small, but you guys are the best in the world.

Shout out to the Muser family! You guys are a great bunch of people!

To the Readers,
The Ever Chace Chronicles would not have continued for so long if it wasn't for all of you who took a chance on a book called Skin and Bones. I grateful to each and every one of you who did and who stuck with me.

Sláinte

ABOUT THE AUTHOR

Susan Harris is a writer from Cork, Ireland and when she's not torturing her readers with heart-wrenching plot twists or killer cliffhangers, she's probably getting some new book related ink, binging her latest TV or music obsession, or with her nose in a book.

Susan LOVES connecting with her fans!
www.susanharrisauthor.com

Thank you for reading *Arsonist's Lullaby*; I hope you enjoyed my book!

Want to be the first to know when I release new books? Here are some ways to stay updated:

- Sign up for my email list so you can find out about new releases.
- Like my Facebook page.
- Visit my website: www.SusanHarrisAuthor.com/
- Connect with me on Spotify

If you loved *Arsonist's Lullaby*, please tell your friends about my book and consider leaving a review. Reviews are like potato chips; you can't ever have enough of them; thanks for reading my book!" ~Susan Harris

www.ingramcontent.com/pod-product-compliance
Lightning Source LLC
Chambersburg PA
CBHW021954190626
46807CB00005BB/2317